Better To Have Loved

Christy Jackson Nicholas

DEDICATION

I lovingly dedicate this book to my parents, without whom this story would never be written, indeed, I would never have happened. I love you both, dearly and forever. I also dedicate it to my husband and friends who have supported me throughout this journey.

TABLE OF CONTENTS

PROLOGUE

1974, Dearborn, Michigan

Kirsten always knew she didn't have a father. She didn't think they were required.

After all, her best friend, Judy, never had one. Judy simply lived with her mother, brother and grandmother, while Kirsten lived with her mother, Julie, and her grandparents. It wasn't anything she believed she lacked until she went to Kindergarten. That's where she learned that fathers were more normal than she had imagined.

She discovered that fathers could be useful. They drove cars and had jobs. Diane's father even built her a treehouse, which Kirsten had always wanted. There was a perfect apple tree in the back yard for such a thing. Sometimes they yelled, as well, but she was used to that from her grandfather. Perhaps she should get a father as well.

She wondered where she might obtain such a thing.

1 – THE GRAND HOUSE

February 16, 1967

Dear Katy,

It looks like fate has twisted my life's tail. I'm writing to you while on a flight to England. Yes, you read right, England! I'll be posting this from there, so you'll likely have seen it on the envelope. But why am I here, you ask? I shall tell you, sister dear.

The children I was taking care of have moved here for the next several months, their mother transferred for specialized training in the Church. Now I'm taking care of Eileen's three children as well as Percy's two children. It's quite a passel—I feel like Maria Von Trapp on some days. And yes, I've taught them to sing My Favorite Things, at least passably well. I had reservations about Eileen and Percy's situation, but I think I've finally gotten to the point where I've realized it's not really my job to judge their love life.

It was like herding cats getting them all packed and settled into the plane. I was surprised to find my belongings all fit into one large suitcase. I guess I'm not much for gathering things anymore. Not after mom gave away all my baseball cards, anyhow. I don't know if I'll ever forgive her for that. There were valuable cards there, including a Roger Marin rookie card. Ah well, such is life!

I'll be in a town called East Grinstead, which is south of London. The name of the house is Saint Hill, a big mansion built for some muckity-muck

1

nobleman. Wish me luck! Perhaps I'll find myself a British boyfriend like you did. Have you two set a date yet, by the way? He sounds groovy, from your description. What sort of music does his band play? Does he have a day job, or is he all about the music?

You mentioned Larry was having troubles in high school. Did you let him know I would beat him up if he dropped out? I should still be able to instill the fear of pain in my little brother, I think.

Give mom a hug for me, and tell dad I'm thinking of him.

Much love,

Julie

*****

1967, East Grinstead, England

Juggling her large battered suitcase and her portfolio over her back, Julie trudged up the gravel driveway to the huge manor house. Her feet were terribly unhappy with the long trip from the bus stop, and the portfolio kept catching the wind, threatening to make her into a kite's tail with each gust.

Saint Hill Manor was palatial. Perhaps it was indeed a palace.

She could count at least twenty windows on the façade. How many rooms did it have? Certainly there were dozens of people shuffling in and out of the place. It was like a beehive of activity.

"You! Girl! Have you checked in yet?" A gruff voice with a London accent called out above the din.

Julie turned around to find an older man with a fringe of white hair around his head pointing a clipboard at her.

"I... no, I don't know where—"

"Over here, quickly now. What's your name?" He started flipping through the pages, looking up at her when she didn't immediately supply him with information.

"Jensen. Julie Jensen. From Detroit." She put down her suitcase and portfolio while he searched for her name. The wind picked up, tossing her thick chestnut-brown curls into her face. With disgust, she pulled them back out of her eyes and repaired the ponytail loosened by travel.

She looked again at the grand house. Would she be in one of the upper rooms? Perhaps with a view across the extensive gardens? She smiled at the idea of waking up to such a view each morning.

"Aha! Found you. You're down in Hayward's Heath. Just a half mile down the path there. It used to be servant's quarters. You're in Unit C. Next!" He dismissed her and looked to an Indian woman in a bright blue sari.

Blinking several times to hide her disillusionment, Julie grabbed her belongings and made her way to her new digs.

The disappointing row of attached cottages all looked the same. Sandy-colored stone with tin roofs, a depressingly small single window cut next to each door. She found the weathered 'C' plate on the third one and knocked.

There was some shuffling inside and a muffled oath before the warped green door flung open. A small, round woman with brown hair looked her up and down.

"Yes? How can I help you?" Her clipped British accent was refined and not unkind.

"I was told this was where I should report... I mean, well—"

"Oh! You must be Julie! I'm Sheila. Come in, come in! Let me help you with your bag. Bloody hell! What have you got in here, rocks?" A swirl of activity with several grunts and shoves later, and Julie was installed in one of the small bedrooms.

There were two, connected to a tiny living area and kitchenette. The place was brightened with several paintings and colorful rugs. Sheila busied herself making tea and sandwiches while Julie plopped down on the overstuffed sofa.

Julie took a deep breath to calm her rising panic. She'd made it to her new place, her new job. She was no longer traveling by plane, bus, or foot. She could relax. Breathe in, breathe out. Repeat. Repeat.

Sheila came over with a perfectly English tea tray, complete with tiny sandwiches, lemon, cream, and scones. How had she whipped all that up in just a few minutes? It must be some sort of strange English superpower.

"So, Julie, do tell me all about yourself. Where are you from?"

Taking one of the scones and slathering an indecent amount of butter on it, Julie took an appreciative bite and closed her eyes for a moment. Breakfast on the airplane had been hours ago, and not very tasty.

"I'm from Ohio, originally, but my parents moved to Michigan when I was fifteen. I just came from Washington, D.C., though. I was living there for about six months..." Trailing off, she remembered her ex-boyfriend, Jeffrey. This new life was an attempt to escape that memory. She cleared her throat and continued. "I started taking care of some kids for a woman who worked for the Church, and she was getting transferred. So, here I am, out of breath and incredibly grateful for these delicious treats." She grinned at Sheila, who smiled back, showing a gap in her front teeth.

"Well, that sounds like a great deal of exhausting travel, Julie! I'm Sheila, and I've been here for about a year. My son, Neil, is three—you'll meet him this afternoon, when he gets out of the crèche. His father is over in the men's dorms. We're both teachers at the Church, giving seminars in advanced theology. We met shortly after we joined. We are quite lucky, actually, as there's just the three of us here. David has to share with five other men!"

Looking around the small apartment… no, it's called a flat in England… she was indeed grateful for small mercies. Six adults in such small a space would have her running and screaming for the hills in no time.

"You can't get a place together? That must be very difficult."

"Oh, we could — but that costs more money than either of us make! We make due. There are all sorts of hidden alcoves and paths in the woods if we want more privacy." Sheila winked and Julie felt her skin heat up with embarrassment.

Looking around for a change of subject, she noticed there were no other doors. "Sheila, I need to use the… the powder room, but I don't see one. Where is it?"

"Powder room? Oh, dear, you mean the W.C., don't you? The toilet is three doors down on your right."

*****

As much as Julie liked Sheila, she was glad they weren't in the room much. With two jobs, Julie was kept well busy. During the day, she took care of Eileen and Percy's five children. In the evenings, she worked on artwork for the Church brochures. They liked her work here, though being an American artist might have had a bit of cachet to the British.

She had no idea why, but whenever someone discovered she was American, they were full of questions. Had she met Marilyn Monroe? Had she been to New York City? Did she know their cousin Bob, who lived somewhere in Indiana? Julie decided they didn't have a true grasp of how big America was, compared to their island country. Perhaps people in Europe still had more of a sense of community than Americans did, at least those Americans who lived in the city.

There were certain things she had needed to get used to, like the tiny rooms, outdated plumbing, and the food. The food ... oh, yes, the food. Boiling everything for ten hours does not improve the flavor in the slightest, but she wasn't a good enough cook herself to offer advice to the professionals. Not being close enough to walk to anything outside of town and having no transportation was another problem.

All the inconveniences were countered, though, by the constant stream of people. Some were in for an hour, others were in for a month. Since this was the international headquarters for the Church, people came in from all over the world. She'd met people from all over Europe, Brazil, the USSR, Japan, Australia, even one man from Saudi Arabia. She couldn't imagine the tenets of this new religion was popular in some of these countries, or really, in any country with a communist philosophy, but they must have influence, after all.

There was no shortage of interesting men to talk or flirt with. There were frequent parties in the big house on the weekends. Some were large, formal events which were sanctioned by the Church, with conferences, fundraisers, important guests, all sorts of rules. Others were groups of friends getting together in one of the many large ballrooms for music, games, or chatting.

While it wasn't the bizarre world Washington, D.C. was, this place had an interesting flavor to it. It was an odd mixture of old world charm and new world hope. As if changing this old palace into a modern facility was a physical act of transformation for the community, to radiate out to spokes all over the world, drawing in the best and the brightest to this glowing center. Well, "centre." It was England, after all, she needed to remember her spelling.

Eileen and Percy had taken the kids out of town for a trip to London. Julie wished them joy. She had been to London just the once so far, having no real wish to repeat the experience soon. It was grimy, loud, crowded, and she didn't care for it at all. She wondered why her sister, Katy, had such a deep, abiding passion for the place. True, the shopping was amazing, but she wasn't a huge fan of accumulating things, so shopping was often a chore at best. She often planned her shopping trips like a surgical strike—go in, get what you need, come out. Julie much preferred the smaller, charming villages, with little cottages and warm, cozy pubs for all to visit. She liked the picturesque country roads, with ivy-covered stone cottages and ruined castles she could sketch. She preferred the rolling, gentle hills in the countryside, or the old growth forest, so lush and full of life. It was idealistic of her, but she could imagine retiring in such a place someday.

Since she had the day off, Julie decided she'd do a little exploring around the place. She hadn't had a lot of time to wander around the rambling buildings.

The manor house itself warranted some time to study and explore. It was a daunting prospect at first, but she eventually stole some time to wander.

She was already familiar with the kitchen, the dorms (which were downstairs), and the teaching area, as well as the main ballrooms. It rambled from room to room, with décor which looked horribly tacky and ostentatious to her simple, midwestern tastes. There were gold gilt, bright-painted cornices everywhere and huge oil paintings, classical statuary in every corner. If she turned around too fast, she would knock over thousands of pounds worth of intricate Rococo art.

Passing through the uncomfortable opulence, she decided to begin instead with the underground areas, under even the servant's hall.

The rooms were dank and dark here. She had brought a flashlight, or a "torch" as the cook had called it, using it to explore the storage rooms. Having read many books about castles and fantasy novels as a child, she took the opportunity to look for hidden passages and false doors, but was disappointed in this goal. There was a real dungeon—a hole which was used to store old files—but she had been down there, retrieving records. No mystery there.

Several hours later, tired, with eyes tearing from the dust, she emerged from the dungeons, as she deemed them, deciding she would have better luck on the opposite end of the spectrum—those rooms which would have been the lord's chambers. She knew where they were. No one lived in them, but they were storage to more of the church's documents. As those documents didn't contain anything confidential, they weren't locked up. She had been in a couple times researching projects, finding old advertisements for inspiration.

She was examining the geometric wooden carvings around the mantle of the huge fireplace, touching the edges of the mirror. There was an odd arabesque design there which seemed out of style with the other decorations. It was sort of art nouveau and curvilinear compared to the squared bits everywhere else, catching her attention. Vines with large flowers lined the one edge of the mirror. She touched them, perhaps harder than she intended to …. and heard a click. Julie dropped her hand, looking around, as if someone was watching her. A cool breeze blew against her legs. She looked down, seeing a panel behind the fireplace that had swiveled out, revealing a dark passage. She had found one! She was excited and nervous at the same time.

She crouched and made her way past the empty fire grate and into the passage. She did her best to close the panel most of the way. She had grabbed a book from a shelf and, apologizing to the book for using it in this abusive manner, placed it like a wedge to keep it from closing. With her escape route secured, she turned her flashlight into the passageway to see what she could see.

If the storage rooms had been dank and dark, this passage was even more so. There were cobwebs and dust everywhere. The passage was about six feet tall and four feet wide, and perhaps turned ahead. There were shapes along one wall, draped with a grimy white fabric. She peeked under one corner, finding several open grid crates with bottles inside. A hidden stash of wine, perhaps? A rare vintage whisky?

The bottles were grey with dust, but one of the crates was opened and only half full. Julie lifted up a bottle and did her best to wipe the label clean enough to read with the flashlight. It looked like whisky. It said 1934 Glen Grant—it must have been the year it was bottled. She knew next to nothing about whisky, except the Scots and Irish both produced it, that it was better when aged, like wine. She looked at the crates, estimating there were about sixty bottles under the dust. Well, it was hidden treasure, of a sort. She wondered if anyone even knew it was there.

Placing the bottle back in place, she tried to arrange the cover back to the way she had found it, but there was no hiding her marks in the dust. She blew here and there, though, softening the marks, so it looked more random. She continued her explorations down the tunnel and around the bend at the end.

There were bits of old furniture here and there, many of them broken. A chair missing an arm, a table with three legs, a sideboard with one door on the casement. She decided they must have been put here, intended for future repairs, then forgotten. She decided to dub it the Tunnel of Forgotten Furniture, grinning at her own silliness.

The tunnel floor angled down after she turned the corner, as the rough flagstones beneath her began forming ledges, like shallow stairs. She walked down with care, aware a fall could render her immobile, and no one knew she was here. The thick walls around her meant yelling for help would be futile.

With this comforting idea, she heard a noise. It seemed like a clattering, then several clatters, as well as voices. She stopped to listen, straining hard to make sense of the words, thinking it was noise from the kitchen. She reviewed a mental map of where she should be in the house. She must be above the kitchens, as she didn't think she had descended two stories from her entrance.

Julie heard a different noise, then, one which left a river of ice where her spine had been. It was a low, horrible moaning, as if someone was in intense pain, pain which would not go away. It was a girl's voice, she decided, too high pitched to be a man's, or even a grown woman's. It undulated up and down, not loud, but close. It would have to be someone in the tunnel. It was not muffled by stone wall. She moved her flashlight to the right and to her left, keeping her back flat against the wall, searching for the girl.

The noise from the kitchen began again, and the moaning was gone, like that. She was still ice cold. She could see nothing with her flashlight. There weren't even any pieces of abandoned furniture in this part of the tunnel, nor any abandoned crates of whisky. She decided she had had enough of adventure and exploration. She hurried back up the tunnel, through the entrance in the hearth, and closed the door, collapsing into the chair near the window once she was safe. She breathed in the sunshine streaming into the bay window, working to calm her nerves, breath by breath. Her body was tingling with the after-effects of adrenaline. She stayed there for a long time.

*****

1974, Dearborn, Michigan

Kirsten was feeling her lack of father keenly today. Kirsten did have a father figure—her grandpa was stern and strong, working as an engineer in Detroit. Her grandma was the nurturing type, 'Oh, dear, did you skin your knee? Let me cook you cinnamon toast and it will be all better.'

But after fighting with her mother, she needed someone else to turn to, and grandpa wasn't that sort. Grandma would merely make cookies. She needed advice.

She curled up with her favorite stuffed animal, a dolphin she had gotten at Seaworld, and cried.

It had been a silly fight, on the face of it, about cleaning her room, but it had made her mad and frustrated.

Her mom lived with her on the second floor, with their own bedrooms and bathroom, while her grandparents lived on the first floor. The basement was partially finished into what she saw as a huge playground. It had a craft kitchen for her mom and grandma, a laundry room, even a man cave for her grandpa. This doubled as a guest room, with a storage room filled with wondrous things.

What she didn't yet realize was she was cosseted and spoiled at her house. She had few chores other than keeping her room clean, but she didn't even do this so well. She had lots of play time, the freedom of a safe, middle-class neighborhood. Her friends lived a block away, and there was a nice park across the street with a playground.

Her mother was being unfair about her room. It was her room, wasn't it? Why should anyone else care about how messy it was, or how many toys were on the floor? It was a big room, with lots of places for toys. She wasn't done playing with them all, so she didn't put them away, it was that simple. But still, her mother yelled.

*****

1967, East Grinstead, England

Eileen and Percy had the kids, so that evening, Julie dined with the main group in the dining hall. She asked Sheila if there were any local ghost stories. She had grown up nearby, so might know if there was a haunting the area.

"Oh, yes, there is indeed. A tragic tale, of course, but it's the best sort, don't you think?"

"I suppose it depends on if you are part of the tale or not, I would think." Julie smiled her question.

Sheila settled into her seat for the story, looking very much like a round bird, fluffing her nest and settling on her eggs. "Ah, quite true. Well, let me tell you this particular tragic tale. It took place about two hundred years ago - and isn't this always how such tales begin? As it turns out, there was a girl. She was perhaps fifteen years old, the eldest daughter of the Lord. Of course she was in love with an unsuitable young man. He was the son of the cloth merchant in the village, so her father was dead set against the match. He had arranged a match with the son of a wealthy banker in London."

"And did she elope with her lover?" Julie found herself caught up in the tale already.

"Well, she had planned to. She had packed up provisions, gathered as much coin as she could find in the house, having gone out to meet him. However, she had never shown up at the rendezvous, according to her intended. They never discovered what happened to her. However, it is said she may have gotten lost in the many hidden passages in the house, trying to find her way out to the servant's quarters. It's what they had been built for, you see, to allow the servants to come in and out of the lord's rooms without being seen on the stairs. She haunts the passages to this very day, so they say." Sheila ended her story with the finality of an experienced bard, expecting to be praised for her skills.

"How many passages are in the house?" Julie decided to ask about practical matters instead of thinking too hard about what would have happened if she had gotten lost in those same passages.

"Oh, no one knows. The old lord had forbidden the servants to use them any longer, so they've remained closed since ... so they say." Sheila ended her story with a flourish of her hand. She loved telling tales, fairy or otherwise, and it showed in her presentation.

Someone had been in there, at least according to the dates on the whisky in the crates. But this was not common knowledge. Perhaps their presence was unknown to anyone else.

The conversation turned to more general subjects, to Julie's relief. The cold shiver returned to her spine as Sheila told her tale. She ate her stew, mopped it up with the homemade bread, trying to think of sunny days and spring breezes in the park.

There were several people on the stage, including a couple of guitarists, a female singer, a young man playing a recorder. Perhaps it was a tin whistle? They played a series of tunes, including one attractive, dark man who did a solo rendition of Harry Belefonte's Day-o!, while playing the guitar. He was good, Julie decided.

They played several tunes while Julie nursed her drink and sat in a corner. She wasn't a dedicated wallflower, but she preferred smaller parties where she knew most of the people. She also didn't care for the sweet, white wine much, but it was better than the punch in the ice swan. It had a fake coconut flavor she didn't like. She was grouchy from being so antisocial.

When the man with the tin whistle moved into a solo, the sound seemed to pierce straight through her skull. The party was loud, Julie decided. The noise was pounding in her head like a drum. She needed to get away for a while. She had met wonderful people since she had been here, more tonight, but she craved alone time. She extracted herself, drink in hand, wandering with studied nonchalance into the next room.

She was not alone, but there was only a group of people in here, chatting near the hearth.

"Oh, I'm so sorry, I didn't mean to interrupt."

The group had stopped talking when she came in, looking at her. It was the room she had been in when she found the hidden passage last month. She had avoided the room since her little adventure. 'Ghosts', really? Such an inane notion for a modern woman.

"No need for apologies. Do come join us." David, Sheila's husband, beckoned her over. He was with four others, none of whom Julie had met before.

"May I introduce Julie Jensen? She is one of our artists, staying near the house. Julie, this is Priya Bamji, from Bombay, Isabella de Santos, from Valencia, and Colum McKenzie from Perth. They have all come for one of my seminars next week."

"I'm pleased to meet you." Julie shook hands with each one in turn. Priya looked at her with liquid black eyes, a short, coffee-skinned thin woman with luxuriant black hair, perhaps in her mid-forties. Julie thought she was the woman behind her in line that first day, but it had been such a whirl that she couldn't be sure. Priya wore a colorful sari of orange and pink, with had a red dot on the middle of her forehead, which Julie had only ever seen in National Geographic magazines. Her handshake was strong and her smile was wide, showing gold on one front tooth. Isabella was tall, sturdy, with dark, curly hair, swept up into a mass on the back of her head, about her own age. Julie now understood what was meant by the term 'flashing dark eyes'. Colum gave her a firm handshake, a medium-height, stout man with reddish-brown hair and a wealth of freckles. He was perhaps thirty.

"We were discussing the global reach of the Church. Have you met many people from other places in your time here?" David was always a polite conversationalist, making sure to include everyone when he could.

16

"Well, tonight I think I've met people from every continent except Antarctica. I've met people from Norway, South Africa, Uruguay, Japan and Tasmania. I knew this was going to be a big production, but I had no idea how big. If I had known, I would have dressed with more care." She made a show of looking down at her garb—a simple dark green dress with ruffles on the edges, with a single jade pendant. The elegant sari Priya was making her self-conscious of her plainness.

"Don't be silly, lass, ye look lovely. The green sets off the reds in yer hair," Colum reassured her.

She flashed him a grateful smile. "Are you new arrived from Perth, then? I presume it is Perth, Scotland, rather than Perth, Australia, from your accent?"

"Aye, that's true. I've arrived this morning on the sleeper train from Edinburgh. Have ye been here long yerself, then?"

"Not so long. I do artwork for the Church as well as childcare for two of our other teachers. I'm versatile." She couldn't help but smile at him. She loved the thick Scottish accent, with its rolled "R"s.

"And how long have you worked for the Church?" Isabella inquired, with a touch of educated Spanish accent.

"Oh, less than a year. I began in Washington, D.C. How about yourself?"

"I have been an employee for two years now. I help out at the Valencia office. We are growing, though slowly. It is difficult to counteract the lassitude of Spanish momentum." Isabella looked as if she regretted her own lack of power.

The music resumed in the other room, so the group stood. As one, they migrated towards the sound, where several couples were already on the dance floor. It was a different set of musicians this time, and one was an accordion player. Reason enough to vacate, in her opinion.

Julie didn't want to be back in the noise. She was less bombarded while she had been in the other room, but the noise was threatening to give her a headache. The swirl of strangers, combined with the harsh sounds and the bombardment of decorations, colors and buzz was overwhelming her. She made her apologies and left, finding an exit to the house this time, away from the press of people.

She walked through the cool night air. The evening was clear, but not as cold as it should be for March. This was a good thing as she had neglected to bring any sort of jacket or wrap with her when she made her escape. She took in a couple of deep breaths, sensing the night and reveling in the quiet and peace of the universe. She smelled the fresh, green scent of the nearby trees, the faint hints of acrid wood smoke on the wind, which smelled like sandalwood incense. Looking up into the night sky, she saw the moon was almost full, shining its light upon the undulating lawn and formal gardens to the right. To the left she saw the outbuildings, noticing one had a light on.

These buildings had, at one point, been servants' quarters, stables, a blacksmithy, other buildings required to run a large estate. Many of them still performed similar functions, housing materials for the gardeners, maintenance men, etc. This particular shed, though, she wasn't familiar with.

She came closer, seeing a cluttered and disorganized work bench through the open doorway. The young man who had sung the Belafonte song was hunched over an instrument which looked elaborate and electronic. His thick, dark hair, which was shaggy, kept falling over his square face. He looked up as she crossed the threshold.

"Hello, I hope I haven't disturbed your work? I heard you sing earlier tonight. I quite enjoyed it, until I had to escape all the noise. Are you a professional musician?" Julie had always had a deep, abiding attraction to musicians, much to her father's chagrin.

The man straightened up, wiped his hands on a clean-looking rag on the bench, coming over to her. He wasn't tall, perhaps about 5'10", but taller than she was, with a solid build. Not muscular, but not scrawny, either. She noticed then he had soulful brown eyes. He had on jeans and a white turtleneck sweater on. What was it with her and turtleneck sweaters on men?

He held out his hand to her. "I'm Paul. I'm glad you enjoyed my performance. No, I'm not a professional, at least, not a professional musician. I guess I'm a professional electrician. And a teacher, and a traveler. I'm confusing you already, aren't I?" He had a disarming grin.

She put out her hand to shake his, but he took her fingers instead. Bowing low over them, he kissed her knuckles with a feather touch of his lips.

"Your servant, madam."

She giggled, nervous.

"Pleased to meet you, Paul. I'm Julie. I'm an artist and a nanny, though I suppose I can't really call either my profession. Are you new here? I don't recall having seen you before?" It was more of a question than a statement. She was rambling, but she wasn't sure why. A strange odor floated on the air, metallic and unpleasant. Was it one of the instruments on the workbench? Perhaps soldering?

"I got here a couple days ago, but I'd been busy with coursework myself. I flew in from Minneapolis. I'm a new employee there, shipped off for training here. There's a new electronic mixology machine I'm supposed to be learning how to maintain. I was overwhelmed by the party myself, so I decided I'd escape and get work done out here in the quiet."

"I was escaping as well. I do hope I'm not disturbing you ...?"

"Oh, not disturbed at all. Well, not bothered, at any rate. Most would agree I'm disturbed by nature." He gave her his disarming grin again. "Would you like to keep me company? It won't be too long, and I can finish off this project. It's an oscilloscope."

"Pardon my ignorance, but what exactly is an ... osilly-whatsit?"

His chuckle was low, pleasant, and not in the least mocking.

"It measures voltage, electrical signal changes. The Church uses them to help measure changes in your electrical impulses when you talk—sort of like a lie-detector test, though they prefer the term 'truth-detector'."

It sounded Orwellian. "Do they … interrogate people with them? Is that even legal?" She hadn't heard of such practices.

"No, no, no, they use them on an entirely volunteer basis. It's part of a new technique they're thinking of using."

"Oh, that sounds more innocuous, then. I was getting concerned." She remembered the book, 1984, having read it in school. The Church's practices did seem reminiscent of "Big Brother." This wasn't the first time she had experienced qualms about practices like this in the Church, but she was often able to rationalize them.

"More innocuous than the sort of thing the Catholic Church does, at any rate." He didn't seem to be saying this to Julie, though, more to himself. She sensed there was bitter history there, but it didn't seem like the right time to delve into it.

"But this isn't the machine you are sent to learn about, though?"

"No, that's a sort of mainframe computer, meant to analyze a color down to its basic components and hues. I'm an all-around repairman and mechanic extraordinaire, I suppose. I've been to specialized training in Chicago, Detroit, Omaha, etc. Once I learn a thing, I go teach it to others. A traveling trainer, if you will. I love the teaching of anything."

They devolved into a discussion about the different techniques used by the Church, which Julie had encountered in her layout work.

"And you are a musician as well? I heard you singing in the house."

He smiled, making laugh lines crinkle at the corners of his eyes and his mouth. Did she detect a dimple there? "I love music. Folk music, for the most part, but I'll dabble in anything. I'm not a huge fan of Rock 'n' Roll, though—I find it the sort of music that often leads to treble."

He paused, with a too-serious look on his face. She had been punned. She groaned theatrically, then laughed.

"Don't tell me that fell flat? Don't I measure up?"

"Oh, please, stop! You're killing me here." Julie laughed while she placed her hand to her forehead and rubbed.

He grinned and said, "I'm addicted to puns, I'm afraid. You might want to escape now while you can, this is merely a prelude."

By this time, Paul had finished fiddling with his electronic mess, coming to sit next to her by the door. There had been three rickety wooden chairs there, which he had dusted off with his no-longer-clean rag, offering her as a seat.

They talked of their lives. He didn't give many details, but he did mention he had once studied as a priest in the Catholic Church, then deciding to go to trade school to learn electronics. He loved puzzles as much as puns, he said.

They talked about other things, such as the food offered in the local pub, the differences between American and British plumbing standards. A bizarre conversation for a first meeting, but she was right at home.

Sometime later, she was surprised to discover they were holding hands, then kissing. She didn't have any clear memory of what had led to this, but it was an electrifying experience. She didn't notice the crick in her neck, or the cool of the March night coming in through the broken window. She didn't notice the flickering of the lamp above the workbench. All these details she would recall later, but right now, it was the kiss and nothing more.

*****

1978, Dearborn, Michigan

Kirsten was at home, sorting her things. She wanted to take everything with her, but mom had given her a limit. She had given her three largish boxes to fill. She said clothes didn't count towards the total, but her toys, books, and puzzles would have to fit into those three boxes. She had *lots* of toys. Legos, puzzles, books, games, stuffed animals, all sorts of things.

The books had to be first—though she did go through and leave the younger ones. She had been reading before she had begun school, to the dismay of her teachers. She wouldn't need the Golden Books or the Dr. Seuss any more. She would bring the Nancy Drew, the Little House on the Prairie books, Trixie Belden, Encyclopedia Brown, definitely those old Fairy Tale books Grandma Jensen had given her.

She loved to read, it was her first choice as an activity. Julie said she believed it was because she was an only child. Reading didn't require a friend.

She also loved showing off how well she could read, because her teachers were always so impressed. In first grade, she kept going through the standard readers until she was seven or eight ahead of the rest of the class. They had talked about having her skip second grade, but Julie squashed the idea, thinking she should stay with her age group. Still, they made sure she had harder stuff to read in school, so she wasn't bored. They did have her tested, and she was reading on an eighth grade level when she was in second grade. Handwriting, though—she wasn't good at that. She could read and write cursive, having taught herself in first grade with a book from the drug store, but it was messy. Her first grade teacher had said there was no reason for her to know it so young, but Kirsten mentioned she had a children's book which was written in cursive. The teacher, the no-nonsense sort, insisted she must be lying. When Kirsten brought in the Babar the Elephant book her mother had bought in Europe, the teacher apologized. Kirsten understood then she hated being accused of things she hadn't done.

After the books came the arts and crafts stuff. The Pentel markers her grandma's friend Uncle Richard gave her— he worked as a salesman for Pentel, bringing her fantastic big sets of markers. They were good markers, with a pointy tip, but a soft side for larger lines. Each color was listed in the cover of the tin container, in English, French, Spanish and German. The top cover was always a painting—soft and drifty images, like water lilies or sunsets. All her construction paper, the glitter, pencils, drawing paper. Should she bring her Silly Putty? Would it be craft or toy? No matter, she wanted to bring it. Besides, it was tiny. She also had a collection of drawings her Uncle Jeff had made her on their annual family trips to Canada. He always drew out cards for her and her cousin Kelly to color in.

Games—Definitely the cards. Uncle Larry had taught her how to play poker, and grandma played Gin Rummy with her. Great-grandpa Jackson played Concentration with her, but he had his own cards, with the big numbers on it so he could see. Puzzle books, Games Magazines, picture puzzles. Wow, those take up a lot of space. Okay, maybe she should leave those—the ones with missing pieces. Sorry, Monopoly, Life—she was running out of space. She hadn't even got to the toys yet.

Toys. What toys should she bring? Jump rope, that was easy—it took up no space. Roller skates? Too small for her now. She was pretty much over dolls, but she wanted to bring her stuffed dolphin. Mom had gotten it for her when we went to Sea World a couple years ago. And her bunnies. She had two stuffed bunnies. She didn't remember where she got them, but one was brown and one was grey. The grey one was missing an eye. Both were worse for wear, but she slept with them both every night.

Leaving the dolls helped a lot. She had several Barbies, as well as the Dreamhouse, van, clothes. She would leave all her Fisher Price toys, as well. My dollhouse! Grandpa had made it, and she loved it. She had added wallpaper and carpet several times, remodeling. But it was so big, it wouldn't even fit in any of the boxes. Maybe mom would make an exception.

She had a photograph she wanted to take, a black and white snapshot. It might be her father, but she had never gotten the courage up to ask her mother. It was a handsome man, with dark hair and a mustache. He had a black turtle-neck sweater on. She made sure to pack that, hidden in one of her books.

Well, that was three boxes filled. She wanted more space. Maybe she could fit things into her luggage without mom knowing? She stuffed a couple minor things in the spaces in the boxes, putting aside another pile of things she might be able to sneak in. Kirsten looked around the room, still seeing so many things she wanted to bring.

When Julie saw the results, she laughed.

"Those boxes are so stuffed, they're bulging at the sides, Kirsten."

"You didn't say they couldn't."

"I know, Hon, I know. Still, if we tape them well enough, they should ship alright."

"I'm not taking them on the plane?"

"No, dear, I am sending them in the mail. They will take longer, but they'll get there okay."

Kirsten was glad she hadn't agreed to put Troy or Darryl in them. They wouldn't have liked being stuck in the boxes for so long. Besides, she wouldn't have had as much room for her own stuff.

Oh. Mom, I have another question."

"What's that, dear?"

"Do we have to go to YOUR Ami? Can't we go to MY Ami? Do I even have an Ami?"

*****

Valencia, Spain May 15, 1967

Dear Katy:

My adventures continue, this time to Spain! Eileen and Percy are taking a seminar in Valencia, Spain. Valencia overlooks the Mediterranean Sea, and it is everything I ever dreamed Spain to be. And more! The food is amazing. I wish I could speak more than a few words of Spanish, but you know I never had much of a talent for languages.

After meeting so many exotic people at Saint Hill, I decided this would be almost provincial, but I am still amazed at all the differences I see. It's truly amazing and broadening. The music is enchanting and makes me want to dance. Have you ever seen Flamenco? So much energy!

I had met a sweet man back in England, named Paul. Remember, I wrote about him in my last letter? We shared a lovely evening and an even nicer kiss, but then I had to travel with Eileen. He'll probably be gone back to Minneapolis by the time I return next month. Why do the good ones always have to go away?

How are mom and dad doing? I miss them. I miss you. I even miss Larry! It's lonely here in Spain, even though it's so beautiful. Perhaps because it's so beautiful, it's lonelier, since I have no one to share it with.

Love to you, sister mine,

Julie

Julie walked out on the balcony and breathed deep of the warm, humid, salty air. She fancied she could see the island of Majorca in the misty distance, across the sea. She needed a respite, no matter how brief, from the screaming tantrums inside the apartment. All five children were behaving as if she had killed their favorite puppy, refusing to settle down, play nice, or even to stop crying. The day had been sticky and warm, but the sun was now setting across the sparkling sea. Only more relaxed, she took one more deep breath and returned to her charges.

Both Eileen and Percy took a sales seminar, which was being taught at the convention center on a cruise ship owned by the Church, and currently docked in the harbor. Julie had been on board a couple of times, but she preferred not to be. She was prone to seasickness, even when the boat was in calm harbor waters. She was supposed to have had a bunk on the ship, but when Eileen had understood how impossible it would have been for her to care for the children when she couldn't even care for herself, she had found a place for her in town.

Julie didn't know anyone on land. Anyone she knew from the church was on the ship most of the day, so she was isolated and lonely, despite the constant company of the five children. She had been teaching history today, at least to the ones old enough to understand what she said. She tended to teach to Gary, Carrie, and Grace while bouncing either Chris or Angela on her knee. She loved teaching history and art to the kids. English and math, not so much. But she did her best.

After much coddling, cajoling, and cursing (silent, of course), Julie got all the kids settled down. The two youngest had cried themselves into a stupor, but were now sleeping. Julie told the tale of "The Little Mermaid" to the older kids, who were now rapt in fascination at her story. She had always loved the Hans Christian Andersen tales. They were useful now she was a nanny.

Grace had fallen asleep about halfway through the tale, one hand entangled in her baby-fine, straight hair. Carrie was nodding off as well near the end, but Gary's blue eyes were wide and he was bright-eyed and bushy-tailed, not in the least interested in sleep. She got him a snack, since supper had been several hours before, opening her book to read while he ate. She hadn't been able to draw much on this trip, as any time she brought out her pad and pencil, the children decided it was craft time, wanting to scribble all over her expensive art paper. She kept them well hidden after the first time, contenting herself with reading in her precious spare moments.

Julie had the book open on her lap—a book on elementary mathematics, to help her giving lessons—but she stared at it without reading anything on the pages. Why did Paul need to return so quickly? It wasn't fair. They had gotten on well, even finishing each other's sentences. He was charming, attractive, a musician, and interested in her. Ah well, it was what it was. Perhaps having a partner wasn't all that it was cracked up to be. She had seen enough of broken partnerships with Eileen and Percy. Both were already married when they got together, and they fought a lot, often in her hearing, about their ex-spouses. She didn't want to be part of that horrible mess.

Julie had never considered herself to be particularly righteous, but she had grown up in a middle-class family in the Midwest—her values were on the conservative side of today's mores, but she still didn't think it would be right to break up a marriage.

She applied herself to the book with determination, but it didn't last long. Mathematics was not her strong point. Her Geometry teacher had made her promise not to take any higher math classes when he had passed her. He told her she should have failed, but as long as she wasn't going to use it in the future, he was reconciled in letting her go on. And here she was, trying to teach young children in the evils of math. At least the basic stuff was pretty easy. She had no idea how she was going to deal with teaching fractions and percentages when they got to that point.

The doorknob rattled with a key. Eileen must be coming by for her evening visit. They seemed to come by less and less lately. Julie often had her weekends free, while Eileen and Percy took the children to go sightseeing around the town and beach, but during the week she didn't see any adult but Eileen. They kept the pantry well-supplied with food for her and the children, so she wasn't complaining, but the constant conversations with toddlers and young children were leaving her starved for intelligent conversation.

"I'm afraid only Gary is awake any longer, Eileen. The rest of the kids went to sleep about an hour ago." Julie kept her voice quiet, not getting up from her chair as Eileen came in, impeccably dressed as always in a robin's egg blue polyester pantsuit.

Gary came in from the kitchen at the sound, with jelly from his sandwich smeared on one cheek. Julie did get up then, wiping his face for him.

"Hello, my darling. Were you a good boy for Julie today?" Eileen picked up her eldest child at arms-length, almost as if she was picking up a puppy that had been peeing on her shoe. Julie had long since come to the conclusion that Eileen was not the most maternal of mothers, an impression that hadn't improved with their trip to Spain.

"We learned about mermaids today." Gary said, sounding both

interested and sulky at the same time.

Eileen arched her eyebrow at Julie, as if disapproving of such a frivolous subject.

"After supper, I told them the tale of 'The Little Mermaid.' It helped settle them all for the night." She didn't need to justify it, but she was defensive. As if Eileen had ever told them a bedtime story.

"Well, it's fine. A small bit of mythology never hurt anyone, I suppose." Eileen did smile at Julie, but it didn't reach her eyes. "Are you coming down to the ship this Saturday, Julie? There is a big party planned. Percy and I will have the children there, as they have someone to run a nursery during the festivities."

"I'll give it a try, Eileen, but can't promise anything. You know how I am on the water."

"I have a gift for you, I think. It's one of the reasons I came by. There's this new nasal spray my friend Charles swears by. Will you give it a chance? It would be nice for you to get a chance to enjoy yourself."

"Thanks, Eileen, I will," Julie said, thinking that she might have misjudged Eileen, tired and cranky as she was from the kids' behavior. "What time should we be there?" She wasn't looking forward to getting all five children ready and down to the ship by herself.

"Oh, we'll come and help get the kids, Julie, they are too much to transport across the harbor by yourself." Eileen was playing with Gary's hair, fixing strands here and there from their tousled state into relative order.

Julie was a lot more charitable towards Eileen than she had been for the past month.

The party started off slow, but picked up steam as dusk approached. Julie wasn't feeling well, as her stomach was protesting the ship's movement, despite Charles' nasal spray nostrum. She walked outside onto the deck, and breathed deeply of the salty ocean air.

Standing near the rail, Julie watched in wonder as the sun set low on the sparkling sea. She watched it touch the water, sending sparks of crimson and orange across the glittering surface of the ocean.

She sensed someone standing next to her, and turned slightly to see a tall, attractive black man with white-tipped sideburns. He was watching the ocean as well, enraptured by the beauty.

When the sun finally dipped below the water line, and the sky was alight with painted clouds, the man turned to her, inclined his head, and walked away, still silent.

She didn't know who her mystery man was, but she was glad to have shared this moment of grace and beauty with him.

*****

Julie swallowed again, hoping to settle her stomach. While the nasal spray did help take the edge off, she was far from happy about being on the sea. The waters were calm, but she still suffered. It was as if the former ferry ship was being lashed by a furious sea, tossed like a piece of flotsam before the storm.

Images like this were not helping. She visualized a calm, sandy beach she had visited in Michigan. Gentle waves lapped at her feet in her mind's eye. Seagulls screeched and argued, the sweet, solid sand beneath her helping her anchor her soul. She took several slow, deep breaths of the salty air, opening her eyes again.

It seemed to help.

They were en route back to England. While she was glad to be returning to a place she had more social freedom, she was not glad of the method of conveyance. However, fate was tossing her about, not unlike the sea was now, so she had less control over her situation. Not that she couldn't leave, of course, she wasn't a prisoner. But where would she go? She had saved up a decent amount of money, but she spoke little Spanish. Jumping ship now would be silly.

No, much better than to ride it out and get back to England. Perhaps Katy would have moved there by then to be with her fiancé. She hadn't heard from her, but it had only been a month. Her sister might not have been able to get a letter back in time to the apartment in Spain, after her last one. Maybe there'd be a letter waiting for her in England?

Wouldn't it be a blast, sharing a place with Katy in England? Well, with her and her husband, of course. Hmmm, perhaps not—she didn't relish being the odd woman out. She hadn't lived with couples before, but she had seen others do so. It often created resentment all around. Lack of privacy, lack of social niceties, and all that mess. She disliked messes, particularly if she was in the middle of it.

Julie's stomach rumbled and roiled again. She swallowed several times until she had her guts back under control, at least for the moment. Calm, blue ocean. Safe, sandy beach.

Would any of her new friends still be in East Grinstead? Sheila, Paul, David, Priya, Colum? She hadn't inquired about their plans when she made ready to ship out with Eileen. There was so much to do, helping to get five children ready for plane travel. It seemed like a blurred memory of chaos. She quailed at the thought of having to make a whole new set of friends. Not that she had gotten to be bosom buddies with anyone yet, but at least she had a baseline friendship with a few of them. Starting all over again was too much chaos.

Chaos, no, let's not think of chaos. Calm, blue ocean. She considered painting the calm, blue ocean, with bits of cerulean and indigo, streaks of white and turquoise on her brush. Smooth, calm, straight lines. A beach of sienna, cream and white and a thin edge of foam between the two.

At least it would be good to be able to socialize with people who spoke English again. She wished she had facility of language, but the basics of Spanish were all she could retain—hello, how are you, goodbye, thank you, you're welcome. That's about it. Even then, the Valencians had a different accent than she had learned in school. Her teacher had been Mexican, so many of the letters were different in pronunciation.

She saw land in the distance. Were they at Portsmouth already? She sighed in relief that the voyage would be over shortly.

Disembarking was chaos. There were people and porters milling around both on the ship and on the dock, and no one seemed to know what went where. She caught a glimpse of her erstwhile companion of the party, the man who shared the glory of the setting sun with her, but in a flash, he was gone. Then she heard Gary's plaintive wail, and focused on the children.

2 – DANCING PARTNERS

1967, East Grinstead, England

Julie took the hands of the people sitting on either side of her at the large, round table in the center of the ballroom. The single candle in the center of the table flickered with a stray breeze, while the medium moaned low and tuneless, ululating in a slow, primal chant. They were attempting to contact the ghost of the young girl Sheila had told her about. One of the teachers, Imelda, claimed to be a sensitive, so got a group together to hold a séance. Imelda was dressed for the part, with a long, flowing gown and several shawls draped upon her ample frame. She had on heavy make-up and jangling jewelry, as well as a dot painted between her eyes, like Priya had. She had gathered a group of ten people, including Julie, Paul, Sheila, and David.

The room had always had its cold spots, but a strong frisson traveled up Julie's spine as Imelda's voice increased in intensity. It was as if the sound was being injected into her bones. The candle flickered as Imelda began to chant words in a language Julie didn't understand, but sounded familiar. She could almost recognize a few words, but they danced outside understanding, as if taunting her with their meaning. Then the words morphed into English, accented with Imelda's exotic Caribbean lilt.

"Are you here? Can you hear us? Give us a sign of your presence."

The candle went out. It wasn't blown out by a breeze, but it was as if someone had snuffed it with invisible fingers. They were doused in darkness, the frisson returning with a vengeance. Julie fancied the fingers which snuffed the candle were now touching her spine with the ice of the otherworld.

"How can we help you? How can we ease your suffering?"

There was another moaning, but it wasn't Imelda's. It started while she was still asking questions. Imelda fell silent, and Julie heard someone gasp, perhaps Sheila next to her. Perhaps it was herself. The voice was higher, younger than Imelda's. It began almost sobbing, keening, as if someone was in great, constant pain.

There was a breeze now. No, more than a breeze—it was more like wind. It was cold, icy, as it was tugging at her clothing. Julie had an almost uncontrollable urge to let go of her hands and yank her clothes away from the questing hands of icy wind. However, her neighbors held her hands firm.

A loud bang, a flash of bright light, then the double doors to the hallway were flung wide. Eileen and Percy stood in the doorway, lights flooding in like the morning tide.

"What in the nine levels of Hell is going on in here?" Eileen's no-nonsense voice was sharp and commanding, while Julie shrank into her seat so she wouldn't be noticed.

The glare blinded Julie after the darkness of the room. She blinked and dropped her hands from the iron grips of her neighbors. She felt foolish, but still had no way of explaining the things she had witnessed.

"Imelda, are you up to your old tricks again? You never get tired of scaring these poor children with your theatrics, do you?"

Startled, Julie looked at Imelda's face, seeing the truth of it in her eyes, as well as the sheepish smile, before she got her features under control. With dignity, Imelda gathered her shawls about herself and flounced out of the room. The rest of the students milled about before shuffling out, chagrined at being fooled, unwilling to discuss the event among themselves. They retreated —and knew it for a retreat—to their respective rooms.

Later, at dinner, she glanced at Sheila and David as they ate. They looked back at her, with sheepish grins. Smiling back, she had been fooled by the tricks along with the others. How had Imelda done it? A recording, a fan, and a trick candle, were all reasonable explanations. She wondered if Imelda had planted the tales she had heard to give verisimilitude to her performances, sort of a hazing for new members.

Paul was sitting on her other side, noticing the glances. He cleared his throat, stood, holding his cup of lemonade up in a toast. "When you toast to a ghost, you lift your spirits." It all seemed silly. A show, a circus, put on for fun, sort of like a hall of mirrors. The table erupted into nervous laughter, and the conversations flowed.

Then again, Imelda hadn't been in the tunnel when she had first experienced the ghostly caress. And Julie had not yet heard any of the tales at that point. The frisson returned, her steak and kidney pie turned into a congealed mass in the pit of her stomach.

*****

About a week later, Julie was helping set up the same ballroom for a party. She was on a tall ladder, trying to secure bunting to the marble mantelpiece, when her balance shifted, as her perch became more precarious. She shifted, trying to get a better angle, to keep from toppling down onto the hardwood floor. The floor seemed far down indeed, when the ladder stopped wobbling. She looked down, seeing Paul securing it for her.

"Would you like help? Unless you are planning on doing diving practice, that is—it looked like you were doing fine."

"I would appreciate help, yes. If you could hold the ladder I can finish this in a second," she replied primly, embarrassed he had witnessed her clumsiness. She completed her task. More gingerly than necessary, she made her way back down the metal ladder.

"So, how do you organize a space party?" Julie looked down at Paul's face, realizing he must be setting her up for a horrible joke. With a long-suffering sigh, she replied in the expected manner.

"I don't know, Paul, how do you organize for a space party?"

"You planet, of course."

"Ugh." Julie had perfected a look of long-suffering resignation where Paul's puns were concerned. "Were you serious about helping me? We've got loads to do yet. An extra pair of hands would not go amiss. You owe me for that pun, if nothing else." Without waiting for acquiescence, she handed him a bag of bunting. "These are to go all around the room, starting where I finished. If you can do this, I can remove the rugs and placing chairs."

"Rescue a damsel in distress, get pressed into menial labor. I see how it works. I'll collect the reward for my gallantry later, then?" His smile was sweet, but sly.

"Perhaps, if you do a good enough job with the bunting. But I reserve the right to demand further payment." She wasn't about to let him extract a promise from her, but he was intriguing. Julie didn't know what to make of Paul. Evidently he had arranged to stay longer than he had originally planned. He had been flirting with her with abandon ever since she returned from Valencia, and he was good at it. He was charming on demand, full of laughter, puns and exaggerated gallantry. He also had sparkling brown eyes which reflected his laughter, as well as an expressive singing voice. As a matter of fact, he flirted with many of the young ladies, and not a few of the older ones. It didn't mean anything except he loved flirting, though she had glimpsed him stealing a kiss from Isabella at one point. He was intelligent, with a keen sense of humor, though his penchant for puns was sometimes horrible. But she had walked in on him one time while he was in a deep embrace and kiss with a girl she didn't know a couple days ago. She had seen him touch people a lot, hands on shoulders, holding hands, pats on the head, but this had been more than a friendly pat. She then realized how much she had been paying attention at his actions.

She rolled up the rugs, being careful to bend with her knees, as her ample backside, bent over, wasn't the sight she wished to present to Paul. As she struggled to carry the heavy Persian rugs into the storage closet, she pondered that attempt, as well.

She liked Paul, but he wasn't the only young man who entertained her. There was Colum, who was broody, but his freckles danced when she did manage to coax a smile from him. Colum was more wont to spend his evenings with a book and a tumbler of Scotch than to socialize, dance, or even kiss. He was an old school, old world man. They had enjoyed a couple evenings in quiet conversation now and then. They had talked about history and social issues, but he was obsessed with a particular aspect of history which she knew nothing about—the Jacobite Wars—and she was out of her depth whenever he steered the conversation to this era. She didn't care for feeling uneducated or ignorant, but she didn't have any interest in battle history, so she would excuse herself after the subject was broached.

Then there was Terry Holker, a Londoner who had arrived a couple days ago. He was solemn as well, but not a history buff. He loved art as she did, so they had discussed several of the Impressionist artists, as well as the Surrealists. He was slim and not much taller than she was, slight and bookish. His blond, wispy hair always seemed to have been blown into a mess by the wind, even indoors. The poor thing had a terrible squint, despite his thick glasses. He seemed to lack, however, any vestige of a sense of humor. Any attempt at a joke or silliness was met with a slow, owl-like blink of incomprehension, followed by a literal, staid response. She wasn't sure she could enjoy the company of someone who didn't laugh.

And there was her mystery man, the one she had glimpsed at Portsmouth. Had he made it here to Saint Hill? She hadn't noticed him, but perhaps he was living off-campus.

Paul made her laugh. He was gallant, silly, fun, intelligent, and handsome. He was a wonderful musician, which had always been her weakness. But he didn't seem to be the sort to settle down. Did she need someone who would settle down? Or was she willing to enjoy a fling?

Julie never believed herself prudish. Though she hadn't considered it that way, she was part of a generation which ignored, shattered, redefined sexual and societal roles. She was part of the sexual revolution. She was also finally daring enough to move halfway across the world, away from her comfortable home and family in Michigan.

She had also never been someone who jumped without looking. The move to England had been scary enough. How could she risk her heart as well? And Paul seemed like he was a little too rootless to comfort her.

But Paul made her laugh.

*****

1978, Dearborn, Michigan

Life was pretty fun, Kirsten thought. She finally cleaned her room, and her mom wasn't yelling at her. Grandpa wasn't yelling at her, and grandma was teaching her how to play Gin Rummy on Saturday.

Then, her world—as she knew it —turned upside down.

Julie walked in the room, "Have I told you yet, I'll be going down to Miami next month?"

"Nope - are we going to Disneyworld again?"

"Not exactly … I am going down to rent a house."

"Why?"

"Well, because we're moving down to Miami in a couple months. I need to set up the move for Aunt Sandy, you and me. It will be an adventure! We'll live near Uncle George and Uncle Jack. You remember them, right? We stayed at their house the last time we were down."

"But why do we have to move? I like my friends here."

"Well, Hon, there are many reasons. Uncle Jack has a job for me down there. Also, it's much warmer. No more cold winters, which will help your bronchitis. Wouldn't it be nice to not be sick every winter?"

"Can I bring Judy?"

"She might be able to visit, but no, you can't bring your best friend. I don't think her mom would like it."

"Then, I'm not going."

"Yes, dear, you must. We have lots of plans. I'm hoping to have you down there in November."

"I can stay here with Grandma and Grandpa."

"No, dear, you must come to Miami with me ... don't worry, you'll love it."

"I won't!" Kirsten was immovable when she set her mind upon a task.

"Give it a chance, okay? You might be surprised at how well you like it."

Kirsten pouted, while Julie left the room, reluctant. Kirsten tended to pout when she was thwarted, as this always gained her rewards with both her mom and grandma. Grandpa seemed immune, though. He always required other tactics.

The next day, Kirsten was complaining about the plans to her friend, Troy, in their third grade class. He was impressed.

"Can I take your place? I'll even put on a dress."

"Sure. Mom won't even notice, as I'm flying down on my own. She'll already be there. By the time she realizes it's not me, it'll be too late." It wouldn't work, but it was helping her to think about it.

"I could come down in your luggage?"

"That doesn't keep me here, though. "

"Yeah, I forgot. Why don't you want to go? There are beaches and palm trees."

"But all my friends are here …"

"You'll make new ones."

"They're all rich kids, tanned and going to the beach all the time."

Her neighbor, Sharon, went on vacation every Christmas to Fort Lauderdale. She always came back tanned. She was a few years older than Kirsten, and always acted snobby, literally looking down her nose at her. Of course, part of it could be that she was four inches taller, but still.

Kirsten's friend, Darryl, was on board with the idea. He was shorter than Troy, he said, so he could fit into her luggage, while Troy carried it. Oh, how she wished this would work.

If she had a father, maybe he could fix it.

*****

1967, East Grinstead, England

The party was well under way now, with several rooms of the Saint Hill mansion filled with people talking, drinking, or circulating. Julie was in what was known as The Monkey Room, named for the enormous mural on one wall, showing monkeys in various occupations. There were monkeys on a carousel, monkeys cavorting as part of a circus, feathers in their hats, monkeys swinging from what looked like a giant maypole, dangling on various ribbons in a wide circle. The big monkey above the doorway was presiding over two enormous cornucopias, filled with fruits, a huge feather sprouting out of his conical hat. It's not tasteful, but it's an excellent conversation piece.

This was what she was using it as now, in a somber discussion with Terry about the various activities of the simian subjects.

"From what I understand, the artist, a John Spencer-Churchill, was commissioned to paint this … piece … by Mrs. Drexel Biddle. Spencer-Churchill was a nephew of Sir Winston Churchill. I would think such an illustrious ancestry would have given him a penchant for dignity, but this is not the case." He took a moment to take a sip from his whisky tumbler, pushing his glasses back up his nose.

"One's ancestry does not define one's taste, surely?" Julie was trying to tease Terry, knowing it was in vain.

"One's pride in ancestry should inspire one to bridle their unseemly passions, at least in public." Terry said this primly, though he did smile. Julie fancied his smile was more in his own pride at bridling any unseemly passions he might have had. She wondered if there was a story there. She tried hard to imagine what those passions might be, but her imagination failed her.

"And what of your own ancestry, is there anything there to inspire you?" She immediately regretted the question. She had forgotten the English (and indeed, Scottish and Irish) tendency to recount their entire genealogy given half a chance.

As she sipped her wine, she listened with only a bit of attention as Terry proceeded to recount several of his more notable ancestors, or at least those he considered notable. She would have preferred to hear of the notorious ones, perhaps a woman burned for witchcraft, or the proverbial horse thief in everyone's history. The constant stream of boring Ministers, Civil Servants, and Permanent Under-Secretaries were putting her to sleep. She looked about the room, seeing Sheila. She concocted an escape from the tedium of her own creation.

"Terry, I see Sheila there, and I do need to ask her about one of my upcoming projects. Would you be so kind as to excuse me?" Severe politeness was the best tool to stopping an Englishman's drone.

"Certainly, of course, please. We can resume again later."

Not if I can help it, buddy.

She escaped to the cluster of people around Sheila. Priya and Imelda were there, as well as two tall men, whom Julie didn't know. Wait a moment, wasn't that her Sunset Man? She was sure it was, but didn't want to appear too keen, so simply nodded politely to them both.

Priya was once again dressed in one of her beautiful, vibrant saris, this one in a deep, emerald green with silver details. Imelda had eschewed her theatrical trappings of the other night for a riotous colorful kaftan with a tribal design, reminiscent of African prints. Sheila was in a short black dress and pearls, seeming so conservative next to the colorful plumage of her companions. The two men—introduced as Jimmy Cranston and Roger Hubble—were in their forties. Both were dressed in casual office garb. Jimmy, who was from Las Vegas, had dirty blond hair, pulled back into a long, straight ponytail. His long, saturnine face cracked into a smile, with twinkling blue eyes. Roger, her Sunset Man, was black of eye, skin and hair, and smiled even wider, if that was possible. He had a hint of white at the sideburns, was tall and thin, and was from Atlanta. She didn't think she detected any recognition of her in his eyes.

Other than Paul, Eileen, and the kids, there weren't so many Americans in Saint Hill, so Julie was glad of a chance to discuss her home country with those who didn't think it was merely three hundred miles wide.

After a while, she looked up at strange sounds nearby, seeing the stage being cleared. They were preparing for musicians. She wondered if Paul would be one of them. The fact he was rootless shouldn't keep her from enjoying his music, right?

Roger had asked her a question. The group was watching her, waiting for a response.

"I'm sorry, Roger, I was miles away. What did you ask?" Julie hoped her smile would take out any sting from the evident disinterest.

"I was asking how long you'd been here in England."

"Well, I got here in March, so about three months. But I was in Valencia for several weeks, while Eileen was taking courses there." She swallowed to keep the idea of the ship from affecting her stomach.

"Ah, that's where I've seen you! You were on the ship, we watched the sun set together." Roger had a dreamy look on his face.

"Yes, that was me!" She was grinning like a loon, but couldn't help it. "I didn't get a whole lot of time to explore Spain while I was there. I was in charge of their five kids most of the time. It was a tiny center of chaos in the universe. When I did get to the beaches, though, it was paradise."

"I can imagine. I was the oldest of seven, so I had to take care of the whole mob. It taught me a lot about control and the value of instilling fear in others." His bright smile took away the hint of literal interpretation.

"A real terror, were you? Daily beatings and weekly lashings?" She arched her eyebrows in inquiry.

"Absolutely! I had the cat o' nine tails' on my belt at all times." He mimicked a whipping motion with his hand, clicking his tongue. His smile was broad, showing brilliant white, straight teeth.

His eyes were beautiful, liquid and dark. And they showed his smile with laugh lines. He may have been older, but he had a young heart with a brilliant smile.

The musicians were playing an energetic tune. Julie turned around, almost rudely, to see if Paul was there. He was not. Sheepish, she turned back around.

"So, who were you hoping to see?" Jimmy asked her. His voice was teasing.

"I thought my friend, Paul, might be on set tonight." She tried to emphasize the word "friend" without being obvious about it. She failed.

"Oh, your friend, is it. I'd like to have more friends like that. Have you a soft spot for musicians? Roger, here, plays the saxophone, you know." Jimmy jabbed his friend in the ribs with his elbow.

She looked at Roger with renewed interest. "Do you? What sort of music do you like to play?"

"Jazz, mostly. I love the smooth sound. I play with a band a few nights back at home." He grinned again, perhaps at her obvious interest.

"So, you beat young children and play radical music. A real rebel, you are."

"I am. Care to dance with a rebel?" He offered his hand with a flourish.

"I would be delighted." She took it and they headed out to the large dance floor, where several couples had already begun to dance.

Roger was a much better dancer than she was, she decided. Though she loved music in most any form, enjoyed listening to it, and on occasion, singing it, she had little talent for dancing to it. She enjoyed moving to the music, but she didn't have the talent or balance for complex choreographed movements. She was glad the formal dance styles were giving way to looser forms, so she didn't have to memorize steps. He was gentle with her, leading her around but not pushing or shoving. He had nice, warm hands.

The song ended too soon, as the players went on to a slower tune, "A Summer Place." She began to walk back to the group, but Roger kept a firm hand on her waist, taking her hand in his. They pressed closer.

She enjoyed the slow rhythm of the dance, almost transported to another time, another place. A memory of dancing with Jeffrey at a club in DC flashed through her mind, and she pushed it away. She brought herself back to the present with an effort. She didn't want to color her impression of Roger with what Jeffrey did. This was a British mansion and a Church-sponsored party, after all, despite being odder than any other Church she had been part of.

"A Summer Place" ended. Roger stopped as she looked into his dark eyes, locked for a moment before he led her back to the group.

"I can't monopolize you, but I'd like another dance later, if it's okay with you?" He adopted the attitude of a poor, starving orphan asking for more food.

"Of course it's alright. You're a dreamy dancer."

"Must be my musician's rhythm, I guess. I've always been at home on the dance floor. I can tap dance, too." He did a shuffle-step-toe on the wooden floor, with a flourish of his arms when he was done.

"Multitalented, you are. Is there anything you can't do?"

Jimmy jumped in with a resounding "No, he's Mr. Perfect." Julie wasn't sure if it was out of envy or loyalty for his friend.

Roger gave Jimmy a sour look for his praise. "I can't draw a straight line with a ruler. And I'm pretty terrible at any sort of math." His rueful laugh was self-deprecating. "I hear you're an artist, though, is this true?"

"It is—I do artwork for our advertisements here, posters, flyers, that sort of thing." She remembered she had a project she needed to finish the next day. She hadn't gotten back to it after decorating today, as she had intended. Instead, she had rushed back to her room and changed her outfit several times until she had found a look which would do for the evening's festivities. It wasn't anything fancy or colorful, like Priya's costume, but it was comfortable and slimming. She had chosen an A-line dress with subtle vertical stripes in rust and burnt orange tones. She wore an orange coral necklace with a matching set of clip-on earrings. Those had been a gift from her mother.

"What about your own work? Is it anywhere I could see it?"

Julie laughed, "Oh, no, I haven't got a gallery or anything. I do stuff for myself, for the most part. I used to do craft fairs back in Michigan, while I was still in college, but I've no head for business. I'm sure I lost money doing it—"

"Perhaps you need a good manager, then? Or an agent?"

"Wouldn't it need to be someone good at math? I thought you said math wasn't your strong point?" Julie asked, one eyebrow arched.

Jimmy interjected, "I'm good at math," but his efforts elicited no attention.

"Well, I wasn't applying for the job, if that's what you're asking." Roger said at the same time. "It might be a logical step if you wanted to pursue your art."

"I'm happy doing it on the side, drawing for my own pleasure. I like doing stuff for myself. Once you cater to your audience, you aren't creating art—you're creating product. It loses some of its soul, in my opinion."

Roger didn't answer, but looked thoughtful. He stayed silent. Had she offended him? Was he thinking of his own music?

"Did I ... I mean, I didn't ... do you ... do you write your own music?" She sounded like a blathering idiot now.

"I do. And most of it is well-received when I play it. But I have to perform covers of well-known stuff in order to get my audience interested in new stuff, I suppose. I was thinking about if I was 'selling out', but I think I'm safe. I don't change my music if it doesn't get a good reaction. I composed it for myself. I play it for others to share the joy. If they can't share it, too bad for them. I still have the joy of playing it."

Julie smiled. "Exactly. It's how I draw and paint. It's for me, to enjoy and share with others. If they cannot appreciate it, then it's a failing in them, not in my work."

"Yes, you understand, you really do. I think most true artists realize this, whether they try to show their work commercially or not."

"Your music is appreciated, Roger. Didn't you tell me you got a call from that record label before you left Atlanta?" Jimmy got into the conversation again.

"It wasn't a real record label, Jimmy. It was a guy who wanted me to finance his record label. He wanted me to help him buy the recording equipment and everything. He had serious balls."

"Come out to Vegas—I'm sure you could find endless venues out there to play. You should see the crap they've got at the supper clubs. I mean, a few of the places are classy, like the ones the Rat Pack perform for, but the dives have terrible 'talent'. Most of them aren't acts like Wayne Newton or Siegfried and Roy—most of them are sad sacks with an old guitar and broken pipes, playing for scraps."

"And you want me to go out and perform my crap for scraps, then?" Roger inquired with sweet irony.

"No, no, you'd get more than scraps. You could have a career out there."

"I think I'll stick to Atlanta. It's my home. I know the people. I know the vibe."

"Are you here in England long, then?" Julie decided she liked Roger well enough to think of future dates.

"A couple weeks, I'm afraid. I was here for a missionary course."

"Oh, I see." Julie hid her disappointment. Why can't the attractive guys with intelligence and humor stay here? Well, the single ones, at any rate.

The group stayed and chatted for a long time, with Roger claiming his promised dance from Julie before the end of the evening. She was exhausted by the time she made it to the sanctuary of her room, collapsing into bed. Her mind wouldn't allow her to sleep, though. She kept thinking about Paul and Roger. If she could only combine the two. Meld the best of both and create one super-guy she would be pleased to be with. She sighed with yearning, drifting into oblivion.

*****

Julie was able to spend more time with Roger the next evening, chatting with him. Jimmy, Priya and Sheila were in the library.

Priya was asking Roger about his family in Atlanta, while Jimmy was trying to impress Sheila with magic tricks he had learned. Julie sipped her tea and watched all four in amusement.

"Have your brothers and sisters all got families of their own then, Roger?" Sheila interjected, uninterested in Jimmy's poor attempts at prestidigitation.

"Most of them, yes. But the two youngest aren't married. I guess I'm a disappointment to our mother, as I never married. I'm the wastrel of the family, the bad example."

"Just because you haven't married yet doesn't mean you never will, Roger. My brother, Tariq, was engaged last month, and he's forty-five. You never know when true love will step into your life. Everything comes in its own time."

"You're assuming I want to get married, though. Why buy the cow when the milk is free?"

Julie almost choked on her tea. She spluttered and coughed until Jimmy pounded her on the back. She waved him off. She had heard the phrase before, but never in mixed company like this. Her conservative upbringing was showing.

"You object, Oh Artistic One? Didn't you live in DC and Detroit before you came here? Surely you saw all sorts of unconventional pairings?" Roger had a smug smile on his face.

"I did, certainly. You caught me by surprise with the, um … phrasing." Her face was growing hot and red, radiating her own chagrin and embarrassment. She busied herself with mopping up the droplets of tea she managed to get on her slacks.

"So, mere words can make you choke? I didn't realize you were such a delicate flower," Jimmy teased.

"'Delicate', right. I grew up in Detroit. Few things remain delicate in Detroit, my friend." She straightened her spine to appear tough and street-smart, but knew she failed.

"Tough girl, sure, I can see it." The look on Roger's face showed he couldn't see this at all. Julie looked down at her brown corduroy slacks and deep brown button-down shirt with beige scarf, realizing she wasn't exactly the image of a street girl. She shrugged with one shoulder, indicating her defeat in the battle. She didn't know why she had attempted the image in the first place. Roger seemed to excel in needling her. She always had to rise to his bait.

"Do you want to move back sometime?" Jimmy's question brought her back to the conversation.

"Me? Someday, perhaps. I do miss my parents, my sister, my friends, even my little brother. But Detroit is a stark place. Not supportive of the arts, you know. It's a depressing place, really."

"That's the best place for art, I've found," Roger said.

"How so?" Sheila asked.

"Not only is it the sort of place which needs art the most, it evokes the best art. Art should comfort the disturbed and disturb the comfortable. I don't remember where I heard it, but I believe it to be true. A depressed area—like an inner city, or a depression-style farm—needs art to have hope, see beauty."

"Things which are crumbling have the most beauty." Julie said, repeating a phrase she had come across when she was in college.

"Exactly! The new stuff, it all looks the same, no character. It could be pretty, but pretty isn't necessarily art. It's the wrinkled, lined faces of the elderly who show true character, the crumbling blocks of a ruined building which shows how time has defaced it."

"I seem to remember reading about a Japanese tradition called Kintsugi. They repair broken object so the break was obvious, part of the structure. Like broken pottery repaired with gold in the cracks, so it showed." She had seen pictures of this tradition somewhere, but couldn't remember the circumstances. Perhaps her Art Appreciation classes?

"We believe It to be true in India," Priya said, "the older a statue or temple is, the more crumbling it is, we believe it crumbles because it holds the beliefs and magic of many generations. It is therefore more beautiful."

"I like the concept," Julie said. "But most of the holy places in India I've seen pictures of have been well maintained?"

"Yes, maintenance of such sites is a duty and an honor. However, there is a certain subsidence which defies maintenance. This is when we say it has crumbled from the weight of magic."

"How beautifully poetic." Julie was enchanted. She considered the abandoned buildings she had seen in England and Spain with that idea. She wanted to draw, as the idea was inspiring her. She had taken to keeping a pad and pencil with her at all times, so she took it out now and sketched out what she remembered of a ruined Moorish palace she had seen in Spain.

Priya and Roger got into a further conversation about ancient religious beliefs, comparing Indian concepts with those of Mediterranean beliefs which were part of his ancestor's history.

"Whatcha drawing?" Julie was surprised by Jimmy's enthusiastic voice over her shoulder.

"A palace I remembered from Spain."

She worked on the perspective lines of the rambling, squared blocks of Sagunto Castle, a ruin she had visited on one open weekend. It sprawled over the top of a hill, crumbling walls radiating out like clumsy spider legs. The main keep was blocky and strong, like most of the Spanish castles, bits of crenellated wall peeking up here and there among the lush foliage. She added textures to corners, rough stone and dressed masonry here, there, a tease, a sketch, with economy of line. She stopped and surveyed her efforts, looking up to find the whole group around her, fascinated.

"It's amazing, Julie. I'd never watched you draw before. Did you create this from your imagination?" Sheila's eyes and smile were wide, showing a missing eyetooth.

"Oh, no, this is a place I visited when I was in Spain. A castle on a hill there, all ruined and crumbling. The discussion brought it to mind. I guess it needed to escape."

"You certainly captured the essence of it. Is this Sagunto? I've been there before. It's a dry, dusty place, but beautiful all the same. May I?"

Priya moved to pick up the pad of paper to turn it around so she could see it better.

Julie was self-conscious whenever others critiqued her work. It was a process she had never gotten comfortable with in art school. She wondered whether any artist did. Perhaps it's why she never wanted to become a professional fine artist, as her work would be always subjected to such critique. With layout work, it merely needed to fit particular parameters.

"This really looks great. And you did it so fast. Simply fantastic." Even Jimmy was impressed.

"Thank you. It's only a sketch, really. I might use it to create a painting, though I'd much rather have done the painting while I was there. That way I could see the place for reference."

"Can you use photographs as reference?"

"Sure, but only if they are in a similar angle or perspective."

"I have several from my stay there. You are welcome to use them if they will help." Priya then handed her the drawing, while Julie closed the pad over the drawing. Why was it so hard for her to take compliments on her artwork? It had always been this way. Her mother had praised her work all the time, never critical, offering honest critiques to improve. Perhaps it was her father's disinterest in her efforts that made them forever inadequate. Or her sister Katy's skill, though she wasn't envious, simply appreciative.

"Thank you, Priya. That's kind of you. When were you in Spain?" Julie was glad of the opportunity to shift attention from her work. Roger hadn't said anything, but he had looked with admiration on her efforts. This bit of affirmation had made her prouder about her work, perhaps gave her more confidence in her own talents.

*****

Julie and Roger made the most of the little time they had to get to know each other, though it wasn't easy. Her schedule was particularly busy, and she chaffed at the wasted opportunities. Still, they managed to carve out time each evening to walk through the village, have a meal together, and gaze up at the stars.

"Ancient man believed the stars to be the hearth fires of those who had died before them. They were lit to welcome the new dead to the heavens." Roger was full of interesting facts about history and archeology.

"What a delightful concept. Certainly more romantic than flaming balls of gas dancing around each other in the void of infinite space."

"It depends on what you consider romantic, doesn't it?" His hand was soft against her cheek, and she closed her eyes at the tender caress. Their relationship had, out of necessity, moved quickly for her Midwestern tastes, but she didn't care. It was whirlwind and steamy, and it had built-in tragedy. Everything a romantic tale needed.

He turned to kiss her then, under the twinkling velvet sky. It was a slow, sweet, savoring kiss, full of promise and a hint of desperation.

The next day was an idyllic day, really. The sun was warm, and soft, fluffy white clouds scudded across the sky. Julie and Roger had managed time to escape for another picnic. He didn't have his saxophone with him in England, but he could sing, so he serenaded her with smooth, soft folk songs. She sketched him as he sang. She made sure to capture the soulful eyes, and the very soft, kissable lips.

"Can I see?"

She reluctantly handed it over to him for inspection. It wasn't her best work. She preferred working in paints, with full color, but the sketch was passable. The eyes worked well, at least, and she caught his hint of smile. It promised so much.

She was very glad they had chosen a secluded spot.

*****

Roger left the next day. They had at least gotten a few moments in which to say goodbye in private. She had only known him a few days, but they were an intense few days. She was comfortable around him, as if she could talk about anything with him. Their parting didn't have much talking, though. It was silence, holding hands, looking at each other. They bent their heads so their foreheads touched.

"Maybe I'll be back this way again, Julie. Or maybe you could come down to Atlanta some time." He reached up and touched the line of her jaw with his finger, warm silk on her skin.

"Perhaps. I don't know when, though. Sometimes I am like so much flotsam on the Jet Stream, being tossed around on the ocean." She teared up, thinking herself so silly.

"Shhh ... it's alright, sweetling. We'll always be friends. Will you write to me, maybe?"

"I'll do that. I promise."

Then they shared their last, kiss. His lips were soft and lush. He held her chin up with his fingers. And he was gone.

*****

1983, Miami, Florida

My girl is beginning to grow up. She's asking questions I'm not ready

Christy Jackson Nicholas

to answer.

Kirsten was about thirteen now, growing up tall and thin, but her curves were popping out all over the place. While she had never been the most graceful of children, she was even less sure of her movements with this new, strange distorted body she found herself in. Julie remembered the sensation from her own adolescence. Worse, Kirsten was getting curious about her father, thanks to a genealogy project assigned in her class.

"But Mom, I don't understand, you don't even know how old he was?"

"No, dear, we didn't discuss it much. We sort of avoided many subjects of his life."

"But you know astrology. Wouldn't you have asked at least his sign?"

"I hadn't gotten into it yet, then. That was later."

"Oh. Do you at least know what he did for a living?"

"Well, at the time, he was teaching machining classes at the Church."

"The Church?"

"The Church I worked for at the time. We both worked there."

"Well, it's something, I suppose. Did he teach other things, perhaps? Maybe it's why I'm good in math?"

"It must be. You didn't get it from me."

"Don't you like math, Mom?"

"No, my Geometry teacher made me promise never to take math again."

"Ha! Seriously? I love math. Well, maybe not Geometry as much, my teacher is a total airhead. She told us when she first got her microwave, she would turn it on with nothing in it to see what happened. But I do love solving math puzzles. It's why I like Games Magazine."

Definitely growing up. She's learning her own place in the world, already heading down a different path than Julie was at this age. All she had wanted to do at that point was watch baseball and paint—and hang out with boys, of course.

"Do you remember how to spell his name? Maybe I can hunt him down?"

"You will not hunt anyone down, young lady. Remember your actions have consequences. Do you want to disrupt someone else's life to satisfy your curiosity? " Julie was horrified at the idea of the child calling her father, and announcing she was his bastard daughter.

"I didn't think of that." She looked so crestfallen, Julie relented, giving her a hug. Lord, she's almost as tall as I am already.

"Well, at least I have plenty on your side to put into the project. I got the packet of information from Meema. Look, it goes back hundreds of years. Did you see? All the way back to the Firestones in Germany in the 1700s. Does that mean we're all German?"

"Not entirely, no. Grandma's maiden name was Firestone, so that was the direct line Meema sent you. Grandpa is English and Scots, I think, I know there's a McKenzie and a Sutcliffe somewhere in there. And Meema herself is Welsh, her maiden name is Rees."

"I remember. How do you know it's Welsh?"

"Rees was originally spelled R-H-Y-S, I saw it somewhere once. Maybe on some paperwork. Did you ever meet my cousin, Peggy? She does a lot of this research now. She has boxes and boxes of stuff."

"I want to write to her, too, so I can get more stuff. This is cool."

Julie smiled, happy to feed her daughter's passion, at least on her own family line. Better that than she delve into the other side.

3 – PINTS AND PHILOSOPHY

1967, East Grinstead, England

"Oh, do stop moping around, Julie. It won't help matters if you don't get out and do things." Sheila was exasperated with her.

Julie had hardly left the room they shared in the days since Roger left, except for taking care of the kids and meal times. Her routine had been to take care of the children in the mornings until about two in the afternoon, when Percy was done with his current seminar. Then she was free to do as she liked, be it take classes, go out and explore, socialize, etc. She had her weekends free, as well as most evenings, though about once a week she took them so Eileen and Percy could go out. She still did artwork for the Church, but it was getting to be less and less. She wasn't pushing her talents, or asking for more work. Others assumed she hadn't as much time for it, so didn't give her new projects.

"I'm not particularly interested in going out and doing anything, Sheila."

"And it's a load of bollocks. Get thee up, woman, go enjoy yourself. That's an order, that is." And with this, Sheila yanked at the blanket upon which Julie was lying down, forcing her to scramble for balance on the single bed.

"Tonight, you are coming with me. There's a gathering in one of the places in town. I shall not take no for an answer. Get your glad rags on by seven for half-seven." With this final decree, Sheila left.

Julie sighed, resigned to Sheila's efforts. Perhaps a night out is what she needed. She missed talking to Roger so much it ached. She still found it hard to credit they had only known each other a couple weeks.

She pulled out a couple of outfits, but none of them appealed to her. Exasperated, she chose one which looked frumpy. It was a midnight blue button down shirt with a sort of jabot ruffle at the neckline. The high collar was positively Victorian. A long, black, swirling skirt would complete her mourning outfit. She did pin her hair back with a couple of barrettes, but then decided to put it into a French braid instead. It would be out of her face, so she wouldn't have to mess with readjusting the barrettes every half hour.

She surveyed herself in the mirror. She did look grim, like she was the matron of a girls' school, out for a rollicking evening at the library, reading a Jane Austen novel. She laughed at the idea. Fine, she'd change her shirt, at least. She found a top with brighter colors, a flowing blouse with orange and pink nouveau swirls on it, sort of satiny. She didn't remember where she had gotten it. Perhaps in San Francisco? She tucked it into her skirt's waistband, deciding it was much better.

When Sheila showed up, she looked her up and down, giving her a grudging nod.

"I was afraid I was going to have to make you change, but you'll do." Sheila had the manner of a sergeant inspecting his troops.

"I figured as much, so I made sure to spare you the effort." She stuck her tongue out at Sheila. They both laughed as they walked, arm in arm, from the dorms down to the village.

They met David, Paul, Colum, and Jimmy on the way down, and one of the townies named Victoria Riches. She was a prim British girl, about Julie's height and perhaps younger. She was pulling her ashy blond hair into a ponytail, revealing a round face, with a buxom figure. She said "hello" shortly, but it wasn't hostile. Julie had learned the Brits tend to sound clipped by nature in comparison to their American counterparts.

"Are you part of the Church here, Victoria?" Julie asked.

"Not in the slightest. I work at Ashdown House School, helping with their accounting. However, I've been up to Saint Hill many times, before all the moon bats moved in. No offense intended." She didn't look as if she cared if Julie took offense or not, but it didn't sound malicious.

Julie shrugged. "It's a church. They're in business of teaching and converting, not making friends."

Paul snorted at this, and even Victoria giggled.

As they walked down the street, with beautiful half-timbered buildings lining either side, they arrived at a pub called The Dorset Arms. They walked in, found a largish table and ordered pints. Julie didn't particular care for beer, but she enjoyed the cider which seemed to be a normal option at British pubs.

They all talked of the village and the history of the place. Victoria mentioned it seemed to be a hotbed of religious focus, as just about every church in the world had made a foundation in the area.

"The hippies seem to think it's a 'ley line' thing. The priests maintain it is a spiritual centre, so the other religious are attracted to it, even if they aren't supposed to benefit. It has always been a place people get drawn to. I suppose the easily credible attract the gullible."

Julie was finding it harder to ignore Victoria's jibes, though they weren't directed at her in particular, but at religious people in general. She also didn't want to get into an argument defending a religion she wasn't invested in. Paul seemed to have no problem with her statements, though.

"After what the damned Catholics put most of the Western World through, I'm surprised anyone of them have an attraction to what it is sacred."

"Well, the Catholics aren't the only idiots to believe in the inscrutable. Certainly not around here. A lot of heartache and money could be saved by burning the lot of them. You sound as if you've a bone to pick with the Catholic Church, Paul. What's the story there?" Victoria stopped to drink her beer and glanced at Paul, requiring an answer of her inquiry.

"I was raised in the Catholic Church, was even in seminary to become a priest myself. I once considered becoming a monk, but was cloisterphobic." He paused, waiting for his audience to groan or laugh. They all groaned. "In all seriousness, as a younger son, it was a perfectly acceptable option, if one follows the medieval tradition. Eventually, I understood most of the church aristocracy was simply in it for the power. They couldn't answer any of my questions about life. It was institutionalism at its worst, which I wanted no part of. Besides, as a priest … well, abstinence leaves a lot to be desired." He gave Julie a long, leering look. Paul hadn't touched his beer until then, but then he smiled at his joke and drank most of it in one long swig.

"And the blokes up on the hill there are any better?" Victoria was incredulous.

"At least some of them still believe in having power over their own destinies, rather than over others. And there is something to be said for practical theology over other philosophies, such as communism or socialism."

Julie got nervous at the mention of communism. It had been thirteen years since the craze of McCarthyism, but she still remembered her parents' stories about those times. She vaguely remembered news reports on television and radio, about neighbors turning in their friends to escape punishment for themselves. It had turned into the worst sort of witch hunt. She shuddered.

Paul was still talking, "It begs the basic questions of life, really. Are we, as humans, obliged to care for our fellow man to the exclusion of our own care? What is the purpose of our own happiness? And that begs even more questions. What is a soul? What is my relationship to my soul? What happens to me when my soul goes elsewhere? I believe basically that I don't *have* a soul, rather I *am* a soul."

"'We are not human beings having a spiritual experience. We are spiritual beings having a human experience'?" Julie quoted.

"Exactly. Have you read de Chardin's works, then?" His smile was wide.

"No, I'm a dilettante. I must have picked the quote up somewhere random." Julie blushed, and Victoria came to her rescue."

"I suppose I could get behind such a concept. I'm done with most organized churches, though. I've been in several of them. I couldn't get past the hypocrisy of any of them, except perhaps Buddhism. They've got decent ideas, and their followers actually tend to pay attention to them." Victoria was almost done with her beer already, standing up to fetch another round.

"That's the angriest Buddhist I've ever seen." Julie opined when she had left.

Paul laughed. "Angry, but honest. I'd wish for more friends like her, really. Sometimes the double-dealing of societal 'manners' are maddening."

"Agreed!" They all toasted this, with the last swigs of their mugs.

When Victoria returned with refreshed pints, the conversation moved on to related topics, such as Sir Arthur Conan Doyle's firm belief in Spiritualism, the ghost stories of the local countryside. Julie avoided giving her account of the abandoned tunnels of Saint Hill, but kept her ears open in case anyone mentioned anything akin to her experience.

After a while, she noticed Paul was no longer among the group. His pint glass was gone, but she hadn't noticed him leave. She had no time to look for him, though, as Jimmy had asked her a question.

"I wouldn't say aliens are impossible. There have been so many rumors and sightings, could all the stories be hoaxes?"

"Where do you think they'd be coming from? What do you think they'd look like?" Sheila wanted to know.

"Aren't most of the recorded sightings of a thin, white body with enormous eyes and no hair? Sightings of actual creatures, not ships, I mean. It could be a Jungian archetype, I suppose. A thousand years ago, we would have termed them Gods rather than Aliens, setting up a shrine in their honor. The ancients, of course, begged them not to destroy our crops with furious vengeance and all that. Maybe they've been visiting for a long time, so the Gods of past civilizations are simply interpretations of those visitations?" Julie shrugged, thinking the theory had merit.

"But ancient Gods aren't tall, thin white creatures with enormous eyes—they are like us, for the most part." Jimmy argued.

"Tell it to the Egyptians, with their jackal-head and falcon-head Gods. Or the Aztecs, or even the Greeks, who's Gods changed shape whenever they liked. Even some of our Gods in Scotland had a non-human appearance. Certainly the Wee Folk could have been tiny aliens. " Colum interjected. "Also, Norse elves were tall and thin, bright—they were what Tolkein used as a guide for his elves."

Julie heard a guitar being tuned. Looking up, she knew where she would find Paul—on stage, fiddling with his guitar strings. He looked up, saw her watching him, giving her a roguish smile. Eyes still on her, he launched into a Kingston Trio song, I Am Henry the Eighth.

Of course, this was a song which had always annoyed her, but was perfect for Paul. She gave him a long-suffering look, which made him smile as he sang the words, in a ridiculous, exaggerated Cockney accent.

He had succeeded in getting most of the pub to join in on the chorus, a few even sang the rest of the verses with him. They were interminable.

At long last, the song was over. He moved on to a more somber tune, Last Night I Had The Strangest Dream. This was a sad anti-war song. Julie's eyes prickled with tears before it was done. World War II may have been done for many years, but she remembered not hearing from her father for a long time when they had all feared he was lost. He hadn't returned from the Japan Sea unscathed. He had contracted malaria, had ringing in his ears, as well as aching joints and back. However, he had come back whole and sane, which is more than many of the soldiers and sailors had done. The Brits had lost even more of their young men, as they had been in the war for years before America had joined the fight.

Paul followed this intense performance with another song designed to wring out the soul—Turn! Turn! Turn! by Pete Seeger. He then segued into a lighter mood with Sunshine Superman by Donovan.

He had the whole audience singing, even if they didn't seem to know the words. It was a strong crowd, but had them in the palm of his hand.

He followed in the maxim of leaving when on top, as he took a break then. He brought his guitar and half-pint of beer to their high-top table, making a show of swigging the remainder of his glass. Another pint appeared—homage from the audience, it seemed. He was well-paid for his efforts in entertainment.

"Well? How did I do?" Paul was out of breath, hoarse from his singing. He wasn't the least bit anxious about his performance, but he did like to be told he did well.

"Wonderful. Well done."

"Bravo!"

"Brilliant!"

Julie gazed at him, knowing she looked like a love-sick doe. She didn't care.

*****

Paul came to Hayward Heath to pick her up for their date. She had chosen, rejected, and re-chosen a dozen outfits, scarves, jewelry sets, and shoes in the two hours before the movie. This was to be their first real date, the first time they had gone out as a couple without other friends along. She had decided on a dark green knee-length flowing skirt, with a clingy sea-foam green blouse which she hoped showed off what assets she had to sufficient advantage. She had chosen a thin forest green scarf to go around her neck, not wanting to block the bits the low-cut blouse showed off. It was chilly, though, with all the ventilation, so she brought along a white cardigan sweater. She didn't care for green herself, but it set off the bits of red in her hair. Julie preferred the warm colors—brown, red, gold, orange.

He looks nervous. It was the first time she had seen him in such a state, but there he was, fist clutching on a bouquet of pink and white wildflowers, a couple drooping down around the sides of his hand. He was dressed in a white turtleneck shirt, a light brown suede sports jacket and matching pants. He had done his best to tame his dark hair, but light wisps defied his efforts when the evening breeze came.

"I hope thistle make you feel cherished." It was a weak pun, and from the sheepishness of his smile, he knew it. Julie rolled her eyes and took the proffered nosegay. She invited him in as she searched for an appropriate vessel in which to keep them.

She found a crystal vase in the kitchen, splashed water into it, making a show of arranging them on the sideboard.

"What was the name of the movie we're going to see tonight? A foreign film, isn't it?" She hadn't been a huge fan of foreign films in the past, as the effort of reading the subtitles as well as watch the images often gave her a headache, but she wasn't about to let him know.

"Mondo Cane," he answered. "Jimmy recommended it. "It translates into 'A Dog's World', I'm told, in Italian. It was nominated for several awards."

The movie was strange and graphic. Julie didn't have many clear memories of it, as it was choppy and flashed from scene to scene with no discernible pattern. She remembered flashes of fishermen in Australia shoving sea urchins down the throats of sharks, dogs being skinned alive for a feast, make-up being put on corpses for a funeral. It seemed to be a documentary about strange rituals around the world, but it was strong. After a while, Paul had gotten up to go to the bathroom. She watched the movie while he was gone, but soon she decided he had been gone a long time.

She got up and found the men's room. Several men walked out, so she got up the nerve to ask one of them if he remembered a man in there of Paul's description. The man said the bathroom was empty. Where could he have gotten to? She sneaked in a look after they left. Indeed, it seemed deserted.

Did he simply leave her there? It seemed rude, most unlike him. She sighed and began to walk home. Her anger and indignation seemed to grow with each step. She had been abandoned. Her rage and wrath was slow to ignite, but caught on well now, ready to burst into flames at a feather's touch.

She heard a car stop next to her. When she turned to look, it was Paul's car, but not Paul driving. Jimmy was in the front seat.

"What ... why are you in Paul's car? What's going on?"

"Paul is okay, but he's in the hospital. Come on in, we'll go. He called me from there, so I walked down to pick up his car. I have a spare set of keys."

He careened through the narrow, winding streets of the medieval town, arriving at the rambling hospital on the edge of the community.

They made it through the endless maze of dim, antiseptic green corridors, lit by harsh fluorescent lights. After several inquiries, they found Paul, hooked up to an IV, looking sheepish.

"Julie, I am so sorry. The movie was too intense for me. I feel horrible at leaving you, but I walked outside for air, then passed out. Someone called an ambulance, so here I am. As soon as I came to, I had someone bring me a phone so I could call Jimmy to find you. Please say you aren't mad?"

Her anger had dissipated the instant she had heard Jimmy say 'hospital', so it was now long cold. It hadn't been the most auspicious first date, but she couldn't hold this against him.

"I don't blame you one bit. If anything, it got worse after you left. I can't believe it was up for awards. It was horrible. Hey …" Julie remembered what Paul had said earlier. "Jimmy, you were the one who recommended this stinker. Why the hell would you do that?"

Jimmy shrugged. "I thought it was pretty good, ground-breaking cinema, and all that. I didn't realize you were so squeamish, old man." He punched Paul in the arm in the time-honored male manner.

"Not the sort of movie for a first date, at any rate." Paul managed a feeble smile.

"Shall we try again in a few days? I might be strong enough then." He made his voice sound old and decrepit.

"I promise I'll be gentle with your frail self." Julie smiled. She kissed him, gentle and chaste, on the cheek. Then they were off, leaving him to rest.

*****

Julie threw another rock against the ancient stone wall and derived considerable satisfaction from watching it shatter into cream-colored bits. She threw another.

She had never been so outraged, so confused, and so hurt in her life. How dare Paul trifle with her heart in such a way? It was beyond cruel.

It had happened the night after their first horrible date.

David had just sat next to Sheila at the communal dinner tables, his mass of unruly, curly black hair pulled back into a long ponytail. Their son, Neil, sat on a booster chair between them. He was trying to decorate his own hair with half-eaten biscuits, while everyone laughed at his antics.

Sheila brandished a wash cloth. "Neil, you are much too old to be wearing so much of your dinner. Let mummy clean your chin, dear."

David grabbed the cloth from her. "Here, Sheila, eat your own dinner. I'll handle this wee hellion."

With a grateful smile, Sheila dug into her own roast, mopping up some of the meat juices with a chunk of Yorkshire pudding. She was just licking a stray drop from her thumb when Neil let out a screech of protest.

David intervened again. "Now, now, stop the sirens, young man. How about some soup?"

Paul smiled and asked Sheila, "How long have you two been married?"

"Four years now, Paul. How about you?"

Julie stopped her fork halfway to her mouth, the baked beans dripping in a congealed glop onto her plate. She waited for his answer.

His eyes flicked from Sheila, who looked horrified, to hers. She saw the guilt and worry plain on his face. Her face heated and she felt the rage rise inside her. Married? He was married?

"Julie? Julie, I had meant to tell you last night—"

She didn't care. She pushed away from the table and her chair clattered to the tile floor behind her. She escaped the now-hushed dining room, aware of so many eyes boring into her back.

Pushing out into the chilly evening air, she stopped and took a few deep breaths. Twilight was beginning to embrace the town in a brisk blanket of cerulean blue. She needed to walk. She needed to think.

Married. He was married. And what in God's name was he doing flirting with every figure in a skirt? How dare he trifle with her heart in such a way? Julie stomped along the path, satisfied at the crunch her boots made on the gravel. Her head could hear nothing but the screaming pain of betrayal and confusion.

When she finally stopped and looked up, she found she was at the pub. With a shrug, she opened the heavy wooden door and stepped in. She'd never visited alone before, but this was certainly a grand time to start.

Victoria was working behind the bar, and Julie closed her eyes in relief. Much easier to vent to someone she already knew.

After several pints, Victoria started asking the tough questions.

"Are you in love with him?"

Julie almost choked on her cider. "Love? I don't know what love is, Victoria. I thought I was in love with Jeffrey... but he..." She couldn't' continue.

"He what, Julie?"

Drumming her fingers on the mahogany bar, Julie didn't answer.

"Julie? What did he do to you?"

"Nothing. Nothing bad, I mean. He... well, he left me for someone else, and it hurt. It hurt horribly. And I was alone, in a strange city, with no job, no friends, nothing."

"Was this in Detroit? I thought that was where your parents lived?"

"No, no, I had followed him to Washington, D.C. We had both worked for the art department of a car company in Detroit who was moving offices to DC, and we followed. We got this tiny, grimy apartment, but we had each other. And then... then he met Sandy."

"Sandy?"

"Yeah, Sandy. She was a good friend of mine, actually, from high school. She had gone to college in New York, and came to visit. They got along together. Too well, it turned out."

"He slept with your friend? What a bloody bastard! Did you call him out?"

"Call him out? What's that in American? No, he just left. He moved off to New York to be with Sandy, and I was left with an apartment I couldn't afford on my own and no friends." It felt good to be talking about something other than Paul. The older betrayal almost felt comforting. She knew how it had ended, and had made some peace with it. Paul was another, fresher, rawer situation.

"What happened then?"

Julie shrugged. "One of the women I worked with at the car company got me involved in the Church, and I started taking care of her kids. She quit the company and worked full time for the Church, and when she moved here, I came with her."

Victoria filled another pint and slid it across the bar to her. "So you ran away. And that was that?"

"That was that. Now I don't feel like I can stay here."

"What options do you have?"

Another hard question. What options did she have? She could always move back home. But her father had never approved of her career in art, and that would be admitting defeat. She could ask for a transfer to another location, but where? Or she could stay and face Paul again. That didn't seem a very attractive option.

When Julie didn't answer, Victoria said, "I've got an idea for you."

Julie looked up. "I'm listening."

"I've a cousin in San Francisco. You could transfer there. Your church has a branch there, do they not?"

They did.

Julie put in for a transfer that evening, and it was granted. She managed to avoid Paul for the three days it took to make arrangements, and then she was gone.

*****

Julie hadn't managed to get a flight all the way to San Francisco on such short notice. The best the church could do was to Houston, unless she wanted to wait another week.

Victoria once again stepped up to the plate and helped. She called her cousin, George, to have him pick her up at the Houston airport. Julie protested that it was too much to ask, but Victoria would not be dissuaded.

"It's all I can do to help mend a broken heart, Julie. You, go and enjoy yourself. You've done precious little of that, and you need some more. Have some fun in the Wild West."

The flight itself was incredibly long and made Julie anxious. Was she making a horrible mistake? Or simply taking control of her situation? Perhaps she was simply running away again.

The dusty motel seemed deserted when she finally arrived, tired from an extra six hours of time change.

Sleep hadn't come with the night. She had tossed and turned, imagining fantasy scenarios which would never happen, thinking about her past and her future. The next morning came much too quick.

Well, time to buck up and change your life, Julie! She told herself with caustic pessimism. She hoped George would be pleasant company, at least. Just as she made this unconscious plea, she heard a quick 'shave and a haircut' knock at the door. It was zero hour.

When she opened the door, she saw a tall, thin man, about her own age, with a thick mustache and beard. He was smoothing down black, wavy, thick hair into his bowl cut. He was wearing a black turtleneck sweater (again with the turtlenecks?), with dark slacks with what looked like ankle boots. Was he a beatnik? This could be interesting, after all. He had a broad grin and his blue eyes looked gleeful.

"Are you Julie?" He sounded hesitant.

"I am, and I'm pleased to meet you." She held out her hand to him, feeling awkward.

He took her hand, but before she knew it, he was hugging her. She was surprised at the intrusion, but he was an excellent hugger. She needed a good hug about then. They held on tight for what seemed like a long time, then letting go.

"Better?" He arched an eyebrow at her, as he held her at arms' length.

"Yes, okay, thank you." She was flustered and shy, all of a sudden, but he kept looking into her eyes, as if searching for the truth.

"No, sorry, I really am better …. "She took a deep breath. "Okay, let's do this." Julie went to grab her suitcase and large purse, fighting back an unaccountable urge to cry.

"Please, allow me." George grabbed the case before she could grip it, so she shrugged and grabbed the grocery bag of other stuff, the books and craft supplies which hadn't fit into her suitcase. There were advantages to traveling light, after all.

*****

1985, Miami, Florida

Kirsten woke up, anxious, at a strange noise. Was it a bang? What was it?

She heard voices in the living room, craning her head to look around the corner from her room. She saw her mom, her Aunt Sandy, and a man she didn't know, all sitting around the glass and rattan coffee table. The sounds echoed in the large white room with its tile floor, distorting them. The words sounded fuzzier than they should, though.

Hearing her Aunt Sandy slur in a sing-song voice, she could tell they were all pretty drunk. Her mom looked like she might fall out of the overstuffed chair, while the guy on the couch was falling into Sandy's lap as she tried to keep her wineglass from spilling.

Julie sighed, shutting the bedroom door to keep out most of the sounds. This wasn't the first time she had found her mom and Aunt Sandy with a strange man or two after a night out on the town. They'd be gone by the morning, but sometimes she woke up to find one asleep on the couch, stinking of alcohol and filth. At age fifteen, she knew well what they had been up to, but whether they had slept with her mom or her Aunt, both women were discreet enough to make them sleep on the couch afterwards, or leave.

Her mom had never dated anyone, but Aunt Sandy had had a steady string of boyfriends, though none lasted long. Her cynicism and bitterness drove most of them off in short order. They always managed to find more, though. Kirsten wasn't even sure if her mom slept with any of them—it could be Sandy was the only active one. She liked to think so, though she had no proof of this.

She dressed, getting ready to go out. She had seen the latest acquisition still on the couch, but no one else was up yet. She would escape to the library, as she so often did after school. She was still trying to research her genealogy, having requested information to be sent via an interlibrary loan. Her mother didn't know she was pursuing her father's line. Kirsten decided it was better this way.

Several hours later, Kirsten pushed herself away from the table in frustration, heaving a big sigh. She pulled back her thin, long, dark brown curly hair into a pony tail and twirling the point with her finger, a nervous habit she had had as long as she had remembered. She couldn't find any trace of her father. She had, at one point looked at phone books from the city her mother said he was from, looking for any similar name she could find. The trouble was, she had no idea how the name was spelled. Her mother was no help. She had written a letter to the East Grinstead Branch of the Church a month ago, but hadn't gotten an answer yet. She used her best friend Tiff's address so her mother didn't see it.

Kirsten gathered her papers, handed the phone books back to the librarian with thanks, walking the mile home. She needed to think, which she did best while walking.

If she couldn't get hold of her father via this method, what was her next option? She had no idea. She had written to the now-defunct branch of the church in his town, but discovered, while one lady remembered him, no one else knew him. He hadn't been a member since 1971, so those records were long gone, destroyed or lost. The one woman who remembered her father had a vague notion he had moved to Dallas at one point, but wasn't certain. Kirsten had included the Dallas/Fort Worth phone books to her search, which she had looked at today. She already had gathered twenty names and numbers from the previous phone books. These had added another thirty names and numbers to her list.

She imagined how she might make the phone calls without her mother seeing a huge long-distance phone bill next month. No one else there, so the calls would be obvious. The Dallas ones would still elicit questions. Maybe she could save money from her paycheck at Arby's, offering to pay Tiff's mom for long-distance calls? It might work. Could she ask Aunt Sandy for help? While they had all lived together for several years, she never warmed to her mother's best friend. They got into frequent fights and power struggles. She didn't think Sandy would be of any help in this quest.

The calls shouldn't take long each, perhaps a minute to discover if she had the right name. If she found the right one, though, it would be a longer phone call, she hoped. What would she say? How would he react? What would he be like?

Kirsten had often imagined her first meeting with her father. Somehow it had always been a face-to-face meeting in her mind, not on the phone, but she had to consider the latter possibility. She didn't want to be disappointed in him, so she had convinced herself of the likelihood he wouldn't be interested in acknowledging a bastard daughter. He had a family of his own, so wouldn't want to be part of her life. He could be a jerk, an ignorant redneck in a white pickup truck and missing teeth. Kirsten figured if she convinced herself of the worst, she could only be pleasantly surprised if he turned out better than this image. She was great at this sort of self-psychological warfare.

With a plan in mind, she turned into her house, grateful to see last night's visitor was gone, all trace of him had vanished. She put her papers away in her school books, beginning her list of chores for the day.

****

1967, On the road

As they got on the highway and headed southwest on Interstate 15, they began the process of getting to know each other. George talked about his father, a dentist who had been set on a son who would follow in his footsteps. He had been a pilot in the Air Force in World War II, until he had been injured and discharged. He talked of his degree in music, which he pursued with his father's express disapproval. His mother had worked as a nurse in the war, helping soldiers in Hawaii. He had a brother and sister, born after the war, and still in high school. His older brother, Fred, was out in California.

"What instrument do you play?" Julie loved all sorts of music, so saw anyone with the ability to play to be a magician, though it gave her a twinge of pain, thinking of Paul.

"Guitar, banjo … anything stringed and designed to strum, really." George answered. "I'd show you, but then my driving might suffer."

"No, no, keep driving—I'd rather live to hear it another day." Julie assured him.

"So ... tell me about yourself, Miss Julie. What brought you to this point? What are you running from?"

"I'm not running away from anything. I'm ... I'm sort of lost, I guess."

This was true, so far as it went. She certainly couldn't go back home.

"Mmm-hmm. Sure, and I'm not running away from anything either. Be honest, my dear. Everyone's running from something. Let's see if we can ferret it out. What's your dad like?"

Julie remembered her father, a big bear of a man. She shoved away the twinge of homesickness.

"He had been a sergeant in World War II, on a PT boat in the Japan Sea. I was born while he was shipwrecked in Key West, at the naval station there. A hurricane had slammed his ship on the way to the Panama Canal. He is an engineer for Chrysler now, which is why we moved to Dearborn."

"Strong man? Yells a lot?"

"Do you know any sergeants who don't?"

"Fair enough. What about your mom?"

"Mom is the gentle sort. She's an art teacher in high school. A peacemaker."

"So there are a lot of wars for her to sort out, obviously. Have you got brothers or sisters?"

"Katy, she's two years younger than me, also an artist. Lari, he's sixteen. He's a brat."

"Of course, he's a younger brother, right? It's the law."

She giggled, thinking of her sister, whom she missed very much.

"What was the last war about?" George kept digging for the answers.

"College. Both mom and dad approved of me being an artist, I'll give him that. But I couldn't handle the math requirements, so I quit. Everything was pretty much a mess. My father wanted to kick me out, since I was no longer in school. My mother argued with him—and she doesn't argue, at least not where we could hear her. Finally, to stop the shouting, I left. I went to live with my sister in her place for a while. That's where I met Jeffrey."

She stopped then. She didn't want to talk about him, but George seemed to sense it.

"And this is what brought you to DC?"

"Yes. And when Jeffrey… left, I got a job with the Church, and taking care of a family of children. They moved to England, so I went with them. Then things in England got a bit complex."

"And Cousin Vicky called for the cavalry, so to speak."

Julie laughed. To hear the prim and proper Victoria called 'Cousin Vicky' in a Midwest accent was just so surreal. The laugh got a bit hysterical before she finally squelched it with a sigh.

The conversation moved onto other things. They talked about the war in Vietnam, the US troops, all the demonstrations about the war, such as the one last month in San Francisco. Julie mentioned Muhammad Ali refusing to fight in the war. George brought up the first artificial heart in Texas. Julie brought up India's first female prime minister. They discussed the tensions between the US and the USSR, and the Cambodian Civil War. Then they decided to talk of lighter subjects, such as the marriage of Elvis Presley and Priscilla Ann Wagner. Then they talked of the final episode of Mister Ed. They drove on in silence for a while, as if talking horses were a sobering and reflective subject.

She must have dozed off, because she startled awake when she sensed him braking. She looked up, anxious, but she saw it was a tree branch which had fallen into the road. It must have been a while, as the sun was blazing high and bright. The car was warm, sticky with humidity and trapped heat.

She had never taken a road trip this long before, and they weren't even halfway through. She had gone up to Canada for summer vacations with her family, but it was only a four hour drive from Detroit, to the lake where her family owned an island with several cabins. Her trip to DC had been in bits, stopping in Ohio to visit both sets of grandparents, then in Virginia to visit one of Jeffrey's cousins. She was enjoying herself, as George was entertaining company, if on the goofy side for her tastes. His capers almost reminded Julie of her little brother, the ultimate class clown. She refused to let herself compare him to Paul.

"Whew! It's getting warm. Can I turn down the window?" Julie mopped her forehead with her sleeve, finding nothing else on hand for the job.

"Sure, hold on," George cranked down his window, keeping his eyes on the road, as she did the same.

Julie told him about her time running the Rocky Colavito fan club. She talked of her little sister, who was also a wonderful artist. She spoke of her best friends, Gail, Helen and Sandy. Gail was now married with a baby, Ross. Gail's husband, Jan, was an auto mechanic. She was immersed in her new family. She described the work she had done in Dearborn at a local needlepoint shop, painting patterns onto canvas for sale. She spoke of Sandy and the apartment they had shared in college.

George gave her a sidelong glance when she mentioned Sandy.

"What?"

"You screw your face up when you talk about Sandy. Did you have a fight with her?"

"No, not precisely. Well, she and Jeffrey… "

"Aha. Have you talked to her since?"

"Not really. I wrote her a letter when I was in England, but she never replied."

"She doesn't seem like a great friend to have, if she isn't there for you when you need her." He was almost laughing at her.

Julie shrugged. "She helps me see past my rose-colored glasses. She was my closest friend in college. When I first moved out of my parents' house, it was with her. We were close … but it's true, we don't see eye-to-eye on many things. Perhaps we complemented each other. Her pessimism modulated my optimism, and vice versa. We helped each other out."

"Alright, alright, no need to get in a huff." George raised his hand in defense, but he was grinning. He was teasing her. It made her warm inside.

They were pulling into El Paso. She couldn't imagine how George was staying up, considering he had been driving for many hours before he picked her up. Perhaps he had stopped to rest before he had arrived at her place.

They decided to stop for a meal break, as it was getting towards late afternoon. George pulled up to a dusty roadside diner, giving Julie a quizzical glance. She shrugged—it was about as good as they were likely to find. It didn't look promising, but they were tired, hungry, and there was nothing else for miles.

When they walked in, they heard all the conversations fade out. Everyone was looking at them. Men filled the diner, dusty and dirty in work clothes, sitting at the counter. Julie stood out in her cream sweater and blue scarf, as if it was a crime to wear bright, clean, new clothes. She looked at George, but it didn't seem to bother him at all. He took her hand, held his head high, walking over to one of the cracked red booths next to the dust-smeared window.

An older woman in a faded pink slack suit and an almost white apron came to their table. She had her blonde hair piled high, with large plastic pineapple earrings swinging from her pierced ears. She was snapping her chewing gum.

"What can I get you, folks?"

"Coffee. Lots of coffee. And a menu?" George grinned at her. She grinned back.

"Sure thing, Sugar. Be right back."

They were no longer of interest to the line of workmen, or they were on a timed break, as they went back to eating their burgers and chatting to each other in muted tones. The muttering rose and fell like a strange wave of dust.

The waitress came back with a couple of mugs with black coffee and the menus. There wasn't much choice. Burgers, several other sandwiches, such as egg salad, ham salad, chicken salad, or tomato soup. They had milkshakes, pie, as well as ice cream sodas. She decided the burger was the safest, well done, with French fries.

George told her he was covering meals. She argued with him, but he insisted.

Julie sipped at the black coffee. There was no sugar or cream, but she preferred it black and bitter. She had taken a couple bites of her burger, but it was greasy and made her stomach churn. The fries were good, though. George was attacking his egg salad sandwich with gusto. He poured the ketchup all over his fries, making a huge mound of mess. Julie believed there were two sorts of people in the world—those who poured the ketchup on the fries, and those who dipped the fries into the ketchup in a controlled manner. She was firmly in the latter category. She looked at his mess in disdain.

"So, you never told me why you were going out to California. What's the story?" Since he wasn't driving now, she didn't think asking him might distract him.

"Well, I finished my degree, so decided I'd go and see the world before settling into the humdrum life expected of me. My dad's a doctor, so he expected both Fred and I to follow in his footsteps. You know the routine. But I studied Creative Writing instead—and he was not happy. I have had a couple poems published in Chelsea Magazine. Have you ever read it? It's a New York publication." Julie shook her head as he continued.

"Fred has a job out in San Francisco. He has his hands full with his wife and kids, so I asked if I could come out and help out with expenses, as a roommate. He's got this snazzy Victorian house a block from Haight and two blocks from Ashbury. It's a great place for poets and other creative types. There are all sorts of coffee houses and places to share my work. That's about it."

George then had asked how she knew Victoria, so Julie explained how she had met her at the pub in East Grinstead.

"And she's your cousin? But you aren't British?"

"Ha! No, our branch of the family came over several generations ago. We do keep in touch with our family across the pond, though. It's a large family. Her brother moved over here about ten years ago and got his US citizenship. He lived near Fred in San Francisco."

"Lived? Did he move away?"

"Yeah. He's gone off on a hare-brained idea to Canada. He has a crazy notion he needs to leave the States because of Vietnam. Like they would come here and invade? Insanity."

"I don't know anything about the war. I only heard bits on the news at my parents, but I've not had a radio or TV since I moved out. I don't read the newspapers much. Is it likely, do you think?" Julie hadn't considered the possibility.

"No way. They don't even have a navy. The Pacific is huge, a lot of ocean to cross, and they are a tiny country. Sure, we've sent troops over there, but I'm sure it will all be over soon." Julie was becoming reassured, but was still uneasy. Her brother is sixteen, so would be of draft age soon. She shoved the idea out of her head, mopping up the last of her ketchup with the last few fries.

"Are you all done? We should be getting back on the road."

Julie swigged the last dregs of her now cold coffee, ate a few more bites of the soggy, greasy, burger. She wiped her mouth with the napkin, gathering her things. George left cash on the table for the bill. Once again, they were the subject of intense scrutiny for the few workers who were still eating at the counter. She was glad to leave the place. It hadn't been much of a meal, but at least it was fuel.

*****

After eleven more hours on the road, they were both so tired they were loopy. By the time they passed a sign that read 'East Mojave Scenic Area,' they were strung out and beat.

The sunrise had been brilliant, painting the stark beauty of the desert mountains with vibrant tones of peach, gold and crimson. With her artist's eye, she named all the colors she had seen. Burnt orange, sienna, aqua, cyan, cinnamon ... and many colors she had no name for, but were beautiful to behold.

The spectacular sight had revived them. She kept sitting backwards in her seat, trying to see out the back window as the wonders were revealed with the rising of the sun. She settled on seeing what happened to each side, watching the long shadows in front of her. She itched to paint, to record these unusual colors, this bizarre scenery which was new to her. She did pull out her sketchpad, but nothing stayed in sight long enough for her to capture more than a quick sketch.

Despite the momentary high the celestial tableau afforded her, she still fought to keep her eyes open. She decided to sing. It wasn't such a crazy notion. Sing a song they both knew and it would keep them both alert. Besides, she had done well in the high school Glee Club. She could at least carry a tune. Shy at first, she sang the first lines of a particular song, inspired by the sight of the rising sun.

"You are my sunshine, my only sunshine …"

George looked at her in surprise. Had he been dozing? Good God, she hoped not. It was a scary notion. But he joined in, their voices growing bolder.

"You make me happy, when skies are gray

You'll never know, dear, how much I love you.

Please don't take my sunshine away!"

They went on to other verses, gaining volume and energy as they did so. Soon they were singing at the top of their lungs, beating on the dashboard and dancing in their seats as they belted out the chorus. Julie hoped the car would survive such abuse. When they were done, they laughed until they cried.

"Good idea, Julie. That got my juices flowing again. What's next?"

"How about a long song, we've got a long way yet. A song with endless verses. 'Ninety-Nine Bottles of Beer on the Wall?'"

"God, no! I'd find a beer bottle and knock you on the head before it's over. I detest that song."

"How about 'On Top of Old Smokey?'"

"Bingo! Much better, yes."

"On top of Old Smokey, all covered with snow ..." Julie began.

At the same time, George sang a different line.

"On top of Spaghetti, all covered with cheese ..."

They both stopped singing, giggling and laughing until George was snorting, unable to control the car. He managed to pull over to the side of the long, straight road. Luckily, they were in the middle of nowhere, so there was nothing around for miles. They grabbed a bag of potato chips from the back while they were stopped, getting control over themselves—or as much control as they could.

*****

George drove through the night as Julie went through her repertoire of songs. Most were folk songs, such as "This Land is Your Land." Some were Rock and Roll, like The Beatles or Fats Domino. She even sang a couple hymns she remembered from childhood.

Her parents were Presbyterian, but didn't attend church often. She wasn't attuned to the religious beliefs they taught her. Of course, she believed in being kind to others—she didn't think the Christians should have the monopoly. But she didn't believe a bearded man in heaven cared about people worshipping him. It made him sound as petty and petulant as the ancient Greek gods. She had done intriguing research into other belief systems, chatting with George about them as the night faded into a bright, clear morning. It was one of the main things that appealed to her about the Church she worked for. The higher power wasn't defined as such, simply a spiritual presence.

"I don't think I believe in an afterlife, or the devil, or any of that." George said, in response to her comments. "I think we have this one life to live, so we must do our best while we can. Anything more is superstitious claptrap, designed to keep us institutionalized under the church."

Julie decided she did believe in an afterlife, but damned if she knew how she defined it, or what else she might think about God. It was different from what she was taught in Bible class.

There was a revolution going on among people her age. One of the hotbeds of this revolution was their destination—San Francisco, a home of poets and musicians in this movement. There was a huge subculture growing which questioned the status quo, the expected behavior of the 'good family', along with all the appearances associated with it. It sounded exciting, so was looking forward to seeing it for herself.

They looked around them and saw so much nothing, they began

imagining things on the horizon. It was flat, desolate, dry, deserted, so lonely there. In order to pass the time, they decided to make a game out of their surroundings. She looked out to the right and swore she saw a shape on the distant horizon. When she pointed it out to George, they guessed what it was, each guess becoming more and more outrageous.

"An outhouse," George guessed.

"Out here? Whatever for? I think it's a stand of cactus."

"A jackelope warren"

"What in the name of all that's holy is a jackelope?? "

"The creature who lives out there. Perhaps it's an alien homing beacon."

"We're in California, not Nevada!"

"It doesn't matter, who said there was only one?"

"Okay, why leave it out in plain sight, then?"

"It's cloaked—to look like a jackelope warren. Disguised."

"Perhaps as an outhouse?"

"Exactly."

On this note, she handed him a cup of water, poured from the jug they had bought when they got supplies.

*****

A couple hours later, the heat of the day was making Julie drowsy. She had been nodding off a couple times, but kept jerking herself awake. About the fourth time, she looked at George, realizing he must be worse off.

"Shall we sing again?" She suggested.

"How about poetry, instead? I think we already sang all the songs we know."

"Hmmm ... Oh, I know ..." Julie began reciting one of her favorite poems from childhood:

"Twinkle, twinkle, little bat!

How I wonder what you're at!

Up above the world you fly,

Like a tea tray in the sky."

"What the hell was that??"

"Have you never read Alice in Wonderland? The Mad Hatter recites it to Alice."

"No, I must have missed that one."

"Where are we, anyhow? Any clue?" Julie grabbed a package of crackers they had in the back, handing him a couple to munch on.

"I think we got into California about an hour or so ago. At least, it's what I thought the sign said. It was faded. I wasn't paying all that much attention. I was hoping it wouldn't jump out into the road in front of me."

"Did you think it would transform into a jackelope?"

"Perhaps. Or an alien. The froggy type."

"I thought there were solely lizard types?"

"'There are more things in heaven and earth, Horatio, than are dreamt of in your philosophy'"

"Do I look like a 'Horatio'?!"

This set them into another fit of hysterical giggles, which kept them going for much longer than it should have, had they not been sleep-deprived.

As they approached the famed city of San Francisco, home of the Beat Generation, the Golden Gate Bridge, and music festivals, they emerged from the drunken haze the lack of sleep had put them in. Fred had given them directions from downtown, so they searched for a way to the skyscrapers. Making several wrong turns, they found Haight. A couple blocks down the road, they found the Victorian house with the correct address.

Julie had never seen so many Victorian houses before. Some were ramshackle and long abandoned, while others looked fresh and restored. Others were painted bright, in horrible colors like lime green and day-glow pink, but most were more traditional, white, grey, or pale blue. They all had beautiful, huge porches with decorative railings, gingerbread detailing on the edges of the high-peaked roofs.

The yards were small but fenced. The parking looked like a free-for-all on the street. They managed to find a spot not too far from Fred's house, while George struggled to fit his car into it—parallel parking was not his strong suit. He might be better at it when he hadn't been awake for at least two days straight.

Dragging themselves like zombies from the car, they were stiff from sitting much too long. Despite the rest stops they had taken for bathroom breaks and to stretch their legs, their bodies complained at the abuse. They didn't even bother grabbing their bags, but trudged up the wooden steps to the door, and knocked. It took several minutes, but they heard stirring inside. It was early evening on a weekday, but Fred worked odd hours. Perhaps he was asleep already?

The door finally opened. It must be Fred. He looked much like his brother, George, though he was shorter and heavier. He looked much older, though in truth, there was only about five years' difference between the two. His hair wasn't as dark, but his eyes had the same gleeful glint. There were lines on his face, but they were laugh and smile lines. And he laughed like Victoria had.

"George? Is it you? You look like hell! Come in, come in. Who's this?" His face changed once he recognized his brother, from cautious and wary to welcome and warm. All of a sudden, Julie was at home in this strange place.

Fred pulled them in, asking all sorts of questions without giving them any chance to get a word in. While George liked to talk, he wasn't a machine gun with his words like Fred was. He was, after all, beyond fatigued.

Julie didn't bother trying to say anything beyond 'hello' when George introduced her. She was so tired. All she wanted was to lie down and sleep for a month. George must have been just as exhausted, as he asked Fred if there was a place they could crash, in his words, 'like, right now?'

Fred led them to a spare room, which had two single beds in it. Julie didn't bother undressing, though she did wash her face in the bathroom down the hall. She had dirt and grime from their trek through the desert, wanting at least a part of herself to feel clean before she slept. Then she pulled off her shoes and socks, crawling into the bed. George was already snoring in the other bed. Never before had a bed offered such comfort, so welcoming, so ... she was asleep before she even completed the idea.

*****

A blaring noise frightened Julie awake, a car honking outside. She was unsure of where she was. It was dark, and she heard snoring. Bit by bit, the pieces falling into place. George. Desert. California. They had made it to California. They must be at Fred's house. She remembered Fred as a vague force of nature and welcomes. How long had she slept? She looked around for a clock, but saw none. It was too dark to make much out of the shapes around her. She eased her way out of the toasty warm, comfortable bed. Her muscles protested with pain, so she went slowly. She also didn't want to wake George.

She made her way to the one window in the room, drawing the curtain to one side, so she could peer out into the street. The car had stopped honking, but there were other sounds. It had rained. She heard the swish of car tires as they rode down the street. It was difficult to see more, as the window was blotchy with raindrops.

George was attractive, despite—or perhaps because of—his beatnik look. He was goofy and intelligent, two qualities she admired. Perhaps she would enjoy this adventure much more than she had imagined. She already felt like she had known him all her life. And it might help take her mind of Paul.

She went back to her bed, lulled by the rain, settling back into the blessed arms of Morpheus.

4 - SANCUTARY

The next morning dawned hazy, with mist coming down from the mountains and through the sleepy streets. Julie woke, ready to wrestle saber-toothed tigers … or at least, a contented housecat or two. She stretched, creaked, moaning with stiffness and pain as she did so. She washed her face and hands, did her best to brush her teeth with her fingers, and brush out the wrinkles out of her disgusting clothes. First order of business would be to retrieve her bags and change into an outfit which didn't smell like a locker room.

The other bed was empty. Julie walked out into the hall, lost. She had been in such a drunken daze last night, she had no clue where the front door might be, or where George and Fred were. She listened for a moment, catching male laughter down to the right. She followed the sound. She also smelled the wondrous, savory odor of coffee. Her stomach decided to wake up and remind her rather with a shout that it was empty. The chips and crackers from the day before had been quite insufficient.

She opened a door near the end of the hall, finding the men in a large, bright kitchen with black and white tiles, white appliances, with a shiny diner-style table on one wall. The chairs were even diner-style, with plastic red poufy cushions and chrome backs. She smelled burnt toast with the coffee.

"Julie! Come in and meet Fred proper-like." George was all smiles, looking miles better than he had the night before.

"Fred, this is my friend Julie. She kept me awake the whole drive. She serenaded me with sweet songs, recited poetry, and made me laugh."

Fred took her hand and brought it to his lips in an elaborate, gallant gesture. Julie had never encountered such a thing outside of films. She blushed and stammered a meek "thank you."

"Is that coffee I smell? I would murder for a cup."

"Of course! Here, let me get you a clean mug." Fred scrambled in the cupboard above the sink and brought out a large black mug for her. He brought a carafe of coffee from the counter and poured. "See, no murder required! Would you like milk or sugar?"

"Oh, no, I prefer my jet fuel black, thank you!" Julie relished the hot, bitter drink on her tongue, sensed it caressing her throat. Ah, nectar of the gods.

"Would you care for breakfast? I finished making George eggs and toast. How do you like yours?"

"However you like them. I would eat boiled boot if cooked with enough salt."

"One boiled boot, salted, coming right up!" Fred said.

She took a more careful look at him, since she was no longer a pre-caffeinated zombie. He still looked much older, but she could see laugh lines creasing in the corners of his eyes. She noticed they were a deep, soulful brown. He was dressed in a comfortable, threadbare robe with purple paisley print all over it. His feet were bare.

"George, can we get our stuff out of the car? My body has melded with these clothes. I want to change while I can still peel them off."

"Already done, Sleeping Beauty—the cases are in the hallway. I didn't want to bring them in the room while you were still sleeping."

"Ah, fantastic! I'm off to change. I'll be back in a flash."

Julie returned much refreshed. While she would have preferred to bathe—nay, to immerse herself in hot water and suds for a week—hunger was a more pressing need. She could relax and eat now she had fresh clothes on.

"Fred, thank you so much. I'm almost human again." Julie couldn't believe she had eaten those eggs so fast. She was staring at the now empty plate, with no memory of the actual meal.

"My pleasure, my dear. George has told me much about you. Welcome to our home. You missed my family so far—the kids are at school and Karen is off at her mother's this week. You will miss me soon—I've got to get to work in about a half hour. Is there anything I can get you before I go? You and George are, of course, welcome to stay here as long as you like, never fear." She decided he was still a whirlwind, even after calming down from the night before. He was exhausting in his energy.

"Thank you, thank you so much ..." but he was gone, out the kitchen door and, up to change out of his lounging clothes to work clothes.

"Whew, he's a bundle of energy." Julie saw George was grinning.

"Yeah, he was always more like a tap dance than a waltz. I prefer to stop and smell the flowers, rather than run them over with a sports car."

"It takes all kinds, I suppose."

"Indeed. So, what would you like to do now that you are in the Wild West?"

"Wild? I don't consider Victorian houses all much like wilderness."

"Ha! Wait until tonight. The nightlife is … different." George looked at her with sly eyes. "Have you not heard stories of Haight Ashbury?"

"Sure, I've heard stories of San Francisco, but I put much of it down to exaggeration and second-hand stories."

"Tonight we shall go and find first-hand stories, then. Today, we settle in, find our place here, perhaps walk around the neighborhood."

"I should also check into the Church, and find out when I start work …" Julie's responsible nature was taking over. She was making a mental tally of the money she had left, and what she would need to use it for.

"Not today. Today is for enjoyment. Tomorrow, maybe. Next week, better. Let's have a holiday."

"I think today is for relaxing and resting, after our marathon drive."

"Alright, then, you relax and rest. I'm going to go out, get the lay of the land. Need anything?"

"Something to read?"

"The library is this way, my dear ..." George led her into Fred's study.

Julie spent most of the day lazing about, exploring the rambling house, walking in the neighborhood until it rained again. George had gone in to town, so she had been left on her own to settle in and take in the new surroundings. She perused Fred's extensive library, picking out a book on past lives and reincarnation. She found a large bay window with a comfy chair, and settled in for a good read as the steady rhythm of the rain beat a soothing tattoo on the glass.

As the day began to fade, she heard a great deal of banging and shouting outside. Before she could rouse herself from her comfortable nest, the house was alive again. Fred and George must have picked up the two children after work, as the hallway was a riot of noise and stomping.

She poked her head out of the library, almost colliding with a sturdy six year old boy—dark, curly hair a mop above dark brown eyes, and a tiny red mouth, round in surprise.

"Who are *you*?"

"I am Julie. I'm a friend of your Uncle George's. And what's your name?"

He looked back to his father, uncertain how to proceed, but with a nod from Fred, he turned back and stuck out his hand.

"I'm Chris."

"Very pleased to meet you, Chris. And is this your sister?"

Julie had noticed Fred was holding a toddler, perhaps about two, in his arm. She wore a pink frilly skirt.

"Yeah, this's Carrie. But she doesn't talk much."

"Very pleased to meet you, too, Carrie."

The blond girl buried her face in her father's shoulder, eliciting a grin from Julie.

"Well, let me help Fred get these two settled in. Then we'll go out and paint the town tonight." George offered. Julie nodded as the parade passed by the library door and up the stairs.

Back in her room, Julie went through the clothes she had, picking out a colorful blouse and comfortable slacks. While they were going to be much more conservative than what she expected the others to wear, they were at least not as stodgy as most of her other choices. She tied her hair back with a scarf so she wouldn't have to mess with it much, putting on make-up. From her meager store of costume jewelry, she found the silver crescent moon pendant. She had never had her ears pierced, and didn't like clip on earrings, so bracelets and necklaces were the extent of her decoration. Rings were simply asking to be lost.

As she emerged from the tiny bathroom, she almost ran into George, on his way down the hall. She needed to figure out how to stop this from happening.

"Almost ready?"

"Sure, let me put my make-up bag back in my room, and I'll be all set. Where are we going?"

"Downtown Hippieland! Bring your rose-colored glasses."

******

George and Julie walked, arm in arm, down the three blocks to the corner of the infamous Haight Ashbury. As they approached, the setting sun colored everything in a brilliant orange glow, as if the buildings were about to burst into flames. She heard music and laughing everywhere. She saw more people hanging out in front of the storefronts.

The riot of images assaulted her as they walked on. Bright colors, riotous patterns and hair everywhere. She saw pinks and yellows, oranges and aquas. She saw paisley and tie-dye, psychedelic patterns which looked like optical illusions from an Escher poster. She saw long hair on both men and women, with woven headbands. There were flowers everywhere, painted on faces and woven in braids. She had walked into an alien world, so far from the Dearborn neighborhood she had lived in at her parents' house. She almost thought she was drunk.

Julie sniffed the air. There was an odor in the air she had not noticed before. The pungent smoke smell of pot. She knew the smell—she had smoked it with Sandy before. But never right out in the street. She was amazed at the bravery of these people. Perhaps she wasn't drunk, but she was getting a contact high, right out here on the sidewalk, of all places.

She slowed down, stumbling on the pavement. George turned and gave her a quizzical look.

"Are you okay, Julie? Did you trip?"

"No, no, simply overwhelmed, is all. I'll be fine, but give me a moment."

"Sure. No rush at all. Want to duck into this shop?"

Julie looked up and saw a storefront with a sign overhead which said 'The Psychedelic Shop' in curvy, oozing letters. The sign was painted in purples, almost looked like it was moving, though it couldn't be. The display window was filled with tie-dye t-shirts and skirts. She blinked to see the images burned on her retinas when she closed her lids.

"Perhaps there's someplace to sit down? These are new boots, so I'm not much used to walking in them yet."

"Of course, come in. Let's see if they've a stool."

The shop was jam-packed with things. The first things she saw when she did a quick survey were the bean-bag chairs in one corner. She made a bee-line for those, plopping herself down with a big sigh of relief. She had been reeling.

George was looking at her with concern, but she nodded to him with reassurance. He gave her a half shrug, moving to look about the store.

Julie looked from her vantage point near the floor, noticing glass cases along two walls. It had all sorts of glass pipes and strange contraptions which looked like they belonged in an alien's toolbox. She avoided looking at the wall with clothing on it. The mass of clashing colors assaulted her artist's eye, giving her a headache. All of a sudden, she imagined herself old and stuffy. She would have to loosen her straight-laced tendencies if she were to fit in this city. She hoped she was up to the task.

She moved her gaze to the walls, where all sorts of posters of musicians were plastered at various angles. Big Brother and the Holding Company, The Who, The Mamas & the Papas, The Beatles, The Animals, Jimi Hendrix Experience. She had heard of most of these, but a few were new to her. Many were done in the same melting sort of font the sign outside used. More Escher-like optical illusions were in the backgrounds as well.

Well, these people weren't afraid to break the basic rules of color and composition. Julie was certain this freedom applied to other areas, as well.

She struggled to her feet, out of the grips of the amorphous mass of the beanbag chair, looking around for George. He was peering into one of the glass cases at the alien torture devices.

"What are those," she whispered to him.

"I think they are water pipes. You use them to smoke."

"Smoke ... pot?"

"Well, they certainly aren't for smoking hams." George grinned at her meek whisper.

It did the trick—she giggled and hooked her arm back into his. Shaky at first, they went back out into the busy street.

Julie was once again assaulted by the noise and throngs of people, but she kept a firm grip on George's arm. She wasn't as overwhelmed as she had been. She was using him as an anchor, but he didn't seem to mind, and she was relieved.

They whirled through and around groups of people who were talking, singing, playing guitars and other instruments. It was like a waltz in time with the ebb and flow of conversation and music. Snippets came through the cacophony.

"...but he said he was already sleeping with her, so ..."

"...the sound is really groovy, man, can you believe ..."

"...so the colors were beautiful ..."

"...like flying in the air above the clouds ..."

As they made their way down the street, she heard louder music, more organized than the little pockets of performers she had been seeing and hearing. Was it a park farther ahead? Fred had mentioned a place called Freedom Garden. Perhaps they had a band set up for everyone to hear. She couldn't see over the mass of people.

She glanced at the shops as she went by, seeing glimpses of music stores, bookstores, bars, and clothing stores. A couple places were dark or boarded over, but most of them were a riot of light and activity. She saw one bar with a poster outside advertising poetry readings, another with a band list.

It was difficult, sometimes, getting around the knots of people. Several times she had been touched or brushed by others, whether by accident or on purpose, she did not know. Now, however, someone grabbed her arm. She whirled to see who was assaulting her.

She saw intense blue eyes staring at her, topped with a long, matted mass of dirty blond, frizzy hair. The young man was looking into her eyes as if searching for the secret to life itself. He said nothing, but merely stared at her. George noticed she was no longer walking and came around to confront the man.

"Hey, man, no need for that. Let the lady go." George tried to pull the man's hand from her forearm, but he held on with a vice-like grip. He had on a kaftan of bright blues and greens, dirty jeans and sandals.

"She's beautiful, man ... you can't keep such beauty all to yourself, man. Share the love, right?" The intruder proceeded to put his other hand around Julie's waist, trying to extricate her from George's arm.

Julie gave him a cold look and said, in the firmest tone she could manage, "I'm quite happy with my escort. Let me go, now!" Still, he held tight, tugging on her. She tried to jerk her arm away from his grasp.

George dropped Julie's hand from his arm, and she panicked, but he only did so in order to use both hands to remove the blond man's grip.

"The lady asked you to leave. Do it now, or I shall make sure you do." George wasn't being belligerent, but he was being firm with the man. All of a sudden, the blond stopped looking at Julie's eyes, swiveling his head, almost in slow motion, to George. As his eyes went wider, Julie noticed how glassy they looked, how dilated his pupils were. She was willing to bet he was on at least one mind-altering substance, but she had no way to guess which.

Just like that, he melted back into the crowd. She could yet sense the sharp grip he had had on her arm, thinking it might bruise tomorrow. She turned to George, a look of amazement on her face.

"Does this happen often, do you think?" Her voice was shaky, but she hoped it didn't sound as rattled as she was.

George gave her one look, taking her into his arms. She was in no mood to argue, but managed not to sob as the adrenaline drained out of her, leaving her arms and legs like jelly. She was much safer there, inside his shell of protection. She was content to remain there. After a few seconds, she considered herself silly. She took a deep breath. George sensed it, holding her out at arms-length.

"Better?"

"Better. C'mon. Let's move on in case he changes his mind and comes back."

"Madam?" He hooked out his arm for her to take with a quirk of his eyebrow. She took his arm with ceremony and aplomb, as well as a grin. They walked on, into the crowds and noise.

*****

Much later, after many sights and sounds, both foreign and domestic, they made their way back to Fred's house, the sound of sitar music buzzing in their ears. Julie went into the bathroom to change into her night clothes—a simple set of pajamas, light green and faded. As she went into the bedroom they were sharing, George was standing by the window, looking out into the night and moonlight.

When she stopped in the doorway, he turned, walking the three steps to her. He took her hand into hers, gazing into her eyes, almost as intense as the drugged blond man had, but with much more care. He grinned as she reached up to kiss that grin off his face.

She had meant it to be a playful gesture, a peck. But he held her face in his hands, keeping it much longer than a friendly kiss would have been. When they parted, she opened her eyes to find him peering into hers with question, invitation, and deep desire.

He kissed her forehead then, but it wasn't a patronizing gesture. It was gentle and sweet. He moved to her cheek, then down to her neck. It sent shivers up her spine to feel the roughness of his chin on her tender skin. He saw her shiver.

"Are you okay, Julie? Would you like me to stop?"

Did she? Was this what she wanted? He would stop if she asked. He wasn't the drugged crazy man they had encountered in the park. He was George, her pal, her chum. Her lover? He wasn't Paul, but perhaps that was best thing about him.

Sleeping alone wasn't what she craved. She put her hand up to his cheek, stroking it with the palm of her hand. It traveled down to his chest, then farther. She let him know, with her hands, that she didn't want him to stop.

He watched her hand travel down his chest, looked up into her eyes, cupping her chin in his. He closed his eyes as he touched his lips to hers, a butterfly touch. He opened his eyes again, with a slight smile. It wasn't his normal goofy grin, but a sweet smile, one she ached to kiss again. So, she did.

Together, they closed the drapes in the window, enjoying the intensity of the night.

*****

Julie awoke, confused. She panicked before she remembered where she was, why she couldn't move. She and George were on the floor between the two single beds, and she was wrapped up like a burrito in a tangle of blankets. There were several pillows here and there, but not in any logical placement. George was still asleep—his warm, steady breath misted on her back. She remembered the night, smiling. She figured George would be a fun lover, but he was a funny lover as well. There were comical moments as they figured out how to best use the space they had. Hysterical giggling ensued, hastily shushed, as to not wake the house. In the end, she did her best to keep everything quiet and secret, but she wasn't sure she had succeeded. At least the kid's bedrooms were upstairs.

She extricated her as best she could, to get ready for the day. She had no idea what George had planned, but she needed to look around for a job.

She made it out to the kitchen with a sigh of relief. Fred must have already left for the day with the kids. She made herself coffee and toast. Fred had been thoughtful enough to leave the Yellow Pages on the table, open to 'Churches'. Well, it's the best place to start. She looked up the address of the local branch and wrote it down.

Julie decided it would be best to get her art portfolio out—the one she used for job interviews, to show the past work she had done. While the Church had no issues with transferring her, she wanted to make a good impression on her new supervisors. They hadn't been able to assure a permanent transfer, but at least three months was good enough.

Julie rifled through a couple drawers in the kitchen, looking for a map of the city. Then with a smack on her forehead, she looked in the Yellow Pages. It had a map of the metropolitan area.

Since she couldn't go out until George could drive her, she decided to play with the images she had in her mind. She pulled out a sketchpad she had in her stuff, drawing the images she remembered from the night before. A girl dancing, flower behind her ear, with layers and layers of fringe dangling from her arms and torso, swirling in a dynamic circle. Her long, straight hair following the fringe in the swirl. A young man sitting, playing a strange instrument which George had called a 'sitar'. He had a macramé headband on his tangled, almost matted hair. He had on a ripped t-shirt and torn blue jeans, with leather sandals.

As she was working on the detailing in the sandals, the shadows on the ground underneath, she heard George stirring in the other room. She put her materials away, heading back to the room. Peeking around the doorway, she admired his long, lean form, stretching on the floor, still obscured in strategic places by the blankets.

"Up and at 'em, Sunshine!" She flung open the drapes, letting in the bright sunlight. It showed all the dust motes floating in the room. She heard a long, low moan coming from the floor.

"Uuuhhhh, I think it's illegal in the state of California to be so cheerful in the morning," he groaned.

"Morning? It's almost afternoon. I'm glad you're up—I need to change into my professional togs and get in touch with the Church soon. May I beg your services as a chauffeur today? Or shall I surrender myself to the vagaries of public transportation?" Julie couldn't help smiling as she watched him.

"Come back to bed, there's no hurry."

Julie was tempted, but she was also determined. "Oh, no, mister, that's no bed—it's a hard, uncomfortable floor, and I've got things to see and people to do … or something like that."

"Well, I suppose I am open to bribery, then. A sweet kiss and a cup of coffee might purchase my services … at least for a time." He was the epitome of gallantry.

Julie settled down to her knees, giving him a chaste peck on the cheek, but she figured this wasn't going to be the end of it. Sure enough, he tackled her down onto the floor, kissing her firm and with purpose. Several minutes later, she came up for breath.

"Now, George, I really do need to get on with this job thing. I can't live off of you and Fred forever, after all. I don't think I'm cut out to be a kept woman."

"Who said anything about keeping you?" George grinned to reassure her he was joking.

*****

1998, Miami, Florida

Kirsten had continued with her genealogical research over the years on her mother's line, turning the passion into a hobby. She had managed to extend the line, filling out places all over the tree, once electronic sources became available. She had subscribed to a magazine which catered to the obsession, Everton's Genealogical Helper, going through each issue. She searched for information on the several 'brick walls' she had found. She still hadn't managed, for instance, to find where her Jensen line hailed from. Scandinavian, yes, but there were several options—Denmark, where she was born? Norway? Sweden? Perhaps even Iceland? All she knew is the family was already in the United States by 1760, but that's where the trail ran cold. She was stuck on a common name—John Jensen. There were too many in the records to determine which one was her ancestor.

As she flipped through the most recent issue of Everton's, she happened to glance at an ad which promised to find lost relatives. It was a name, an address, and the offer. If they found nothing, she paid nothing. If they did find information, she paid a hundred dollars.

This was a lot of money to her. She was twenty-eight, working full time while trying to finish her graduate degree in accounting at night. She shared an apartment with her boyfriend, struggling from paycheck to paycheck. It was expensive, but it might be worth it.

She had looked, of course, in the various resources she had come across over the years, for any clue to her father. But the information was so nebulous. The Church in East Grinstead had replied to her query, having at least verified the spelling of his name. However, they could give no other information due to privacy considerations. Her research into various phonebooks had come up with nothing. She had no other avenues.

She wrote to the man in the advertisement and gave him all the details she knew. Perhaps, just perhaps, this might bear some small fruit.

Several days later, she received a phone call from the researcher, letting her know it might take a while, as he did this part time. It involved a lot of writing and requesting records. She understood, having done this sort of research herself. She thanked him and wished him luck.

She waited on edge for several weeks, but heard nothing. She moved on to other things in her life, almost forgetting the matter.

*****

Her visit to the Church had been... mixed.

The local branch was a rather fancy façade, with glass windows and soaring architecture. It was obviously a newly-built place, and the airy atmosphere reflected an eager spirit.

The receptionist, who couldn't have been more than seventeen years old, showed her to the art director's office. That's when it started feeling off.

Bradley Tibbets, so the name plate said, was the Director of Advertising and Marketing. He stood up when she entered, offering his hand out. His skin was clammy, and his handshake limp. It was difficult to extract her hand from his, and the alarms started going off in her head. This was a slimy man. She'd met some before, but he already felt like the worst of the oily, used-car-salesman personalities.

"So, what brings you to San Francisco, Miss Jensen?" His over-bright smile did not reach his pale green eyes.

She had come up with an innocuous-sounding excuse, with George's help. "I have a friend in town who has not been feeling well. I was thrilled to discover I could transfer here to help her out."

Tibbets nodded, and he pushed his brown hair back a bit, looking her up and down.

"I'm sure I can find some work for you, my darling. When can you start?"

Julie looked down at the artwork portfolio she'd brought. She handed it to him, but he just stared at it. "What's this?"

"My portfolio, so you can see what sort of work I do?"

"Oh. Well, no need for all that. HQ wouldn't have transferred you if you were incompetent. Tomorrow morning at 8am?"

She nodded, and he escorted her out, one hand on the small of her back. She tried to walk faster than him, so he would stop touching her, but he maintained the contact. When she finally escaped, he managed to get in a pat on her bottom. What a slime.

George tried to cheer her up by suggesting a nice dinner out, but the sear of mooching guilt pained Julie. Her independent streak was annoying at times. It made it almost impossible to accept gifts or generosity guilt-free.

"How about cheap and cheerful instead of nice and expensive? It would make me less ... dependent."

"Bingo! Your wish is my command, my lady. Cheap and cheerful it is. How about the pizza joint we saw, the one that looked like a diner?"

"That would work fine. Thanks, George."

This place was a far cry from the dirty, dusty diner they had eaten at on the way to California. The place gleamed—it was black and white all over the floor and ceiling, with bright red booths and silver tables. The odors of garlic and baking bread were strong, lifting Julie's spirits as they walked in. She wanted to go change into one of her fifties style skirts and neck scarves for the occasion. She would need saddle shoes to complete the picture.

There was a large jukebox in the corner, flashing bright lights and playing "A Hard Day's Night" by The Beatles. There were about five other tables occupied with groups or couples. No one paid them much attention, as they made their way to an empty table near the window.

George had to catch the waitress' eye for her to come by with menus. She got them a couple glasses of Coke and George ordered a large pie with mushrooms and pepperoni for them to share. Julie protested they'd never eat it all, but he assured her they could take home the rest.

"Do you want to try to find a different job?"

Julie considered it, but she was too weary to do that now. After the long trip from England, and across half the country, she couldn't even consider hitting the pavement at this point.

"No, no, I'll give this one a chance. It's difficult to get art jobs, especially if you're new to the area. For art jobs, the best way I've found is to get your work noticed somewhere, by someone, maybe a write-up in a newspaper or magazine, create some reputation before they have a chance to be prejudiced. It doesn't always work. If you're there in person with a printed recommendation, people find it more difficult to dismiss you out of hand, especially if they can see you do good work."

"I suppose it makes sense. I imagine it would be the same with musician jobs, too—bring your instrument, play, and let them hear what you can do. Of course, most of those jobs are found by the job-giver seeing you play at a concert or bar." George looked thoughtful. "Perhaps I should play here and there."

"I thought you were only staying a month?"

"I might be convinced to stay longer. There are … attractions to this place, after all." His grin was wolfish, in a caricature of a leer. He stroked her arm as it lay on the table, a feather touch. It made the hairs on her arm stand up, giving her goosebumps.

Julie blushed and ducked her head. This is ridiculous. She wasn't usually coy or shy. It's not as if George was her first. She steeled herself to look up instead—right into the large pizza pie which was descending to the table in front of them, steaming and aromatic.

*****

The next morning, to her surprise, Fred was still in the kitchen when Julie made her way in, having left George sound asleep. He looked up from his coffee and paper when he heard the door squeak, looking her up and down.

"Well, you look ready to kill. Off to your new job today?"

"Did George tell you of my delightful prospect yesterday?" Julie gave him a rueful grin.

"He did, and if you decide it's not worth it, I might have a solution. We could use someone at the local branch of my own church to do layout work. It's what George said you do—interested?"

"Well ...sure. But ... where do you work?"

"A company based in North Dakota, but we have branches all over the country. I'm starting up the branch out here."

"What sort of work will it be?" She was nervous at the idea of working for a big company, but she was sure she'd be able to pick it up in short order.

"Mostly flyers and posters we will be giving out and mailings. Internal promotional materials for our members. It's not full-time, perhaps thirty hours a week, for $2.60 an hour, but it could change as we get going. We're slated to open doors next year. Right now it's a messy office, I'm afraid, but we'll find space for you. I work there as sort of an ambassador to the other groups." Fred proceeded to go to the sink and rinse out his now empty coffee cup.

"Don't you want to see my portfolio? To see if I can do the work?"

Fred gave a careless shrug. "George said you were good. I trust his judgment"

"If this turns out to be a dud, I appreciate the option." Julie had poured her own cup of coffee, blowing on it to cool it down before she sipped it.

"Great, just let me know."

"Fred … I do thank you. This is truly kind of you. Now I'm even more in your debt, though."

"Yeah, I know my brother mentioned you were feeling … moochy. You aren't, of course. Hell, you've only been here a couple days. Official mooching begins after a month, you know."

"I didn't, but I'll keep it in mind." She smiled at him over her coffee cup.

*****

Arriving in that glittering office, Julie thought perhaps it wouldn't be so bad after all. Perhaps she wouldn't have a great deal of contact with Tibbets. Alas, he was waiting for her as she arrived, and brought her into the marketing department.

In contrast to the sleek reception area, the marketing offices were full of dust and mess. Julie saw piles of boxes, files and papers. Underneath them all, glimpses of desks and chairs were scattered about for structure.

The first person she noticed was the woman. She was tapping a pencil on the pad of paper she held in her hand, standing tall and slim in a smart pink business suit. She shook her head as she spoke, making her immaculate bouffant of blond hair wiggle.

"This is Julie. She's transferred over from East Grinstead. She's an artist, and ready to tackle our layout work. Julie, this is Tamara Lange. She is one of our promotion experts." Tamara gave her a cold look from head to toe, then nodded to her in grudging acceptance.

"Tony is our advertising sales manager." The slightly-hunched man Tamara had been speaking to was nodding with a thoughtful look on his face, his wavy brown hair, bobbing as he looked up to her. He was wearing a typical office uniform with a button-down shirt and slacks.

Julie made the round of handshakes, welcomes, smiles and assessments, as Tibbets left. She was glad she had decided to dress smart, as Tamara's elegance made her frowsy in comparison. She stood taller and straighter in reaction, despite the fact she had decent posture. She lifted her chin, smiling ruefully to herself at her defensive response.

Tony showed her to a cluttered desk in one corner, doing his best to relocate the boxes and files which had been on it. He made sure she had supplies—pencils, paper, ruler, stapler—and recommended she list what artistic supplies she might need for her layout work.

"May I see what I would be working on? Perhaps an example of what your finished products look like so I can get an idea of the standard? I don't want to waste too much of your time," Julie asked in a meek voice.

"Nonsense. My job is mostly in bits and spurts. Right now, I've nothing I need be doing. I can help you settle in all you like, never fear."

As Julie sifted through the brochures, pamphlets, posters and flyers Tony had dug up, she noted they had a sleek, slick style. This was a Church with money and power, and not afraid to show it. The stuff at the British branch had been a bit... paler, calmer, less aggressive. They tended to produce sober, simple flyers, not this glossy, professional stuff. Lots of photographs of beautiful people enjoying their life, possessing smiles with dazzling white teeth, all around them text written with loaded words, designed to attract and entrap the reader with sensuality and allure.

She could learn a lot here about such work.

She sensed rather than saw someone approach, coming up behind her. She turned around and saw Tony.

"How are you getting on? Need anything? Perhaps a cup of coffee to clear the dust?"

"Oh, coffee would be precisely the thing. Where is it?"

"Come on, I'll show you"

Julie followed him down a hallway and around a corner into an unfinished room which served as a canteen. There was a silver coffee maker on the counter, perking away. Tony poured them both a full cup, rinsing out the maker before started a new batch.

"It's one of the rules—if you take the last bit, you brew another batch. This is a never-ending need here, trust me!"

"I can well understand it. Coffee is one of my few vices."

"There are worse things to be addicted to, I suppose," He flashed a sly smile.

"I'm sure there are, especially here in the City of Sin. However, I think I'll stick to the coffee for now."

"Sugar? Cream?" Tony pulled out dry Coffee-Mate non-dairy creamer. She had tried the stuff exactly once, and had almost gagged.

"Oh, no, thanks. I prefer mine black. Thank you for showing me where to get it, though. I'm sure the information will become invaluable. " She smiled at him, blowing on her cup before she sipped it. She turned to return to her desk.

"We do get a break around lunchtime. May I take you out for a sandwich? There's a nice place a couple doors down."

"That would be delightful, thank you. Noon?"

"Sure, see you then."

*****

The café, called Hofbrauhaus, was nice, she decided. And, despite his penchant for disgusting non-dairy creamer products, so was Tony. They talked, discovering a common interest in art and science fiction. They talked about Salvador Dali and Robert Heinlein before their food arrived. He was quieter and shier than George, but they had a few things in common, enough to base a friendship on.

She was enjoying her Rueben sandwich while he had tomato soup and a grilled cheese. About halfway through the meal, Tamara came over, asking if she could join the party.

"Have you been in the Church long?" Tamara asked her with raised eyebrows. Julie puzzled at the odd inflection in her question, but had no idea what it might mean.

"No, I got involved in Washington DC, less than a year ago. I worked doing art for them, and taking care of one member's children. When that member, Eileen, moved to England, I followed along. Then my assignment ended, and I managed to get a transfer here. I've a friend who is ill, and I was glad of the opportunity to help her out." She decided she had no need to go into the complex history there. She didn't think it would be a good idea to appear so reckless to her new employers.

"Oh, I see! And how do you like San Francisco so far? Have you been able to see much of the sights?"

"Not really. George took me around the first night after we arrived, but the next day I saw a lot of downtown—while I was looking for a job, at least. I've not even seen the Golden Gate Bridge yet." She gave them a shrug.

"Be sure to climb up Coit Tower, as well. It's a fantastic view from up there. And there are many places outside the city to visit, too. We've a beautiful city—might as well enjoy it." Tony sounded like he belonged on a tourist commercial. "Are you from DC, then?"

"Yes, well, originally I'm from Ohio, but my parents moved us to Michigan when I was ten. I had been doing layout work in DC after college. I had moved out there with a friend." Julie hoped glossing over the reasons for moving to DC was sufficient to discourage further probing into the matter. She was like a leaf floating on rapids in a river these last couple of months, but perhaps she could settle roots down here, at least for a while.

The group ate their lunch with idle chatter. The locals shared stories about the area, the problems of opening up a new office, funny stories about Tibbets. Julie was awkward discussing her new boss.

She finished off her day by looking around for any art supplies she might be able to use, making a list of things she wanted to have. She then made a shorter list of the basics she truly needed, asking Tamara to whom she should give the lists. She mentioned Tony did the supply shopping, so she might consider going with him to pick out the specific tools she needed. When she asked Tony when he was planning to go, he suggested first thing in the morning. She nodded and said she would meet at the office first.

Unfortunately, Tibbets insisted on accompanying them. Julie did her best to walk on the other side of Tony, and out of grabbing range.

Julie had been amazed at the number of things on offer at this specialized store. Of course, she had been to art stores in both Michigan and DC, but they had been tiny places—carved out of larger stores, or converted almost as an afterthought to offer art supplies. But this place ... it was almost as large as a warehouse. It wasn't all art—much was given over to office supplies, shipping and packaging, that sort of stuff. But the art section had a whole section purely for calligraphy, another for stenciling. So many canvas and paint options, her head swirled. She was a kid in a candy store. She had to restrain herself, reminding her inner child she was shopping with someone else's money.

She had gathered the items on her "needs" list, pricing them out. She asked Tony if there was enough in the budget, so he approved more. She went to the stenciling area, knowing she would be doing layout work.

Lost in thought, she didn't realize someone was behind her until she turned and almost crashed into Tibbets. He had been standing right next to her. It made her uncomfortable, but it didn't seem to rattle him at all. He leered at her, and moved off to get his own purchases before they left.

5 - PSYCHADELIA

August 2, 1967

Dear Katy:

Hello, sister mine! I've been out in the Wild West for three weeks now, and haven't yet found a gold mine, so our early retirement plans are still on hold. What I have found, though, is a job and a place to stay, at least for now. It's a different world out here, Katy. There are artists and poets, musicians and dancers everywhere you look, every night in the streets. It's bizarre, as if I'm living in a twisted nirvana.

How are your classes? Have you had to take Life Drawing yet? Watch out for the teacher, Mr. Settins, he's on the grabby side. I think it's why he teaches that class. He's a lech.

I'm doing layout work for the Church here, and its interesting work. They've got a decent budget, so I can do a few creative things. They aren't so rigid in their thinking about options, either.

I've found a good friend in George, but unfortunately, he's due to head back home to Michigan soon. Luckily, I've found a few other friends here, including his brother Fred, the people I work with, like Tony, and the aforementioned artists and dancers. I've also started going to this one sort of studio apartment, where they have 'art-ins'. Each week, they whitewash the walls. Then, they invite anyone in to paint them however they like—pictures, abstract, whatever. They let people see it all week, then do it again the next week. Sort of drive-by gallery art. I got the nerve up to take a section of one wall last week, and drew a wizard in an invisible cloak in an autumn forest, sort of a Tolkein-esque scene. Long white beard, pointy hat, staff, etc. You can see the foliage through the cloak.

I'd best sign off now. Give my love to Larry, Mom and Dad, Gail and Helen. Perhaps when you have a school break you can come visit me in the New Bohemia.

Much love,

Julie

On the weekend, she and George went out for a night of escape. Julie liked her new job fine, enjoying the people she was working with. But the sense of this city was so alien to what she was used to. Detroit and Washington DC were more business-oriented cities. They worked, and they worked hard, in those cities. They were industrial, as well as industrious. This city, though, while there were many people working, had a much more relaxed vibration about it. Enjoyment seemed to be an essential ingredient in life, and this was a new concept to her. Her father wouldn't have approved. He was very much of a mind that hard work was its own reward. It didn't seem … right, somehow, for a city to be so happy with itself. She was dismayed at how much her own father's attitudes had infected her own.

She needed an escape from this unease, so she had asked George to take her outside the city to see the sights. He took her around to the rocky shores along the coast. They drove up the Pacific Coast Highway to the Muir Woods. Walking through the forest calmed her. They found a quiet spot in the shade. George laid out a large blanket so they ate a picnic of fruit, cheese and bread among the trees, bees buzzed around them and the wind soughed through the leaves.

After they had sated themselves, in both food and body, they lay among the dappled sunlight for a long time, refreshing their souls.

She had brought watercolor supplies with her, in case she was inspired. After a while, she got up and set up a station to capture the light and color among the trees. Golds and greens, sepia and umber, with the occasional dots of yellow and white wildflowers. Washes of pale blue sky and silver clouds. George came to watch her, but she wasn't as self-conscious as she often was when someone watched her work.

Satisfied with her work, she laid the paper out to dry in the warm summer sun, turning to George.

"Well, I'm refreshed. Up for round two?"

George smiled and took her hand.

*****

Julie looked in the mirror, putting the final touches on her make-up and hair for their sojourn. They were off to the park again, near Haight Ashbury, for a Saturday evening of fun. George had friends he wanted to hook up with to watch a concert. She had met them before last weekend, so was looking forward to fun. She even put flowers in her hair, purloined from a bush along the street.

The flowers reminded her of the gardens behind Saint Hill Manor in East Grinstead, which in turn reminded her of Paul. She squashed the memory and blinked the tears from her eyes.

She had expanded her wardrobe in the month since she'd been in California. She had purchased caftans in tribal designs. While the colors were bright, they were still tasteful enough not to offend her sense of color. The outfit she was wearing tonight was in her favorite palette, browns and golds with bits of brighter yellow as accent. She had a copper colored hairband and wore her thick hair long in the back. I look like a proper hippie. And she giggled at the idea of a "proper hippie", a true oxymoron if she ever heard one.

They walked arm in arm down the street towards the park. George was dressed in a new jacket which had fringe coming down all along the arms, in strategic places on the front and back, in a V pattern. Others were walking towards the park, like moths being drawn towards a flame of fun.

Julie wasn't as overwhelmed any longer, having come almost every evening since the first night. She was beginning to learn how to ride the wave of frenzy and peace, another contradiction. She had enjoyed all the new, bizarre music she had been hearing, trying the interesting drinks and smokes she had been offered. There was fantastic new art (and not so fantastic), as well as people who were colorful, in all aspects of the word.

The music group they were going to listen to was a new one, called Jefferson Airplane. She had heard of them last week, as they were listed on a poster for the big festival coming up at Monterey. George had promised to take her, but she was excited to be able to preview one of the artists, so to speak.

They ambled through the park, because people were packed in tight, over-welcoming to strangers. One young man with long brown hair and glassy blue eyes came up to her, placed a daisy behind her ear with gentle hands. Julie tensed, as did George, remembering the previous assault, but the drifter offered no worry. He drifted off, with stars in his eyes and a bunch of other daisies in his hand, perhaps for other random women. A large blond woman with heart-shaped glasses came to them and kissed George on the mouth, then Julie, spinning off to someone else.

When at last they found the tree at which they were supposed to meet their friends, they waited and people-watched on the seething crowds before them.

"Look at how long that guy's hair is! He must have been growing it for years." George pointed to the left. Julie craned her neck until she saw his subject.

"Wow—it's longer than mine ever was. I didn't realize the hippie thing had been around so long."

"He was probably a beatnik before. That began sometime in the fifties, didn't it?"

"You tell me. You're the one who loves those black turtlenecks."

"Turtlenecks do not a beatnik make. I like the way they look on me," George did his best to look haughty, but Julie chuckled.

"Sure, sure … oh, wow … look at her. She's belly-dancing. What are those in her fingers?"

"I think they are called castanets. She looks amazing. I didn't realize the back would bend that far back." George turned his head to one side as the dancer bent farther back. Julie wasn't sure she cared for the interest George was taking in the dancer, so looked for a distraction from the limber young lady.

"Hey, isn't Summer over there?" Julie raised her arm to wave at one of the friends they were meeting.

"It is, and Jonas and Otter as well." He joined Julie in her gesticulations until the group saw them. They waved back.

As the group converged and greetings were exchanged, Otter pulled out a bright red handkerchief out of his pocket and opened it with care, revealing a piece of paper, perforated into smaller bits, each bit with a strange picture printed on them. He had six of them.

"What is it, Otter?" The man had a love of trying all sorts of new things. This must be his latest acquisition.

"LSD. Acid. Everyone want a hit?"

Julie had heard of LSD. She searched her memories for any of the side effects, but all she could remember was it caused hallucinations. According to the stories, it's what made Jimi Hendrix and Jim Morrison such famous poets and musicians. Perhaps it could do the same for her art? It wasn't the first drug she had tried, but from what she heard, it might turn out to be the strongest yet.

"Okay, I'm game. George? How about you?"

"Sure, but let's make a pact, first. The five of us look out for each other. No wandering off on your own in this crowd. We'd never find ourselves if we got lost in this. Deal?"

Everyone agreed, taking one. Otter took two, explaining he'd had it before, so he knew how to deal with the effects. Besides, having one left meant he'd have to trip alone in the future, which wasn't as much fun.

Julie tensed herself after chewing the little piece of paper for a while, swallowing it. Other than her own tension, she experienced nothing strange.

"It takes a while to set in, Julie. Relax ... you will feel it in a half hour or so." Otter was looking at her, putting a hand on her shoulder.

They all decided to sit down under the tree to people-watch. It was safer than moving around in the throng of people. This was also where the musicians were supposed to play in about an hour, so there was no particular need to move at that moment.

George held her hand, but dropped it to point to a man dressed in vibrant colors, who was leaping his way through the crowds. He reminded Julie of a mountain goat on an alpine peak, bouncing from rock to rock. She then glanced at her hand to examine it closer. She had done detailed study drawings of her hands in art class, but she had never before understood how fascinating all the tendons and muscles under the skin were. She flexed and relaxed her hand, studied the lines in her palms, examined the texture of her skin. The play of tendon and bone beneath her skin was fascinating and alien. When she clasped her hands together, it felt bizarre, as if she was somehow detached from the act, her skin numbed and separated from her body.

She turned to share this with George, but when she looked up, she forgot her intent. She was glad she was sitting down with her back against a sturdy tree. The waves of color and people undulated like a heaving sea, the very mass comingling, breathing as one, in and out, in and out, like a giant alien creature of peace, joy, and eternal, universal love.

Julie wanted to get up and dance, be part of this incredible journey, this one-ness of nature, but she was rooted to her spot. The tree was holding her there as though she were part of its root system. This was fine—she liked being part of the tree. She closed her eyes and reached down into the roots, into the loamy, thick, cool ground, down into the dirt, past the squirming worms and to the solid bedrock.

She breathed in deeply, then let her breath out with a long, shuddering sigh. Opening her eyes, she rose again from the deep, into the bright, cool, thin air. She was reborn, blossoming, new and shiny.

Next to her, she saw George breathing deep as well, staring into the crowd, transfixed by what he saw. Otter was also frozen, but Jonas and Summer were entwined next to the tree, their hands exploring each other with reckless abandon.

Something shifted behind Julie's ear, a heavy thing which didn't belong. She put her hand up to her head and touched the daisy which had been placed there, a thousand years ago.

She pulled the daisy out and caressed its petals, one by one, the soft, silky, smooth, fragrant petals. She placed them against her cheek to stroke their essence. She caressed the soft fuzz along the stem, thinking of her body hair, prickling with gooseflesh along her arms, as her own stem fuzz. She handed the flower to George for his examination, wanting to share her profound discoveries with him.

He turned in slow motion, looking at her as if he'd never seen her before. He put a hand against her hair, stroking it down to the ends. Fondling the ends between his fingers, he pulled them up to brush her nose. She chuckled at the tickling sensation, grinning. He leaned over and kissed her. The kiss took forever, and no time at all.

Sometime later, they heard music. The band was playing close by, deep tones vibrating through Julie's bones. The music was strange and haunting, the heavy guitars whining up and down in a wave. Julie wanted to get up and dance, but when she tried, George kept her down.

"We have to keep together, remember? Let's all stay put. It's safer that way."

"But I must dance. I think if I don't dance, I'll break."

"Well, okay, we'll get up and dance, but stay near the tree. The tree is our safe place. It's our home, it's our refuge. Don't leave the tree." George looked both worried and transcendent at the same time.

"I shall be like Buddha and be one with the tree." Julie agreed with solemnity and got up to dance. She danced slowly, her feet in place, swaying her upper body in time to the slow guitar waves. She heard the singer above the noise of the crowd.

"One pill makes you larger,

and one pill makes you small …

And the one that mother gives you,

won't do anything at all …"

Julie imagined herself growing and shrinking with the waves of sound, as the crowd sound grew and fell with the rhythm. It was almost a physical wave rushing over her, the tide waxing and waning with the music. Despite his earlier admonishment, George got up and danced with her, his hands on her waist to anchor them both. Otter got up to join them, dancing as one, swaying and waving with the tangible sounds.

Much later, as they were sitting once again around the tree, they began to come back into reality. The crowds had died out, and the music was long done. Jonas and Summer had finished their own explorations. Had they made love right there? Julie believed so, but she couldn't bring to mind the memory itself. They weren't sleeping, but were clinging to each other tight, hands caressing and touching.

Julie ached to have a pencil in her hand, or charcoal, or paint, or even mud, anything she could use to create, to draw, to paint the images. Flashes of inspiration were cascading through her mind. She resolved to have supplies the next time she did this, as the images were going so fast through her she couldn't grasp one to keep it in her memory. Flitting, fleeing, swift as doves the visualizations came and went through her creative center.

Flashes of memory of the evening began to come to her as she became more grounded. She recalled others had joined her in the dancing, but George, sometimes Otter, had kept one hand on the tree as a physical anchor, keeping them from drifting into the chaos. The sounds were still a mélange of noise, but they were stripped of their three-dimensionality, no longer buffeting physical forces. At one point she was certain she was dancing with Paul, but that couldn't be possible. Paul, Paul, a memory from a thousand years ago. She pushed it away.

Summer and Jonas sat up, languorous, stretching. It seemed like an excellent idea to Julie, so she gave a mighty, full body stretch—and it was delicious. She kept stretching, moving, bending. It was an almost sexual pleasure to do so. She was dancing again, but with her own soul.

"I think we should head home, Otter. Will you folks be all right?" George took Julie's arm, but she didn't want to go yet.

"But we are still having fun. We are part of this amazing creature, this universal alien."

George looked at her askance. She imagined what she said would make no sense to someone who hadn't been in her head for the last several hours. She laughed at herself.

"Sorry, I went down strange paths, I guess."

"I guess so. But yes, I think we should finish this trip up in a more controlled area. Does that sound okay?" He stroked her cheek with a feather touch. She put her hand on his as he did so.

149

"Yes … yes, that sounds … wonderful …"

They thanked Otter for the trip, took their leave of Summer and Jonas, wending their way back to Fred's house. It seemed to take a prolonged time, even though it was four blocks away, but it was an entire adventure in itself. She kept looking up to see the dancing stars, twinkling in the velvet dark sky. When she did so, she would stumble and trip, so George had to remind her to watch her steps.

When they did reach their room, they got into the beds. They had long since moved them together to form one larger bed, tying the legs together to keep it from moving apart. The sheets were so sensuous and cool on her bare skin, she wanted to abandon herself to the sensation. She kept squirming and moving around under the covers.

"Keep doing that, Julie, it will make my part much easier."

"And is it normally a difficult job?" She teased him.

"Not at all … but this way I won't have to move at all, just let you wiggle your way home, so to speak."

His skin against hers and the hair on his chest was scratchy and rough. She was fascinated with the texture. She touched every inch with her hands until he took her wrists and moved them farther down.

"If you're going to get stuck in a fascination loop, there are better subjects for your attentions."

"Indeed there are."

They finished the trip in an intense study of each other's bodies, wrapped in a fog of isolation and sexual joy.

*****

Julie shifted the mockup photographs around, not pleased with their current layout. She offset and angled them. Yes, it was better, it looked much more interesting this way. She tacked down the mockups in their spots, plotting out the text, using her ruler, stencils and pencils.

"It's looking great, Julie. Is it for the new buyer conference next month?"

Julie almost jumped out of her skin at Tamara's voice. She had been concentrating so intently on her project she hadn't heard the older woman come up behind her.

"That's right. Tony asked me to put it together so we would have time to send it to the printers."

"What are you doing for lunch today? I've found a quaint little sandwich shop a couple blocks away. Would you like to join me?" An invitation from Tamara was more like a royal command from the Queen, so there was only one acceptable answer.

"Of course, I should be delighted."

*****

Julie was enjoying her favorite sandwich, a Rueben, while she wondered what Tamara wanted. Though she was always perfectly polite to Julie, Tamara didn't waste time with idle chitchat. If she was talking to someone, it was for a concrete purpose.

Tamara looked up from her club sandwich and asked her, without preamble, "I was wondering, Julie, do you like children?"

This was such an odd question, out of the blue, related to nothing they had ever discussed. Julie was momentarily dumbstruck. She took a sip of her Coke to clear her mouth, giving her time to formulate an answer.

"I like children quite well. Are you asking if I want to have family?" She managed to put only enough quizzical into her response to sound curious but unconcerned.

Her short laugh was clipped and loud. "Ha! No, nothing like that. Well, perhaps vicariously. I need someone to look after my own children, you see. I remember you mentioning you had been a nanny before. I've three young ones, aged two, four, and seven. Barbara, Janet and Donald, in that order. My husband and I have … sought separate paths. Therefore, since I have no desire or means to quit working to take care of them, I need to hire someone to help.

Would you be interested in the position?"

Julie considered it. She did enjoy the work she was doing, but she also loved children. But Tamara was so abrupt in manner, she wasn't sure she could handle it in large doses.

"You could continue to work at the Church, of course—much of the work you do can be done at home, or you could adopt an evening shift, after I've come home for the day. I could pay you $75 a week, as well as your own room, rent-free, in the apartments above the office. Please, do say you will? I have been watching you work, and you do have an admirable work ethic. I would love for someone to instill this in my children."

"It all sounds delightful, and I am tempted. I helped my mother take care of my little brother for many years. I do enjoy children ..." Julie was concerned about her relationship with George, but also knew he would be leaving for Michigan again soon. And the month-long mooching grace period at Fred's house was coming up fast.

"I'll even arrange for you to take classes at the art school for free, so you can further your career." Tamara said this as if it was an offer much too good to pass up, a royal bequest, as it were.

Julie decided it must be time to shift her path. As George was leaving, she would need a new place to live. This was not only free lodging, it was additional income as well. It put a serious dent in her social life, but without George she doubted it would be as active as it had been.

"Tamara, I'd be delighted. When would you like me to start? When can I meet the children?"

"Today is Monday—could you come home with me tomorrow evening, to meet them all? And perhaps we can move you in this weekend." Tamara pulled out a notepad from her clutch purse, writing a couple notes. She flipped to another page and scribbled, ripping it out and handing it to Julie.

"This is my address and phone at home, in case you need it. Thank you, Julie. I do look forward to having you in the household." She held out her hand, formal, so Julie took it, wondering what she had gotten herself into.

*****

July 1, 1967, San Francisco

Dear Katy,

Life has once again shifted, but I think it's still in a good way. I'm still working at the Church, but George has returned to Michigan, as he had planned. I was teary at the parting, but we remain good friends no matter what else has occurred between us. I thought for a while it might be more, but he's great fun to be with. Anyhow, I think I need someone with more substance and purpose for a permanent partner.

I've an additional job now, taking care of three young children for Tamara Lange, one of the employees. She's paying me as well as providing a room above the office to live in. She's even arranging for me to take art classes. I start my first one, a specialized advertising class, next week. I'll let you know how things turn out.

I told you to watch out for that teacher, didn't I? He was a menace when I took his class, to anything in a skirt. Don't let yourself get caught alone with him again, please. I know it takes a long time to gather all your art supplies— cheat, and start before class is over. That way you're not the last one left.

Something strange is going on with the people working here, but I don't know what it is. I can sense tension, and there is a secret no one seems to be talking about, but there are significant glances going around. I don't think it's anything about me, but I'm loath to ask questions, since I'm so new. Low woman on the totem pole, and all that.

So, tell me about your boyfriend. All you've told me so far is you met him in England. Is that where he's from? Details, girl!

Much love,

Julie

*****

Julie was almost pulling her hair out in frustration. Janet was cranky and crying so hard, her little face was a deep, angry red. There was no clue to the reason for her rage, but Julie did her best to rock her into calm. She bounced Janet on her knee, rocking her, stroking her thin, straight, white-blond hair.

Donald wasn't home yet from elementary school, but Barbara had been playing in her room. Bouncing the baby on her hip, Julie went to check in on Barbara, discovering she had taken every single toy in her box—this was a significant number—and strewn them around the room in a chaotic mess. There were dolls, building blocks, stuffed animals, and books all over. She daren't walk in, for fear of stepping on a toy and dropping Janet.

"Barbara! What on earth are you doing?"

"Playing." Barbara was excellent at the art of pouting, setting her face into a determined expression. Her reddish-blond hair was tousled, spiked out in all directions.

"You may play with one toy at a time, Barbara. Put the rest away, now. Start with the books, please." Julie did her best to be firm but polite. She emulated Tamara's manner when taking the children to task, so they would be less confused with orders.

The child argued, but received a level look of determination from Julie. Barbara proceeded to put each book away, with sullen glances at the door after each one. Julie remained there, watching her, bouncing Janet on her hip, until she heard the front door downstairs.

"Keep at it, young lady. I'll come back to check your progress. The dolls are next. " If she didn't give clear instructions, Barbara would always find a way to wiggle out of them. A born lawyer, this one was.

She went down the stairs, expecting to see Donald coming home from school. The bus dropped him at the corner, two houses down, and he was due home soon. However, she was surprised to see Tamara there instead.

"Julie! Whatever is wrong with Janet?" The child was still sobbing and red, though the screeching had calmed down when she went up to Barbara's room.

"She's been horribly fussy. She's calmed down from earlier."

Tamara looked doubtful, but accepted the explanation. While she was business-like in all other things, she was solicitous of her children. "Very well, as long as she's getting better. Is Donald home yet?"

"Not yet, I thought it was him coming in when I heard the door. Is anything wrong? You're home earlier than normal." Julie searched Tamara's face for clues.

"Oh, no, I had a project I was working on and realized I had forgotten my notes. I'll be back out again in a moment." She walked into her library/office, grabbed a file from one of the mahogany cabinets in the desk, bustling out again.

Julie imagined the office had first belonged to the husband, the absent Charles Lange she had heard of but never seen. She wondered what he had been like, why they had broken up. Well, it was none of her business. She continued to rock the child on her hip, pleased Janet was almost asleep in her arms.

*****

That evening, Julie was working late in the office, finishing up a project Tony had wanted for the next day. She was usually done at Tamara's by five, done at the office by nine. It didn't leave her much time to socialize during the week, but she made up for the lack on the weekends. She was deep in concentration on her task when she heard a door close elsewhere in the warren of rooms.

Who could be here this late at night? She had a momentary twinge that it would be Tibbets, and shivered. He did give her the creeps. There hadn't been anything she would call an incident since the art supply run, but she tended to avoid him since then.

Having lived in Detroit, Julie decided to be cautious, hiding herself in case it was someone breaking in. She turned out the desk lamp she had been using, found a spot behind a filing cabinet, waiting.

She heard a woman's voice and a man's responding chuckle. She caught a glimpse of their shadow along the far wall, near the corridor. They appeared to be embracing. Was it a couple looking for privacy, in from the streets? She was about to come out and ask them to leave when she recognized the voices. It was Tamara … and Tony? Tony was married! Well, so was Tamara, but she was separated, so it wasn't so bad, but Tony … she liked him, he was a good friend. She was betrayed by this action, as if being loyal was a prerequisite for being affable. Perhaps she was mistaken in her assumptions?

As she stood there, still in shock, the couple moved on past the doorway. She could see them in silhouette. Tony's arm was around Tamara's shoulders, hers around his waist. She was looking at him with almost simpering eyes. Tamara didn't simper. This was so odd.

They moved on to where Tamara's office was. As soon as she heard the door closed, she gathered up her purse as best she could in the dark, sneaking out of the building. She was careful to close the door behind her without so much as a click of the lock.

Julie was confused and betrayed, for Tony's wife's sake. However, she did know she should not be caught in the building right now. Neither of them would appreciate being found out. Instead, she headed down the street to the late-night café where she often ate dinner, ordered a chocolate milkshake and a Rueben sandwich, thinking.

She never had met Tony's wife. Perhaps they were also a separated? It must be. She hoped it was. She would be less judgmental if they were both 'available', at least in spirit. She was such a prude—this was the time of love, the place for experimentation. Her Midwestern morality wasn't welcome here. Still, it was difficult to surmount.

After about an hour and a half, Julie decided she should get back to finish her project, then get sleep. It was going to be a stressful day tomorrow, especially if the artwork wasn't finished in time.

*****

1967, East Grinstead, England

The leaving was rather bittersweet. She knew it was coming, but the three months went by quickly. Victoria had written to her, to assure her that Paul had transferred away. Back to Minnesota, or somewhere else, she didn't much care. As long as he was gone. Sheila had assured her she still had a position in

East Grinstead, and Eileen had agreed to take her on again as a nanny. It almost felt as if she was taking a step backwards in time. But she had enjoyed her months in San Francisco, and in some ways, it had changed her perspective on things.

For instance, the affair between Tamara and Tony had shown her that not all marriages are right. Sometimes you must break a bad match to make a stronger one. But Paul had never hinted that he wanted to leave his wife. He hadn't been interested in a change, just a fling.

The journey to England was uneventful, and she slid back into her old life without much fanfare or grief. Victoria became a closer friend and confidante, and Julie felt more at home than she had in years.

*****

1968, East Grinstead, England

"I didn't hire you just to have you be unavailable when I need you. If I need you for the children, you'll have to reset your priorities. I did apologize for the short notice, but there's nothing I can do about it." Eileen, when angry, didn't shout. She did get snotty, Julie decided.

"Eileen, if it was a social conflict, I could cancel, no problem. But this is work. I'm on a deadline. They've been giving me more responsibilities, since they're ramping up the new membership drive. I've got to get this artwork done before tomorrow morning. And you know I can't work on art with the kids around. There is no way I could concentrate, much less keep my art supplies from being confiscated or destroyed by curious kids."

Julie was beyond exasperated. She had been told by her she was up for consideration to run the art department in this location. Doing this job well might be the deciding factor. She would have had plenty of time to work on it tonight, though she would have little sleep. But Eileen just now told her she and Percy were going out to an event in London, so would need her to watch the children until well after midnight, when they were due to return. Again, this would have been fine if she had gotten an advanced warning. But Eileen was getting less considerate of her young nanny. Julie had about had enough.

"You know I love these kids as if they were my own, but it isn't fair of you to expect me to have no plans during the evenings. I am here for them during the day, but I need a warning. Did you not know you were going to be out tonight?"

"I did not. Percy did—he had bought tickets to this charity event as a surprise for me. It's an art exhibit." Eileen sounded like the height of nouveau riche snobbery, proud of her rise into the upper echelons of the social elite of London. Julie snorted.

"Then he should have let me know. Look, I'll do my best to find someone to look after them, but I simply do not have the time tonight."

Eileen's gaze got colder than a glacier on midwinter.

"Do not bother, Julie. I shall find someone else. Permanently. Please come back tomorrow and we shall gather any of your personal items for you."

Eileen then strode, quick and haughty, out of the room.

161

Well, this was lovely. Pretty much half her income came from Eileen and watching the kids. She'd been saving her extra money for a while, so had a stash, but not a lot. If the promotion didn't come in, she would have to rein in her entertainment budget, but it was doable. Her lodging was covered by her job, as spartan as it was, so at least that wasn't an issue.

*****

Julie was still shaky with adrenaline, so she gathered herself, retrieved pad of paper and her pastels from her room, making her way out into the town. There was a serene park nearby where she liked to sit and draw. It's what she needed right now. Since she was fired from the kids, she didn't have to worry about having time for the work assignment now. Besides, she would be in no shape to do demanding creative work until she calmed. She knew it for base escapism, accepting it as such.

She found her favorite bench, took a deep breath and closed her eyes, centering herself as they had taught her to do in class. She took several more deep breaths, slow and steady, calming her jangled nerves, spiky anger, and ruffled feathers.

When she opened her eyes, all she saw was the trees rustling in a gentle May breeze, pink wildflowers dotting the grass. She heard the sweet trill of birds coming from the soughing leaves. There was no one else around. She decided this was as it should be.

Julie decided to draw the more unusual-shaped trees near her. One had a thin, low-lying branch which looked like a Victorian swing, so that's what she drew—a young girl, in full swing, with a flowered hat and white, fluffy petticoats billowing around her outstretched feet, clad in white shoes with straps across the top. The girl should be smiling. She took her darker pinks and made a hint of a grin on the girl's face. Turning attention to the hair, Julie decided it was sunny, so she must be blond. She was contemplating making the lawn dappled with sunlight when she heard a sound.

The sound wasn't at all unusual. It was the trees rustling in the breeze. However, it sounded stronger than it should have. She looked up at the sky, noticing it was much darker than it had been a short while ago. She gathered up her materials in haste. There were bits of pastel all around her, as she got messy working with them. A few of them broke as she shoved them all into the cardboard box, with its individual spaces for each color. Her drawing would be ruined with the first drop of rain.

Everything stashed, Julie grabbed her pad and pelted to the house. She stopped, ran back, picked up the box of pastels she had packed and forgotten, running even faster. She stayed hunched over her drawing, trying to shield it from the incipient rain, but at the same time trying to keep it from brushing against her, as the pastels weren't fixed yet. As she made it back to the house, a few large, wet drops plopped on her head. She made it to her room and surveyed the painting, looking for the splotches. No, it was safe. She had made it.

It would have been adding injury to insult to have had her art ruined within two hours of her being fired, she decided. At least now she could replace a horrible memory with a pleasant one.

She truly hoped Eileen's plans were ruined for the night, and she had to stay with her own bloody kids.

As she turned down the hall, she ran right into Paul. He was looking good, tanned and smiling.

She retreated, confused. "What! What are you doing here?"

"Julie! I was hoping I'd run into you. I'd heard you were back." His grin was guileless and maddening.

"You... you were gone. I made sure you were gone."

"I was gone. I was transferred to Spain for a couple months. But I'm back now." He reached for her hands. "I wanted to explain—"

She snatched her hands back from his questing fingers. "You have nothing to explain! You're married. That's the end of the story." The confusion bubbled within her head, making her foggy and sluggish. Why was he here? She had escaped him. It wasn't fair.

"Julie, please, can't we talk about it? Not now, not here, perhaps lunch? Down at the pub? I'll be there tomorrow at noon. Come, please. Just give me a chance?"

His brown eyes pleaded with hers, and she blinked away the tears that threatened to fall. She spun around and walked out into the rain, heedless of the damage to her sketchpad.

*****

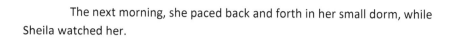

The next morning, she paced back and forth in her small dorm, while Sheila watched her.

"Settle down, Julie. He just asked you to lunch. It wasn't as if he asked you to elope with him."

"He wouldn't be able to. He's married!"

"Yes, and that isn't a crime."

Halting, Julie stared at her friend. "Fornication is! Adultery is!"

Sheila raised her eyebrows. "And has he done any of these with you?"

"You know damn well he hasn't. That's not the point."

"I do believe it is precisely the point, Julie. He is asking you to let him explain. Can you not at least give him that much of a chance?"

"I don't want to."

"I realize that. But it's only fair, is it not? You've never struck me as an unjust person."

Julie let out a deep, angry breath. Sheila was right, damn it all.

*****

"I'll have the steak and kidney pie, please." It was one of Julie's favorites. She loved the savory gravy and flaky pastry of this British staple. "And a pint of cider, thank you."

"I think I'll have the fish and chips, and … a lemonade, if you please."

The cozy little restaurant was almost empty, but they were out early in the evening. Later, as the pubs filled, the restaurant would get more business. For now, though, there was only one other couple dining in the dark room. The walls were paneled with dark wood, perhaps mahogany, while the booths were covered with what may have once been red velvet. The walls were covered with memorabilia from the World War I era, old photographs, recruitment notices, bits from planes and many things Julie couldn't identify.

"You know lemonade doesn't mean what it does in America, right?" She asked Paul.

"Yes, but I like the carbonation. It's an improvement, in my mind."

"Fair enough."

An awkward silence lay over them. Paul reached for her hand on the table, but she snatched hers out of the way and into her lap. She glared at him, and he sighed.

"Julie, my wife and I — well, we have a sort of arrangement."

"What sort of arrangement?"

"She knows that when I travel, I'll be away from her for long months. She has sort of... given permission to me to sow my oats, as it were."

"Sow your oats. Do I look like a field ready to plow, then?" She could feel the heat rise in her cheeks, and lowered her voice. The quiet pub was practically empty, but sound carried easily.

"Of course not. That was a poor choice of words. She... she understands that I would likely meet people who I would like to get to know better when I'm traveling. Can you understand that?"

"I suppose I could understand. That doesn't mean I'm one of them."

He closed his eyes as if praying for patience.

"No, it doesn't. It does mean that you are someone I would like to enjoy lunch with. Will that do for now?"

Julie thought of Tamara and Tony, and their extra-marital affair. If Paul had a pre-arranged agreement, they wouldn't really be hurting his wife. It wouldn't be so bad, would it? Still...

It wouldn't hurt to be friends.

She asked, "Have you eaten here before?"

"I have, but it's been a while. The food is good enough. Basic British fare, nothing fancy, but reliable."

"Fare enough." Julie emphasized the word 'fare' so he could tell she was trying to make a pun. She wasn't as skilled at them as Paul was, if 'skilled' was the right word to use. Her attempt was feeble.

He gave her a sidelong glance, screwing up his face.

"Now you know how we feel when you do it."

Their drinks arrived, so she raised hers in a toast.

"Here's to second chances. May our second be more successful than the first."

"I'll drink to that." Paul smiled, took an obligatory sip, taking her hand.

"I am sorry I left you in the lurch last time. I promise, no more gory movies in the future."

"I appreciate the sentiment very much. " Julie smiled at Paul, his hand was still holding hers over the round table. It was falling asleep, so she shifted to relieve the pressure.

"Does the graphic stuff not bother you, then?"

"I guess not. I don't panic at blood in real life, though I prefer not to deal with it if it can be helped. I'm also able to disassociate enough from movies and television to realize they aren't imminent danger," she theorized.

"Perhaps I should work on dissociative techniques in the future."

Julie shrugged, "Couldn't hurt, I suppose. Might be downright helpful in the future. Like when you have children." She instantly regretted the reference to his marital state.

Paul heaved a sigh, and squeezed her hands. "Julie, my wife and I have a sort of … arrangement. Not an open marriage, but she realizes when I'm away for long periods of time, I might … stray."

"Hmph. I don't think I appreciate the implications to my own status as a stray's bone." Julie retrieved her hand from his grip, despite his attempt to retain it.

"Julie, Julie, that's not what you are at all. You are a friend. A friend I would like to keep. A friend I enjoy being with. If it moves on to being an affectionate friend, fantastic. If not, that's also fantastic. Let's play it by ear, okay?"

Julie wasn't sure she was ready to be mollified. She was still ruffled after her dustup with Eileen the week before. She had, at least, put Eileen's plans into disarray—they had to cancel their trip to London. Her supervisor had been thrilled to move her to daytime hours, with full time work. She was looking like the best candidate for her promotion. Julie was more in charge of her destiny than she had been in a long time. This new-found confidence seemed to make her more edgy, it seemed. She had never considered being the ladder-climbing career sort, but she hadn't tried it before. She was willing to give it the old college try and see how it worked. Perhaps she should do this with Paul, as well.

She took a couple more breaths. "All right. Let's see how it goes. It seems unfair to both me and your wife."

"Friendship should never be unfair, my dear." How could she resist that grin? He was one of those men who smiled all the way, his mouth, his eyes, even his hair seemed to be joyful and entreating.

The waitress came up to them with a huge tray on her shoulder, setting up a tray stand. She was surprised to find her steak and kidney pie not only came with chips, but with a green mess which she figured was mushy peas. She had seen it a few times so far, but had never before been brave enough to try the green mushy mess. She pictured a new alien species which was invading dinner plates all over the land.

She tasted a small, cautious spoonful of the glutinous mass. She blinked a couple times, trying the taste and texture out in her mouth, taking another, larger bite. It tasted like a thick split pea soup, with pepper and other spices in it. It was good. She was chagrined she had taken so long to try the stuff.

Paul had avoided his, but was noting her pleasure in the dish. "Like the mushy peas, do you?"

"I'd never tried them before, but they are pretty good."

"Not my thing. I prefer my food with crunch and texture. The taste is fine, I love peas, but I like to bite my food, not slurp it."

"What about soups?"

"Stew and chili, fine. Cream or puréed soups? No thank you."

"Interesting. I wonder if you had issues dealing with moving to solid foods as a baby."

He looked thoughtful "Could be. I've never been a fan of them."

Julie smiled. "Perhaps now is when I should let you know I make a mean chili?"

"Trying to impress me with your domestic skills already? My, you do work fast." He looked like an outraged Puritan.

"Tease. Merely making conversation." Julie returned, with a quelling look.

*****

As they walked back towards Saint Hill, they held hands. The night was bright, as the moon was full and the sky was clear. Stars sparkled above them in a glittering display of jewels on velvet. Julie breathed in deep of the cool air, smelling the leaves, flowers, the hint of smoke from nearby chimneys.

"Was that a sigh, or are you enjoying the night?" Paul sounded halfway between concern and teasing.

"Enjoying the night air. It's so different here from where I grew up near Detroit. The light pollution is almost non-existent. You can see the stars and smell the trees."

"Minneapolis is the same way, but if you go north, into lake country, you have the universe laid out before you." Paul had a dreamy look on his face. They stopped walking and faced each other. "My family always went up north in the summer, to vacation among the ten thousand lakes. We would get a cabin on the lake, go fishing or boating, and relax into the wonder of nature."

"We do something similar, but up into Canada. Our family has an island, perhaps three acres long, with three cabins on it. We all go up on vacation each summer, doing about the same. There is a family on the mainland, they've been friends with our family for three generations. They have a huge farm, so we get to go pick fresh strawberries and peas, get fresh bread and butter from them. Pure heaven." Julie remembered the annual trips with great pleasure and wistfulness.

Paul stroked her cheek with a tender brush of his fingers. He bent down to her, ever so lightly brushing her lips with his. She caught her breath, and managed to turn it into another deep, though ragged, sigh.

"That was nice." She smiled up at the silhouette his head made against the moon-bright darkness.

"Yes, it was … nice." He bent again to kiss her with purpose.

*****

1968, East Grinstead, England

They didn't have a lot of options for places to have any privacy. They both shared rooms with other people. Though the estate was large, it was busy will all manner of people going to and fro, with no real rhyme or reason to their movements.

Over the course of the next several days, Julie and Paul found stolen moments to enjoy each other's company. They spent time talking, kissing, with not a small bit of physical exploration. However, to take it any further, they would need true privacy.

It took discussion to figure out trysting spots. They decided the bathroom in the B&B where Paul was staying at was the most practical place. It could be locked, and there were a couple people staying there who had a reputation for long visits, so to speak. As unappetizing as this sounded to Julie, she had to agree. Even any sounds they might make could be explained as a normal occupant's colonic struggles. She teased Paul about how romantic the places he chose were, how she would, one day, tell their children about his swoon-worthy gallantries.

They made their rendezvous several days later, when Paul was sure the B&B would be empty, at least long enough to ensconce themselves in their chosen sanctuary. They locked themselves in, standing in awkward silence.

"Isn't this the part where you're supposed to sweep me off my feet, despite our banal surroundings?" Julie asked him, raising one eyebrow.

"It isn't conducive for romance, is it?" He eyed the space on the floor. It was, like most bathrooms in the UK, tiny compared to US bathrooms. The floor space might accommodate them both lying down, but only if they sort of bent. At least it was meticulously clean. His landlady would have brooked no speck of dirt or grime in her house, upon pain of court-martial. He looked for further options, chagrined he hadn't considered any requirement beyond privacy.

"Perhaps the bathtub would serve?" It was a cast iron Victorian job, complete with claw feet, painted blinding white. "We could put down a couple towels, perhaps, on our knees ...?"

"It'll be tight, but it could serve. It will likely be more comfortable than the floor, at any rate."

"Very well. Milady?" Paul reached for her hand, turning it over, kissing her wrist. Julie closed her eyes, sensing the soft, barely-there sensation, surprised at how this tiny contact went all the way down to her toes. It added suspense and anticipation to their contact, knowing, for the first time, they would be able to do whatever they liked.

She opened her eyes to find him kissing farther up her arm, to the crook of her arm. Even though he was clean-shaven, it tickled so much she flinched. He looked up, as if afraid he had somehow done something wrong, but her eyes were closed again, savoring the sensation, trying hard not to move.

Up the kisses went, to her shoulder, her neck. She could no longer hold in the moan of pleasure at these incredible sensations of tickle and ecstasy. The hairs on her arms sprang up, as she suppressed the frisson which climbed up her spine.

She opened her eyes again, seeing his brown eyes looking at her, intent.

"Your eyes are like reflected, still pools on a stormy day, you know."

She closed them again.

By the time his lips reached her mouth, she was more than ready for his now insistent kisses. They held each other tight while kissing, hands fumbling to loosen clothing, caress, touch and stroke.

They made their way to their narrow 'bed', not noticing it wasn't the softest of king-sized feather beds.

*****

Later, after awkward gymnastics and fits of giggles, they curled up together in a sitting position in the tub. Julie was lying back on Paul, his arms around her.

"Well, I think this might be one for the record books." Julie could feel Paul's chest vibrate as he chuckled.

"Oh?"

"How many times do you think such a setting has actually worked for such an act? I'm sure we're trailblazers. Perhaps I should call Guinness and have them create an entry?"

"Perhaps you should not!" Julie was aghast until she understood he was joking.

"Don't worry, I'll keep this as our special secret. Besides, no one would believe us."

*****

April 16, 1999, Miami, Florida

Dear Sir:

Let me open this letter to state that I am looking for nothing from you. I do not need money, nor acknowledgement, just closure, perhaps practical information, if that is all you can give. I have been researching my family for many years, hoping for at least medical background and genealogical data for my own research.

I have reason to believe that you are my father. My mother is Julie Jensen, and she worked for the Church in the 1960s, in East Grinstead, England. She had met and became involved with a man named Paul Stein. As a result of this liaison, she became pregnant with me, and has raised me on her own.

I understand you will have a family of your own. I have no wish to have this family upset by an intruder, so I would request at least information, if I can. Do I have any half-siblings? Is there any history of disease in your side of my family? Diabetes? Cancer? Heart disease? I would greatly appreciate it if you could share such details as you may.

If, however, you are able and willing to acknowledge me, I would be most appreciative. I've enclosed a picture of myself so you may judge for yourself if we might look alike.

Sincerely,

Your daughter,

Kirsten Jensen

Kirsten chewed the back of her pencil and looked at the letter. It read clinical and detached, but it had to be the way to do this. An emotional request would be blackmail, and she disliked such manipulations. This, however, should be sufficient for even the most hostile putative father to accept. She hoped.

She made a copy of it before she signed, sealed and mailed it out. The researcher had gotten back to her, a year later, with information on her father. This was her first use of the information. He had gotten her an address in Missouri (Missouri??), a birth certificate, and a marriage certificate.

Her next step was to use the birth certificate to at least find out more about this branch of the family. It listed her grandparents' names, so she could at least write to the State of Minnesota to get their birth certificates, to continue her researches. If he never replied to her letter, she could at least find out where they all came from.

After her record requests were all posted, she gave her mother a call.

"Hello, this is Julie."

"Hey, Mom. It's Kirsten."

"Who else would be calling me Mom? How are you, hon?"

"Doing okay, I guess. Stressed with the new job, but its interesting work. I'm at a CPA firm up in Jupiter. It's larger than the ones I've worked at before—about twenty accountants, five partners. They are all nice folk."

"That's good, I'm glad. Sandy is threatening to quit her job at the hospital again, but you know her—that's a constant." Julie and Kirsten shared a laugh at Sandy's never-ending complaints.

"What about your job? Are you still doing design work at the architect's office?"

"Well, mostly secretarial work, but yes, Joe sometimes has me working on decorating the plans he creates. I fill in the plants and external pretty bits before he presents it. He sticks to the building parts."

"At least you're doing artwork again. I know you missed it when you were doing the property management stuff."

"I still don't get much time for artwork I LIKE doing, but at least this is something, yes. And this place is much closer to home, as well. I don't have to take the Metrorail to work. I can ride my bike again."

Kirsten couldn't figure out a good segue, so she figured she'd dive right in anyhow.

"Oh, I wanted to let you know—I may have made progress in finding my dad."

There was a moment of silence on the line.

"I haven't found him yet, or anything, but I've gotten a birth certificate and marriage certificate. I can at least find out about his family."

"Oh ... okay, I suppose its fine, then." Julie sounded guarded and hesitant.

"Mom, if I do find him ... I mean, we're all adults now, even any children he would have. I don't want anything from him, and I'll tell him so. I want to know who he is, you know? Fill the ... hole in my psyche. Discover his half of my roots." She doesn't understand. She always knew who her parents were, what they were like. Her mother couldn't understand, deep inside, that there was a part of Kirsten which wasn't complete without this knowledge.

*****

May 20, 1968, East Grinstead, England

Dear Katy:

I'm so sorry I haven't written to you in a while. Things have been hectic around here, now that I've been promoted to be in charge of our art department. I no longer take care of Eileen's children, as we had a difference of opinion on what my priorities should be. I miss the kids a lot, but having the freedom to set my own hours has really helped me advance here. It also allows me my own free time to pursue my art. I've even had my paintings on display at one of the local pubs, getting several compliments on my work.

I'm afraid I've gotten involved with Paul. I think you would like him, despite his silliness and his tendency to pun through everything. He is sweet, musical, and intelligent, as well as dashingly handsome. He's got dark eyes and hair, and plays guitar. I'm sure that would be enough for you to fall for him. He's a true flirt, and I know I'm not the only female whose company he enjoys, but I'm happy to have my part of him. He was joking the other day that each of his harem had a part to play in the world—mine was to bear him children. Can you imagine that? If he wasn't so silly, I'd accuse him of the height of arrogance, but there isn't much he cannot make light of.

How are your plans coming with the move to England? Are you still slated to come up this winter to meet with your fiancé? I would love to be there to meet you when you arrive, so please let me know as plans solidify.

How are mom and dad doing? Any news on Larry? Is he doing any better in school?

Give my love to everyone, and please let Gail know I might have missed her last letter. It's been a long time since I've heard from her.

Love always, your sister,

Julie

*****

She needed more burnt sienna, Julie decided. She used more of the warmer colors than the cooler ones, so she was always running out of her favorite palettes. Perhaps she could create from the regular sienna and mix in black. Not the same, but adding a bit of green did bring it closer. The green reminded her of Paul's eyes.

The scene she was painting was a pastoral one. The landlord at the pub had commissioned her for this. He wanted a view from the back of the pub, across the village park with the hills in the distance. There were a couple of interesting trees here and there, though she did move one closer to the edge of the canvas for composition reasons. She wanted to give the sky a sunny look, but with clouds for character. Today was a good day for it, with clouds scudding across the sky, dark with horded moisture, looking both ominous and atmospheric.

One of them was getting larger. She decided she had done all the painting she should today, before the cloud decided to be more than ominous, dropping its horded rain upon her and her painting supplies. She had gotten quick about gathering up her things, since the weather had mercurial moods.

As she made her way back up to the house, she ran into Sheila and David, walking with their child, Neil, and Victoria. They stopped under an awning as the rain dripped down upon them.

"Were you out painting again today, Julie?" David inquired, polite as all Brits tend to be when on their game.

"I was—Nigel at the pub asked me to paint a scene for him. I was excited to get my first international commission piece."

Sheila smiled, "Surely you've had commissions before? You're a wonderful painter. I especially like the fantasy works you've done." Sheila loved anything whimsical, be it fairy tales, Tolkein books, or science fiction movies.

"Oh, I've done commissions before, but all back in the States. This is the first time I've gotten one since I came over here. I wish this was a fantasy piece. While I love the countryside, I've never been a huge fan of landscape painting. I itch to put an interesting element in the scene, like a stray cat, looking at the viewer, or a cloud shaped like a dragon."

"I'm sure you could sneak a dragon in without Nigel getting into an uproar. He's really a most accommodating gentleman. You pretty much have to be in order to run a successful pub, you know. The customer is always right, and all that rubbish." Victoria had a great respect for a well-run pub, having expressed her opinions about such things many times before.

Julie mused on this, deciding she should be able to. She disliked doing commissions, as her own visions almost never coincided with her buyers'. Wrestling her creativity into someone else's idea of perfection was a painful process.

"I think I could come up with something, Victoria." Julie nodded to her. "Thanks for the notion."

"Oh, did you hear about the hidden treasure up at the house?" David asked.

"Hidden treasure?" Victoria was the one who asked, but the question piqued Julie's interest as well.

"Evidently someone was exploring the hidden passages in the house, and found several crates of ancient whisky in one of the tunnels. They plan on selling it off at Christie's, making a bundle. Likely it will help fund the Edinburgh expansion."

Julie remembered her own quiet explorations several months before, smiling.

"Did anyone know how long they'd been there? Nothing else was found with them?"

"Probably since at least the thirties. They were incredibly dusty, from what I hear. I wouldn't mind sampling the wares, at all, so to speak. Must ensure the quality is good, after all. What else would they find?" David smiled and mimed taking a drink.

"Oh, perhaps a ghost or two ..."

The rain eased, the sound of drip, drip, drip slowing.

"I'm off, folks. Enjoy what's left of your walk." She dashed out, shielding her portfolio from stray drops, despite the fact it should be well-protected by the water-resistant sides.

*****

1968, East Grinstead, England

Julie was moping in her room. She was not the type to mope, but she gave in to the urge on occasion. Today was that sort of day. She hadn't cared for the news Paul had given her after breakfast at all.

They had gone on a brief walk, hand in hand, in the park, before she had to get back to work in the office. He had broken the news to her with compassion, but she hadn't taken it with any grace. She had known, somewhere within her, he must return to Minneapolis, to his life there, to his wife. She was on a roller coaster of despair. First Roger had to leave, and she had done well in getting over him. Now Paul was abandoning her.

Of course, this had to happen, eventually. However, she hadn't admitted such an inevitable conclusion to their affair would happen. Now, she had no choice. She was a practical person, but this time she resisted practicality to wallow in her own misery, her own painful heart. She was tired of being the practical one, the accommodating one, the one who bent over backwards so everyone else got their way.

It wasn't fair. She had found a man who made her laugh and cry. A man to whom she could talk to about anything, made her cherished and precious, and awakened in her a passion she didn't think she had possessed. Sure, she had enjoyed her lovers before, but it was nothing compared to the sizzling reaction she had to Paul and his attentions. She mused on how much of this was due to the forbidden nature of their love, but she decided it was a minor part compared to the overall suitability of their partnership.

Their love affair had lasted several months after the halting, not-so-auspicious beginning. It had grown into a warm and comforting relationship, as well as spicy and daring. It had become a part of her very being. When he left, so would a piece of her soul. What would she do without him? This notion sent her into another black hole of despair.

Sometime later, when her tears had become hiccups and sobs, she heard a rattle on the door. She had locked herself in, not wanting to be disturbed in her misery, but she heard Sheila's voice outside asking if she was inside.

"Julie? Julie, are you okay? Is this about Paul leaving?" She was so sympathetic, so understanding, it made Julie cry again, in full force. Sheila unlocked the door and rushed in.

"Oh, my dear, sweet girl. It's okay, it's alright. Shhh, shhh, shhh." Sheila held her tight, rocking her as she would her child. "I know it hurts, it hurts terribly. I could tell you it will get better, and it will, but I know you won't believe me yet. Shhh, shhh."

Julie had cried herself out and into a fitful sleep. Sheila laid her down, tucked the blankets around her, leaving her to her despair.

*****

Several hours later, Sheila came back in. Julie was still sleeping, so she was loath to wake her. However, everyone had been summoned to a big meeting. She put one gentle hand on Julie's shoulder and shook her.

"Julie? Julie, wake up, dear. Julie?"

Julie moaned and rubbed the dried bits of sleep and tears from her eyes. She blinked, bleary-eyed, at Sheila.

"Julie, Sharplin has called a general meeting—he wants everyone out on the lawn in about fifteen minutes."

"What ... what's going on? This's strange."

"I'm not sure, though the rumors are, of course, flying fast and furious. Why don't you freshen up, while I wait outside for you, and we'll go down together. David's already down there with Neil. I brought you water, as well." She handed Julie the glass of water, tepid and without ice, giving her a sympathetic look, then left the room.

Julie roused herself and went into the bathroom. She scrubbed at her face with soap and hot water, brushed out her sleep-tangled hair, tying it back up in a sloppy ponytail. She surveyed her face in the mirror—the redness had receded and she looked almost presentable. Her clothes were rumpled, but would straighten out as she walked around. She decided delaying would be no good. Taking a deep breath, she drank the water and left.

*****

There were already about fifty people out on the lawn, milling about in groups and cliques, the murmurs and conversations rising and falling like waves. Everyone seemed to have their own theory for the cause of this unprecedented meeting. They heard snippets of conversation as they went by.

"...think Sharplin is dead ..."

"...shutting us down, I'm sure ..."

"...government denied our charter ..."

Julie and Sheila passed several groups as they met David, Priya, Colum, and Jimmy. Julie was glad not to see Paul with them. David was holding Neil in his arms, but surrendered the young boy to Sheila as she approached. Julie tried to get him to smile with a silly face, knowing trying to cheer someone else up would help her cheer up.

"Any theories which are believable?" Julie asked Colum.

"Not with any teeth, no," the Scotsman said, with a half-smile. "There is certainly no shortage of ideas, but most are gae crazy."

The head of the Church, Jasper Sharplin, climbed the dais where a microphone had been set up, near a stand of trees. He was often at Saint Hill, but Julie had only glimpsed him in passing, having had no encounters with him personally. He was sort of a larger-than-life figure, with his thick, square glasses and fancy tailored suit. He stepped up to the microphone, speaking with no preamble.

"There are serious rumors about actions which are to be taken against us by the government. Therefore, we are moving our World Headquarters to Spain. We will try to do this with the least amount of disruption. Our most essential functions will be moved onto the new offices in Valencia. However, there isn't a lot of room there yet. The rest of the administrative functions will move to the new branch Edinburgh. Please coordinate with your supervisors to see where you need to go. Thank you." And he left without any other information. Julie didn't know if the announcement was so short because he was worried, stressed, or because this was his style.

The crowd was buzzing, almost a frenzied reaction to this shocking news.

David looked at Sheila. "Sharplin had always had a tendency towards paranoia about government interference with his Church, but if there were substantial enough evidence to force him move his operations, something must be in the works. Fancy a move to Scotland, my dear?"

Sheila smiled and said, "Wherever the wind blows us, sweetie."

And it was once again time to float along on the flimsy raft she called destiny.

6 - ANOTHER BEGINNING

1968, East Grinstead, England

A week later, she was packing up her clothing and the few belongings she had gathered in her months in England. She didn't collect things much, but she had managed to acquire several items of decoration, gifts from various people, artwork she had liked and purchased on several trips to London. She did her best to protect these with packing to ship to Michigan—it would be better if she pared down her belongings for the next move. She had no idea what her next quarters would be like, or if she would be sharing with a squad of other people. She'd rather her valuables be safe at her sister's place. Katy wouldn't mind holding them for her.

Her throat contracted as she put away the crystal pendant Paul had given her on one of their shopping trips to London. Swallowing, she lifted her head, finished her packing, putting all memories of him out of her mind. He was leaving today. The best thing for her would be to put him out of her mind, remove the barbs he had in her heart, and live on.

She must be strong.

She wasn't so strong, though.

She was so weak, completing everyday tasks were like pushing through an invisible, viscous sludge. Her movements were slow, halting, her decisions were all weighty, and her satisfaction in such decisions, nonexistent. She was glad, for once, she tended to go with the flow of her destiny. For once, she had no choice about moving. Of course, she could have moved somewhere else, not go to Edinburgh. Eileen apologized to her the day before, after barely acknowledging her existence for several weeks. She then invited Julie to be her nanny again, but this time in Valencia.

Eileen knew about Julie's miserable time in Spain, but had forgotten, or didn't care. The latter, was Julie's uncharitable thought. She only apologized to me so I'd take care of the kids again. She is nice when she needs help. Well, this was one decision she didn't have to second-guess.

Julie gathered her cases, three medium-sized bags and the two boxes to send to America. She hefted the large purse in which she carried the things she wanted to keep with her during the train journey. It was almost a portfolio, for which she had searched all over London. It was large enough to hold a decent-sized sketch pad, pencils, a book, even toiletries. This was a long, overnight journey, so she wanted to ensure she had plenty of things to keep her mind occupied, and off ... other things.

Sheila had already headed up to the new place, along with her family. Julie was among the last to leave the Saint Hill Manor, with its outrageous murals and manicured grounds. She would miss the space, the trees, the charming little village. She would miss Victoria, whose honest sarcasm was a refreshing change from the supercilious gushing of the other employees. She would miss the fresh air and laid-back vibe. They would be staying in the city, so she figured it would be like London—loud, crowded, grimy, dense with people and stories.

There was a bus taking them to the train station. She managed to get her stuff out in two trips. Victoria had offered to post the packages for her, meeting her on her second trip. They hugged and promised to keep in touch, though she wouldn't hear much from Victoria—she had already warned she was too insular a personality to keep long-distance friends.

She took a long last look at the manor and surrounding countryside, turned to the bus—only to walk straight into Paul.

Great. The one person she was hoping not to see before she left. And now, she would have to say goodbye in front of everyone, exactly what she was hoping not to do.

Julie did her best to hold all the emotions bubbling inside her from showing on her face. Betrayal, rejection, anger, pride, despair ... all fought for dominance. She wasn't great at hiding her emotions, so she was sure her face was a banner for all to read. Paul was holding still, looking into her eyes, waiting for her to get herself under at least a vestige of control.

"I was hoping I would be able to bid you farewell, my dear."

"And I was hoping we could avoid such a scene." Julie said. For the first time, Julie appreciated and wished she possessed Eileen's frigid inscrutability.

"Julie, Julie ... please don't be mad with me. I do love you, but you know we can't stay together. We must move on, we must part. I will always remember you, with love in my heart and a smile on my lips, my sweet queen of hearts." He took her hand, despite her stiff resistance, bringing it to his lips in a medieval, chaste kiss. She yanked it back, glaring at him. Finally, she relented.

"I ... I will remember you with fondness, as well, Paul. I must go now." Her answer was clipped and stiff. If she let any soft words out, it would be accompanied by a flood of tears. She pulled her hand from his grip, turning away. She controlled her stride to the bus door, careful not to run, as much as she wanted to, keeping herself from looking back when she embarked.

Later, alone in a compartment on the train, she gave in once again to the tears she had held in check for so long. She sobbed in time to the clickity-clack of the train along the rails.

*****

August 20, 1968, Edinburgh, Scotland

Dear Katy:

I know you love London, Katy, but you should take time to visit Edinburgh if you get a chance. It's a beautiful city. I imagined it would be dusty and grimy with centuries of coal dust and Victorian chimneys, but it is surprisingly clean, and the architecture alone is enough to take your breath away. More so than London. The streets are a byzantine mess in most places, but they are fun to wander around. And of course, all those men with sexy accents.

The food is different from what I'm used to. They seem to deep fry everything, but they have seemed to discover the magic of sauces. The English have not yet discovered this innovation, other than the ever-present Brown Sauce and salad crème (mayonnaise!) on their salads. The drinks are heartier up here, as well.

I'm enjoying my time up here. The work is hard, and they are giving me accounting work. Which, as you know my lack of ability at math, is sure to make you laugh. I'm doing my best, though. They are short-staffed, as they've divided their upper echelon between this office and Valencia. Sharplin seems to think the UK government is about to shut him down, so they have the true leaders out in Spain, while this place in Edinburgh are the nominal headquarters to the outside world. Sort of a bait-and-switch operation. It's such a flattering sensation to be disposable bait.

You mentioned you were coming to London in November, so I'll do my best to take a trip down to meet you. Give me a call when you leave. I can't wait to see you again.

More later, I must get back to work. They are keeping me busy here.

Much love,

Julie

*****

Julie massaged her forehead and stared at the numbers again. They weren't making any sense. She'd never liked math, and she lamented volunteering to help out when their official accountant decided to go out to Spain. She had protested she could only help, but they ended up putting her in charge of payroll. People's livelihoods now depended upon her ability to do this, but she was doing her best to bear the pressure.

She worked with the last month's payroll paperwork, trying her best to mimic what the accountant, Corey, had done. She presumed he had known what he was doing far better than she did. There had only been a few changes in the payroll, most of them additions of people from Saint Hill, like herself. The rest wasn't too hard, though trying to read his numbers was a challenge in itself. She took to trying to classify them as artistic symbols rather than numbers. These now danced in her head like a Dali-inspired animation.

She closed her eyes. She was tired, needing far more coffee than she had if she was going to get these figures done tonight. It was already well past sunset.

Several hours later, dead tired and eyes blinking with grit and sleep, she pushed herself back from the old, wooden desk, and gathered her papers. She didn't think it was right, but it was as right as she could make it, at least with so little sleep. She looked at the clock on the wall, realizing it was three am already. At least her flat was a block away.

She shared the flat with two other girls, Charmaine and Holly, but they were away on a trip to the Perth office for a couple days, so she had the place to herself. She rattled the iron key in the flimsy door, stepping in. The room was grey and dark, dust glowing from the outside lights. It was never dark in the city, like Detroit or DC. There was always light in the streets, if not the corners and alleyways. When the mist was in the air, it glowed like fairy dust, sparkling motes dancing among the breezes and sprinkling her hair and face with fairy kisses.

She decided she could do with fewer fairy kisses, and more sleep. Inside her flat, she didn't even bother undressing. She kicked off her shoes— sturdy to deal with the ankle-turning cobble-stone streets—and flopped on top of her covers. She was asleep in moments.

The loud, raucous, metallic ring of her alarm woke her four hours later. Cursing, she slammed her hand down on it and turned to go back to sleep. She had left the paperwork and paychecks on the secretary's desk for the director to sign and distribute. She could sleep in longer.

Several hours later, the noise from the street and the pervasive odor of the nearby Drambuie factory roused her from her stupor. She hated the smell. It always made her stomach roil, the sick sweet aroma wafting into her flat, tendrils finding every alley. She stumbled towards the bathroom and retched into the toilet.

She knelt there, miserable, reamed out and disgusting. This was not a happy place for her. Not the toilet, but Edinburgh. Yes, the city was beautiful, but she had no time to enjoy it. She was working day and night trying to keep up with the work she was given. She hadn't made many new friends as she had no time to socialize. Even Sheila and David were no company as they had been moved on to Perth for several weeks. It seemed the dour Scots Covenanters' distrust of song and dance permeated the rest of Edinburgh, for she had a hard time finding social situations.

Julie got up then, washed her face and looked in the mottled mirror. She looked awful, despite being able to catch seven hours sleep. It would be noon before she showered and got into the office, but she didn't care. A change needed to be made. She would ask Chas to move her from the accounting work.

Julie dressed to suit her mood, in black corduroy slacks and a navy blue blouse. She plaited her hair back into a severe braid. She imagined herself no-nonsense, and dressed to show others she meant business.

When she got to the office, she sought out the director, Charles 'Chas'

Brenner. He was an over-meticulous twit, though he did run the office well. His secretary, Barbara, scrambled as she came in. It smelled as if she had been doing her nails under her desk.

"Did you get the payroll, Barbara? I left it on your desk before I left." Julie asked for forms' sake. There was no way Barbara could have missed it, as she had placed it front and center.

"Payroll? No, I don't think so. Chas was bellowing about it earlier. He was upset."

"I put it right here, Barbara. I swear I did." Julie was confused now, wondering what had happened.

"Oh, here it is. Chas must have put these transfer orders on top, covering them up."

"Whew! I thought I was in trouble again."

"Well, I'll let Chas know we found them—it wouldn't do any good to let him know he was the one who hid them, would it?" Barbara winked at her with conspiracy.

Julie waited outside while Barbara faced the lion's den. After much shouting, arguing and paper shuffling, she came out again.

"All clear, though I wouldn't ask him for any favors. He's not in a good mood."

"Ah, well, yes, then, I'll move on back to work." As determined as she was to confront Chas about changing jobs, now was not the time.

*****

Several more days passed. While the workload eased, it would increase again as payroll came due. Tonight, however, she was determined to enjoy herself. She would treat herself to a pub dinner, a nice evening out, perhaps a stroll along the Royal Mile.

Barbara had recommended a nice place for her to eat—World's End, a historic pub right along the Mile, near the bottom of the cobblestone street. It was a huge place, with several rooms for people to eat, drink and socialize. Like most pubs she had been to, it was paneled with dark wood, had all sorts of odd memorabilia on the walls and hanging from the ceilings. The atmosphere was thick with the smoke from cigarettes, pipes and cigars, whether the current patrons were partaking or not. The odors were overpowering—smoke, whisky, beer, and stale sweat. She hesitated at the front door, not wanting to be sick again, but after a few moments, she was able to continue in.

It was dim and crowded, but she managed to find a place near the bar to sit. This was one of the few places which were both restaurant and pub, and it had been around for several hundred years. It sure smelled like it.

She looked at the stained menu, deciding to play it safe with fish and chips. It's hard to ruin such a thing in the World Capital of Fried Foods. Any pub worth its salt could do fish and chips. She ordered that and a pint of cider, sitting back to enjoy people-watching.

There were several groups of people, though the largest, the loudest, was near the black and white television at the end of the bar. There was a soccer game being televised. It was called football here. The fans were rabid, she had discovered. She heard them cheer for a goal, then subside.

Near the bar, there were a couple old men, nursing their pints, while a younger man, already drunk, was trying to talk them up. Perhaps to buy him another pint.

This place was disheartening her. She was more optimistic than this, but now she seemed to see everything in the worst possible light, rather than give the benefit of the doubt. She took a sip of the cider the landlord had brought to her, trying to think of happier things.

As she made this resolution, there was a disturbance at the door. A flurry of activity revealed itself to be a group of four people entering the pub. It was two men and two women, all about her age, all American. She smiled at the assumption, but she was certain they were, indeed, American. They hadn't spoken yet, other than exclamations at the rain outside. It was their loudness, their confidence, their disdain for everyone else's comfort or privacy which declared them such. Though she tried her hardest to disabuse most people of the common 'loud American' stereotype, she knew the reality when she saw it.

Like a ship pushing through ice floes, this group made their way through the pub and to the bar, ordering their drinks in voices loud enough to be heard in London. Then they snagged a table, where they laughed, told stories, made merry, oblivious to the censorious stares around them. They had asked for Budweiser, and been told it wasn't available. They had settled instead on local ale, McEwan's Scotch Ale. It was apparently up to snuff, for there were no loud complaints.

Julie decided it was better than watching television. Not only was it amusing watching this band of misfits among the quiet and somber Scots, oblivious to the ruckus they cause by their actions and reactions, but it was hilarious to watch the looks passed from person to person within the bar, the not-so-quiet comments about such rude Americans. Julie was ensconced at her table in the corner, watching all the drama unfold. She was glad she had assimilated enough to be believed, if not local, at least not foreign. No one had pegged her for an American, she believed. Once she spoke, they knew she wasn't Scots, but she spoke in a quiet, enunciated tone with no arrogance. Her American accent had become somehow softened by her time here. Most people assumed she was Canadian, or perhaps from another place, just not England or Scotland.

She had about finished her dinner by this time, but didn't want to leave back to her empty, tiny flat. She didn't relish walking back in the rain, either, but it couldn't be helped. Waiting for the rain to stop was a futile wish in Scotland. If it wasn't outright dropping from the sky, the mists and fogs were pervasive. But she had a paperback with her, so she pulled it out, sat back against the leather corner booth, proceeding to escape, into the world of Horatio Hornblower.

*****

Sometime later, she glanced up from the descriptions of a particular vicious storm, realizing her own stomach was churning in sympathy. Perhaps she should skip this section while she was full of fried foods.

The Americans had quieted down, while the Scots were getting louder. Interesting. Drink does grease the wheels of many social situations. Perhaps here, it has succeeded in bringing each group to a happy medium, a compromise of social grace. Julie grinned at the idea of how many world conflicts might be alleviated, if not avoided, if everyone simply drank together more.

A pretty young lady had entered, long reddish-blond hair dripping with the rain. As she removed her cap, she glanced around the room and made a bee-line for the loud Americans. They greeted her with smiles and claps on the back as she pulled up a stool, settling in. When she went off to the bar to fetch a drink for herself, she glanced Julie's way, stopped, blinked, came towards her.

"I'm so sorry to bother you, but haven't I seen you before? Perhaps at the Church?" Her voice was soft and high, difficult to hear. She did have an American accent. Maybe Californian? It did have a west coast lilt to it.

Julie blinked a couple times herself, peering at the young woman. She looked familiar, but faces sometimes swam together in her memory. Best be polite, though. "I think so, I do work there. I'm Julie."

She stood up and put her hand out for the girl to shake.

"Yes, that's right, Julie. I'm Barry. I came in a couple days ago from the States. I thought I'd seen you in passing, the other day. I'm pleased to meet another American. Won't you come join us?"

Julie looked at her erstwhile entertainment and shrugged, deciding it would be more interesting than reading about storm-tossed seas at the moment.

They approached the table while the group looked on with expectant eyes.

"This is Mark Johansen, he's here from Minneapolis." Julie did her best to clamp down a gasp at the mention of Paul's city, shaking hands with the tall, Nordic man with blue eyes.

"Raymond Theroux here is from Montreal." Julie noted the short, dark, round man was older than she had first imagined, perhaps around forty. The woman next to him was also short, with curly, kinky black hair and a round face. "Kimberly Berger is from Los Angeles, like me," Barry said. "And, last but not least, is Tammy Rudell, from Cincinnati." Tammy had reddish hair as well, flying up like a wavy aureole in response to the humidity. She wasn't as tall as Barry, but was thin and carried herself with aplomb. It put Julie in mind of finishing schools, with scores of girls walking about with books balanced on their heads.

Shoving this image aside, Julie introduced herself. "I'm Julie. I'm an artist from Detroit, but I've been here in the UK for almost a year now."

"What are you doing here, Julie?" Kimberly asked, with a polite inquiry.

"I started out doing artwork, but now I'm also doing the payroll and paperwork for them." Julie wasn't sure if this group were all church employees like Barry, or just friends, so she didn't elaborate. She kept her frustration and annoyance out of her tone at the mention of her current torture. "What do you all do?" She looked from person to person, eliciting their personal stories.

Barry began. "I'm a musician and a free-spirit, in truth. I don't 'do' anything. I 'am', if it makes sense." She smiled a sunny, bright smile, the smile of someone happy with life and content with themselves. Julie hadn't often encountered such people. "I grew up in LA, playing guitar and singing with friends. I made it up to San Francisco, hanging out with my friend Peter. About that time, he formed a group with other friends, so I moved here. If I had stayed, perhaps we would have become Peter, Paul and Barry." She smiled, waiting for the reactions.

Of course, Julie had heard of the band Peter, Paul and Mary. Most people had. They were a huge hit on the folk scene, had even made inroads into the mainstream, performing on Jack Benny and getting Gold records. And Barry claimed she was almost a part of this phenomenon?

Almost without noticing, she had been humming "Puff, the Magic Dragon" under her breath. She stopped before anyone else noticed.

She brought her attention back to the group, where Tammy was talking about her life in Ohio, working for her parents' garage. She was in Akron, which is one of the Church's larger hubs. Oh, then they were all part of the Church. She was easier.

She had missed the thread of the conversation, as they were all laughing at Tammy's last statement. Julie laughed as well, pretending she had heard. Raymond spoke up next.

"I was running a hunting lodge in Ontario, but got injured, so I had to retire from that life." He pointed to his leg. Julie noticed one thigh was much thinner than the other. "A moose decided I was a more comfortable carpet than the road. It broke my leg and left me stranded for several days before I was rescued. Part of the flesh had gotten corrupted, so they had to remove a big chunk of muscle. But, I healed, heading to the city. And now I'm here, doing research." There was no trace of the expected French accent from him, but Julie did notice he enunciated his words more than Barry or the others did. Better than she did for that matter.

Kimberly, it turned out, was a nurse. She had worked for a hospital in Los Angeles. "I was low woman on the totem pole. Any time I requested *any* time off, one of the senior nurses would take the time herself. Since she had seniority, my request was denied. After three years of this, I had had enough. I quit, moving in with my friend, Barry." She nodded at her friend.

By this time, most of the pints were empty, so Julie volunteered to stand another round. This was an accepted custom in the UK, but she wasn't sure if the others knew it. The party seldom got smaller, so getting in your round early was more economic. She got everyone's orders and escaped to the bar.

She wasn't isolated in the group, but she was overwhelmed by the personalities. Perhaps she had become so accustomed to the understated actions of the English, these brash Americans grated upon her. She had to damp down the urge to cover her ears when they laughed so loud. She gathered her pints, deciding she was being foolish.

*****

Over the course of the next couple of weeks, she hung out with Barry, Tammy and Kimberly a lot. They were the first friends she had made here. Raymond and Mark had already headed back to the States, as their training was over, but the girls made a habit of going out every couple nights to blow off steam in well-deserved debauchery. They were all working hard, all day and most evenings as well.

The work was difficult, as Julie still struggled with the numbers. She wasn't settling into this position. She wasn't suited to it, but she was never good with confrontation. It seemed easier to plow on than to ask for a different duty. Besides, everything was in flux, so perhaps it would change on its own. And she didn't want Chas to decide he didn't need her and fire her. Then where would she be? Stuck in Edinburgh with no job, no place to live, no options. No, better to put her head down and do her best. At least she got a 'break' with artwork or other non-financial task, which she was much more comfortable with.

Today was one of those days. She was working on a new poster to be put into the colleges and hospitals. She had finished her final mockup, after several tries and rejections, bringing it into Chas' office for approval. He wasn't there, so she left it with a note on his desk, escaping. She'd have time off this evening, and she meant to spend it with the girls. She had no intention of getting caught and assigned another mind-numbing task today.

She made it out of the office and to her flat without incident, changing into evening togs. Any outing in Edinburgh required layers, to combat the changing weather, even if they weren't planning on staying outside. Long skirts would to get muddy, wet hems, so she found a pair of corduroy brown pants, her favorite loose-flowing gold satin shirt. She tied her hair up in a matching gold scarf, grimaced at herself in the mirror, adding added a pendant. She didn't own any real gold, but this was a teardrop goldstone pendant in a fake gold setting. It worked well enough.

They were going out to Victoria Street, where Barry had heard of a club called The Place. Julie was apprehensive as they climbed down three flights of dank, concrete stairs into the basement. It was hot, and she fancied the dampness on the walls was the building itself sweating in sympathy. The muted sounds below hit them full force as the thick fire door at the bottom was opened.

The place was heaving with people and sound. She heard the band, but couldn't see them right away in the dim throng. There wasn't a real stage, but she did see an area where the people appeared taller than those around them. When she squinted, she could see they had instruments. Behind them was an ornate spiral staircase with a glowing red EXIT sign above it. That was a good thing to find.

She didn't recognize the song, but knew it was mod music. Tammy had mentioned a band from Glasgow called The Pathfinders. As the girls threaded their way closer to the music, she heard them better. She liked it, but would have liked to get pints in her before she danced, cool and refreshing.

Julie craned her neck in the reddish, dim light, but couldn't see anything which looked like a bar. Indeed, she saw no one carrying anything looking like a drink. She sighed. This must be music-only, no alcohol. Well, might as well enjoy it while she was there. She saw Barry had her arms flung up, tossing her head side to side, hair spiraling out, eyes closed, swaying to the beat. She had attracted male attention. Kimberly and Tammy were dancing with each other, so Julie began to move, as well. She closed her eyes, which did help to relieve the claustrophobia, experiencing the music thrum through her.

She danced with abandon, paying little attention to her surroundings, swaying to the music, the beat, the guitar. She moved and swung, bumping an unknown body now and then, but moving more, back and forth, around and around. She sensed someone's hair brush her face, a hand around her waist. Then it was gone and there was a wall against her back.

Opening her eyes, she found herself on the edge of the frenzy, with no sign of the other girls. She looked for Barry's hair, a feature which tended to stand out since the girl was tall, but she couldn't see it. She closed her eyes again and danced more.

The music faded, then stopped. The band had moved through several tunes, from one to the other, not stopping in between, but they were now taking a break. The crowd sort of shuffled to a stop, though not everyone. Some people still danced to their own inner rhythms, dancing to the drummers no one else can hear.

She found Barry now, and Kimberly. Tammy wasn't with them, though, so they looked around for her—and found her in a corner with a tall young Indian gentleman, in a close, intimate and intense conversation. They decided to let her be for now, finding a place to cool off.

Kimberly found a couple stools near one wall, so they sat and fanned themselves as best they could. The heat had increased when people stopped moving, as the air became stultifying and still. She was having trouble breathing. She took a couple deeper breaths, experimenting, but everything was fine.

Barry was trying to speak, but the noise level was still high, so Julie pointed to her ear, indicating she hadn't heard.

"I said, 'are you having fun?'" Barry fair shouted into her ear.

"I am, but it is sweltering in here. I might go out for fresh air."

Barry and Kimberly both nodded, resuming fanning themselves with their shirts.

Julie looked to where Tammy was, seeing that the conversation had moved from a verbal one to a much more physical one. She could only tell which limb belonged to which person by the color of the skin.

The music began again. As one, they all moved again.

The beat was stronger, faster this time. Julie got overheated right away. She found Kimberly, tapping her on the shoulder to get her attention, indicating she was going outside. Kimberly nodded, gesturing to wait for her. They waved to Barry, but Barry was in a bliss of dancing, so didn't even notice them.

As they emerged from the bowels of the club, they both took in deep, delicious breaths of the sweet, fresh, cool air, pulling it into their lungs with relish and joy.

"Man, I love the music, but what I wouldn't give for a giant fan above everyone." Kimberly said.

"No kidding. Though I've noticed they don't do ceiling fans here much. They don't seem to care for moving air. I have yet to see one in any of the rooms or B&Bs I've been in, much less the restaurants or hotels."

"Yeah, I noticed that. And the closets they claim are bathrooms."

"Oh, I could tell you stories about the bathrooms here," Julie said in a conspiratorial manner. She had referred to her time with Paul without falling into instant despair. Was she healing already? Kimberly had asked her a question.

"What? Oh, a story about a tryst I had with a guy in England. The bathroom was our only private space." She grinned at Kimberly's shocked expression.

"In these tiny things? How did you not break your neck trying?"

"It had a fantastic, large Victorian bathtub."

"Wow. Just wow." Kimberly's eyes were round with wonder.

Julie smiled. Perhaps she was beginning to live on again.

*****

Julie woke with a moan and a clatter, knocking her clock off the tiny table next to her bed. The alarm hadn't gone off, but she had dreamt it had.

Her roommate, Charmaine, stirred and shifted, pulling her covers up over her head. Holly was gone already, she was often out early. She liked walking the city as it woke up, saying it helped clear her head in the morning.

Julie twisted herself out of her tangle of blankets, sitting on the edge of the tiny cot. She rubbed the sleep out of her eyes, trying to remember what it was she had done the night before which would leave her in such a terrible state. Then she stopped thinking, and ran to the bathroom to worship the porcelain gods.

Please God, kill me now. She'd not had so much to drink the night before. She had no idea why she was so ill, but she suspected it had to do with the horrible Drambuie odor. They had combatted it in the flat, by burning sandalwood candles to mask the sickly sweet, but it didn't work. It merely combined with the musky candle to produce a bizarre mixture of scents.

She settled enough to get up and take a bath. She preferred showers, but it wasn't an option at this place. It was a bath or nothing. She disliked baths, since she figured she was cleaning off the dirt, only to stew in it for a while before trying to wipe off the dirty water. Showers were much more to her liking, but not as common in the UK as in the States.

She had the day off for once, and hadn't needed to get up so early. Well, her stomach had insisted on the morning rise, so she might as well make the most of it.

Julie decided to take a page from Holly's book, taking a brisk, refreshing walk. The weather looked decent enough for now. She dressed in sturdy shoes and clothes, with a jacket. It may be late August, but it was still fresh in the morning and evenings.

She made her way to the Royal Mile, then to Arthur's Seat. She wasn't much of a hill climber, but this was an easy hill, with a set path. She stopped often and sat on the velvet green grass, looking out at the panoramic city laid out before her. By the time she made it to the top, a couple of hours had passed. She was clear and refreshed.

She stayed there for a while, having brought a couple of sandwiches and fruit to snack on, having a picnic while she surveyed the city. The architecture was stunning. The people were nice enough, once you got past their gruff, stolid exteriors. They weren't jovial, until you got several pints in them. Their solemn manner often masked keen interest and intelligence, as well as fierce loyalty and gallantry.

There had been an incident several nights before, where she and Kimberly were walking home from a pub, on the tipsy side. They stumbled against each other on the cobblestones of the streets. One man had come up with them, giving them a hard time, trying to take Kimberly's hand. Before they could extract themselves, another man had come up, inserting himself between the girls and their accoster, shooing him away from them. He then had turned, bowed to them, walking off in another direction, not waiting for thanks or thought of reward. She had looked at Kimberly, then they both laughed in hysterics before moving on towards home.

She took out her ever-present sketch pad, drafting her view of the city. She didn't care for cityscapes, but the architecture of Edinburgh was incredible. So much gothic detail, she loved drawing it. Curlicues and flying buttresses everywhere she looked. It was almost organic, like the Gaudi buildings in Barcelona. She drew with pencils, no color, to capture the stark monochromatic city. From where she was, she couldn't get a lot of detail, as the hill was high. However, she could get the general sense of the imposing castle, Holyrood, and the buildings along the Royal Mile, as well as the docks in the distance.

The wind had picked up, but she only noticed it when she kept tacking down the corners of her page. They fluttered as she was drawing, which was distracting.

Julie decided it was time to go back. She discovered this was chancier in the steep bits then going up, sliding a couple times here and there. She hadn't hurt herself, but did realize she was climbing hills on her own, and no one knew she was there. Don't be silly. Lots of people walk up here. It's not like I'd be stranded for days. Look, there's someone now, walking his dog up the path. Nevertheless, she placed her feet with care, deciding she ought to let someone know the next time she went walking about.

The dog came up to her and, as dogs do, sniffed between her legs. She laughed and pet the dog, guiding his head away, but it made her think. She couldn't remember the last time she'd had her period, so this made her pause. She counted back as the man and his dog walked on.

Had it been more than a month? Sure it had. She plopped down, verifying the math, but knowing she didn't need to. The last time had been in East Grinstead in May, she was sure. And she had been here in Scotland since the end of July. Now it was the beginning of September. Oh, no, she groaned. It must have been in the bathtub. Great, THAT'S a fantastic story to tell my child someday. This was a hysterical reaction to the realization that she was pregnant. Besides, it might not be Paul's after all. It could have been Roger. There wasn't much time between the two affairs.

What could she possibly do. Adoption? Abortion? Keep it? Kill herself? She dismissed the last one right away. She had never considered such a thing before, and she wasn't about to now. A child wasn't tragic, it was beautiful. But how could she keep it? Her father was going to kill her.

She had a quick image of herself telling Paul about the child, asking him to leave his wife for her and the baby, but she shook it off. He was married. Julie had never been one to rock the boat. Seeing herself as one of those selfish women who broke up families was repugnant. She had no idea if Paul had children with his wife, but if he didn't now, he would later. No, better if he never knew. If it was Roger, on the other hand... but she remembered his disdain for his siblings' families. Perhaps he wouldn't wish to be trapped with a child, either.

There had been girls in San Francisco who were single mothers, but they were already living in a commune or in one case, a strange, open relationship with three men. Abortion wasn't legal or safe. Adoption—could she handle it? She would still have to go through the pregnancy and the birth. She then understood why the Drambuie was so sickening to her.

Well, she wouldn't have to decide on adoption until she had the child. She breathed in the incongruous fresh air and grass smells around her, determined this would not destroy her life. She would make plans, but why should it be such a problem? She was part of a Church which could help her. She had friends, a community. She could do this.

Making her way back down to her flat, she decided perhaps she didn't like days off anyhow.

*****

2000, Miami, Florida

Almost a year had passed. Kirsten had heard nothing in reply to her letter, not even an angry retort, saying she had the wrong person, denouncing her as a charlatan and a liar. She would have almost welcomed it—at least it would have been a reaction, which she could have worked with. She sighed. Perhaps her mother had been right. Perhaps she shouldn't have tried to get hold of him.

"What's wrong, Kirsten?"

Kirsten hadn't heard Cathy come in. She was one of the other CPAs at her office, having introduced herself to everyone as the original Chatty Cathy, and she hadn't exaggerated. The woman talked more than any of the other accountants combined. It was hard to get a word in edgewise. She was looking at Kirsten with intent curiosity, her short grey hair swinging around her round face in a bob cut.

"Drifting, I suppose. I am stuck on a … genealogical research problem, I guess. Nothing to do with work."

"I didn't know you were into genealogical research. I love the stuff. I have all sorts of CDs from Family Tree Maker, and Everton's—do you read Everton's? I've even got microfiche files. Have you tried the Mormon Church files? They have lots of stuff on their computer database, as well as microfiche. If you find anything, you can ask for them to send it from Salt Lake City. It's where their headquarters are, you know. Largest genealogical library in the world. I've been there twice. It's a mecca for genealogists. Have you ever been?"

Kirsten mumbled out a quick 'no' while Cathy stopped to take a breath, rambling on about her last trip to Salt Lake City. Kirsten tuned her out, as she had learned to do, but held onto at least one nugget of information in the avalanche. Mormon Church? She had heard of them having files, of course, but didn't realize there was a branch nearby. Maybe there wasn't? She waited for Cathy's next breath to stop the torrent.

"Cathy? Is there a Mormon Church nearby? With a research center?"

"Of course, didn't I say? It's up on Roebuck Road. The family history center is to the right, the church is to the left. They close at five pm, but they stay open late Wednesday nights, until nine pm, so it's the best time to go. The weekends are busy. Bring coins for photocopies, though, unless you like writing a lot. I hope you find lots of great information."

"Thanks, Cathy, I'll let you know how I do." Julie managed to stop the conversation by getting up and going to the bathroom. By the time she returned, Cathy had left, so Kirsten planned her visit for the following evening.

Wednesday, she escaped work by six, a short day for tax season. She found the church without too much wandering around, as it was in a cleared area off a wooded road. The sign outside was new and well kept. She was able to find the family research side with no assistance. She signed in, and read the list of rules near the unattended front desk. She noted some paperwork was free to request from the main center in Utah, but others had fees. Fair enough. She hefted her book bag and walked in, looking for a terminal.

One wall had six cubicles, each with a huge CRT monitor. Only two of them were occupied, so she chose an empty one and pulled out her family tree sheets. She might as well make the most of her time here. She was planning on checking on each of her 'brick walls' to see what sort of information she could fill in.

Lost in a maze of information and possibilities, she looked up to notice several hours had passed, but she was only halfway through her list of projects. She had found good nuggets of information, noting their sources so she could get copies of the relevant birth certificates, death notices, etc. She decided she had time for one more tonight, but would have to come back next week for the rest. She looked down and saw the next item listed was on her father's line.

Back when she had gotten a copy of her father's birth certificate, Kirsten had written to get copies of his parents' birth certificates as well. She had those, so had information on her father, his parents, and both sets of their parents. She hadn't gotten farther than this, but they had nice, unusual names, a boon to any genealogical researcher. She was looking for Fred B. Stein, Johanna Lembeck, Paul H. Ford and Josephine Moraveck. Sure, the men's names were more common, but those wonderful, unique women's names helped. Those should be easy to find. Nevertheless, she prepped herself for disappointment, knowing women seldom made their way into historical records in the nineteenth century.

Sometime later, Kirsten sat, staring at the screen. No mistake, it was there. Fred Bernard Stein had married Johanna Anna Lembeck, in 1908 in Minnesota. There was no doubt about it, these were her great-grandparents. She looked around for a clue to where the information had come from. It was part of a submitted family tree, so someone had compiled it and submitted it to the Mormon Church database. Where was it? There. Sharon Henderson, of Minneapolis, with an address. With shaking fingers, Kirsten wrote down the address.

At home, she wrote a long letter to Ms. Henderson, detailing the account of her mother's adventures in England, her long search for her father. She told of her search which had come across her family tree, begging Ms. Henderson to send information, if she had any, on her father's branch of the family. She hoped the woman had concrete data, not merely a snippet of stray information.

It was difficult to hold onto that hope. She had been disappointed before, after all. But she was, at heart, an optimist, and this was her true strength.

The next few days were tense, but as they passed, Kirsten relaxed. She had gone through this before, with other dead ends. Like when she had first contacted the researcher from Everton's, though she got useful information from him. This information had led to this latest foray.

Tax season was in full swing at work, so she had little energy to devote to worry. She was working long hours, not getting home until well after eight. She flopped down exhausted, watched television, or played a computer game for a while to disengage her mind, then falling asleep, only to do it again the next day. She almost longed for the days she had classes at night, as it gave her something to think about other than tax returns.

7 - ESCAPE

1968, Edinburgh, Scotland

Perhaps this hadn't been such a good idea.

She clung onto her purse as if it represented a lifeline, or at least an anchor. Why had she let Barry talk her into this? She didn't relish walking home on her own, in the dark. Not on this night. She vowed to strengthen her resolve and get a grip. Her belly was awkward and her back ached. Six months pregnant was no time to go partying.

There were crowds of young people, all talking hushed in groups around an ever-growing scrap pile of wood, broken furniture, with other, less-identifiable bits. She hadn't seen such a thing last year, when she was in East Grinstead, but was told it happened all over the UK on this night, Guy Fawkes Night. They burned an enormous bonfire in effigy, to celebrate the capture of a man who plotted to blow up the government four hundred years ago. The group here, on Broughton Road, were made up of teenagers and twenty-somethings, almost all locals. They were rougher than the folks Julie was used to, on the threadbare side. She heard language she didn't understand, but couldn't tell if it was accented English slang, or if it was another language, like Scots or Gaelic. She wasn't sure she wanted to understand, though—whatever they were saying, it didn't sound like they were talking about rainbows and butterflies.

She turned to Barry, to ask if she wanted to stay among this crowd, when movement caught her eye. A parade of sorts was coming down the street, with the young man in the front carrying a scarecrow, or what might pass for one. It was a set of pants and a shirt on a cross, stuffed with hay and rags. There was nothing resembling a head, only the top bit of the cross sticking out of the neck of the shirt. It looked like a parody of the Christ statues she had seen in Catholic churches.

This must be the effigy she had heard of, the one they burn on the bonfire. She stepped back, giving the procession plenty of room as they went by. She glanced at Barry, seeing her eyes wide in anticipation. She was enjoying the show, by her smile. She was rapt in the drama and showmanship of it all.

The effigy made it to the bonfire, which had been built in an empty lot at a crossroads. Julie wondered if it was significant. People were hanged at crossroads, to keep their ghosts from haunting. The leaders of the parade secured the scarecrow more or less in the center of the pile of wood, then backed up, forming a solid ring around the area. Barry fumbled for her hand and squeezed it in excitement and anticipation, while Julie squeezed back.

This seemed so primal, so ancient, hearkening to a Celtic or Nordic primeval past. It could be a call to the gods of fire, or to the spirits of chaos. Or even a simple worship of sun, asking it to return after the winter is over. Who was she to say these beliefs were unworthy, or outdated? It spoke to something seminal in each person's soul, fire did. It was controllable and yet dangerous at the same time. It was man's most useful tool. It was also his greatest enemy. It was comforting and terrifying in turns.

"Remember, remember, the fifth of November." The crowd was chanting, without music or song, but with strength and enthusiasm.

"The gunpowder treason and plot

I know of no reason why the gunpowder treason

Should ever be forgot."

With this, the young man who had been carrying the effigy walked up to the pile of debris, lighting it with a torch. It must have been soaked in pitch or gasoline, as it caught quickly, as flames licked all around the straw man. Pitch, Julie decided—the smell of pine and turpentine was overwhelming as it burned. She didn't know why she hadn't noticed it before. It made her choke, her gorge rising. She backed off, releasing Barry's hand, seeking clearer air behind the ring of watchers.

Barry came to ensure she was alright, but Julie waved her back to the festivities. The ring was all holding hands now, sort of swaying, now walking around the fire, like a giant game of Ring-Around-the-Rosy. A giant, surreal children's game before a primal god of fire. What a strange sight in modern Edinburgh. I suppose we are all still slaves to our primitive urges.

Her stomach decided it had had enough of strange sounds and smells, ejecting its meager contents on the sidewalk. Julie stood hunched over, holding her own hair back, until the wave of nausea passed. She swished saliva around her mouth and spit, disgusted at the necessity, but feeling much better. She rejoined the chanters and partook in their primitive ceremony around the now raging bonfire.

*****

The next day at work, she regretted her late night. Her throat was scratchy and raw from all the smoke and turpentine. She was certain it was the beginning of a nasty cold. She didn't seem to be able to catch a break.

She was having lunch with Barry today. They planned on going to this place down the street, a sort of hole-in-the-wall café which had a lunch counter. It was actually called the Greasy Spoon Café. It wasn't great food, but it was cheap, sandwiches and soups, and it was within walking distance of the offices. Most of the decent restaurants and pubs were closer to the Royal Mile where the tourists went, about two miles away, which was fine for an evening out, but far to walk on your meager half-hour lunch break.

They walked to the café, which catered to seamen and dockers, so it was on the rough side. It was empty today, though, so they ordered a couple of sandwiches, with fizzy lemonade.

"Alright, Julie. What's going on?" Barry wasn't one to beat around the bush.

"Well, I'm in a mess, you see. I was hoping for insight, maybe even advice."

"What sort of mess? Is it your job?"

"No, well, yes, it's related to it, but that's not the primary problem."

"C'mon, Julie. Spit it out. What's wrong?" Barry sounded abrupt, but Julie knew she cared, was trying her best to help. Nevertheless, Julie's eyes burned, her throat closing with tears. She had never been so prone to tears.

"I'm …" Julie lowered her voice to a whisper, "I'm pregnant." She looked up at Barry to see the reaction in her blue eyes.

Barry looked at her. She stood up, brought Julie up out of the chair, and looked her up and down. She placed her hand on Julie's stomach, and her eyes grew wide. Julie wasn't thin and had taken to wearing baggy shirts and dresses. Barry wrapped her arms around Julie. She hugged tight, but when Julie moved to disengage, she hugged tighter. Julie hugged back, so they stood like that for several minutes, until the waitress came by with their sodas.

"Are ye girls ok, then?" She looked at both of them with concern.

"We're fine, thank you." Julie went and sat on her stool, put her straw in her soda, taking a long sip, feeling the carbonated burn sear her throat. She was still holding Barry's hand over the round, silver table.

Julie had control over herself once again. She took a smaller sip of her soda, relishing the lemony sweetness on her throat.

"What are you thinking of doing, Julie? Are you going to keep it?"

"I am thinking I have to, at this point. I don't know yet if I want to put it up for adoption, but I don't think I could do ... the other."

"I don't blame you, hon. Do you know who the father is?"

"I believe so, yes." Once again, she had a flash of an image, her telling Paul, him leaving his wife for her. Julie was going to cry again, so she took a sip of the lemonade. It helped. But was she sure, after all?

222

"And? Does he know?"

"No, and he never can know. He's American, back with his wife." She got it all out in a rush, hoping she wouldn't have to say any more about it.

"Oh. I see. Well." Barry took a deep breath, flung her hair, squeezing Julie's hand. "It'll be fine, Julie, you'll see. All sorts of things are possible nowadays. You'll have me here to help, with Kimberly, and Tammy. We'll be your family."

*****

Of course, Barry hadn't counted on moving a couple weeks later, but her intentions had been good. The Church had decided they needed Barry and her fiancé, Bruce, to work in the Copenhagen office, to help the groups there get more in line with the UK organization. So, at the end of December, they had moved the couple to Denmark. Kimberly had already gone back to California the month before, so Tammy was the only one left of the original group of Dangerous Ladies, as Barry had labeled them.

Julie wished she could talk more to Barry or Bruce about her worries, but most of them had to do with having a baby. They had been trying to have one of their own, so didn't want to rub it in their faces that she would, truth be told, be happier without a child.

She didn't get along as well with Tammy, who was far more interested in finding a new man, her flavor of the week, than in hanging out with a mere woman. She was sowing her oats, wild or otherwise, with a vengeance. Julie wasn't as interested in searching for men, as she had about had her fill with the fickle beasts, so she didn't accompany Tammy on her conquests.

Julie adopted the solitary existence she had first had in Edinburgh, before Barry had blown into her life, living to work, with the occasional break to go out and draw. Her efficiency at everything seemed reduced by her growing belly. It was more difficult to walk the few blocks from her flat to the offices, especially when it was wet, or the few times snow fell. She invested in good, sturdy boots with wide, corrugated soles, to help keep her from slipping on slushy cobblestones or hidden potholes. She took to carrying her sketchpad with her wherever she went, anxious to get away from the office in stolen bits and scraps, to feed her soul with art. Since these chances were few and far between, she did gesture drawings, or quick sketches of people, while she sat at a café sipping tea. She filled up several sketchpads this way over the months. It was a shield for her. If she had a project while she ate alone, she was less desolate. It was something to do, rather than look like she was eating alone. She had her artwork as a companion to keep her on track.

She tried hard not to look forward to the baby. She had begun to refer to it as her little Angel—as it could be a boy or a girl, acknowledging its innocent state. But then, Julie decided if she didn't think about it much, it would be easier to give up for adoption. As it grew in her, her body grew and stretched in response, she caught herself stroking the mound, smiling to herself. As soon as she saw she was doing this, she stopped, scolding herself for unwanted sentimentality. Don't get attached, Julie.

Her determination was strong. Was it strong enough?

*****

Julie looked at the numbers again, then a third time and a fourth time.

She used the adding machine to run a tape and check yet again. No, there was no mistaking it. She had screwed up, screwed up big.

Despite her denials, she had overpaid every single person last payroll. Nobody was going to be happy about this. It meant, in order to fix it, she would have to short everyone's payroll this paycheck. She was not looking forward to her conversation with Chas.

She had been working with the payroll for five months now, but had no better grasp of the complex process than when she had first begun, the ledger books having been dropped on her desk in a puff of dust and ink. They had left her to puzzle out what had been done and what needed to be done. No one had checked her work, trusting she knew what she had been doing.

She hadn't known, of course, had protested as much, but her protests had fallen on deaf ears. Now she would be in trouble for having screwed up. Well, it wasn't as if she could run and hide. She couldn't run anywhere, in truth, being eight months pregnant, as big as a house, and about as nimble as a whale with club feet. She wasn't hiding anywhere in her condition.

She got up, put a hand to the small of her back to alleviate the pain, waddling into Chas' office, damning paperwork in hand, into the lion's den.

About a half hour later, she gathered up her things from her desk. She packed her personal belongings, nodded farewell to Barbara, and left. She wondered how much of her firing had been due to her mistake, and how much due to the fact she wouldn't be able to work in a couple weeks, anyhow, due to her baby.

She held the tears back until she got into her flat. She hated the fact she must cry, but she knew no other way to release her frustration. She had known she was likely to be fired. It hadn't made it any easier to take when Chas had exploded in her face, called her an incompetent cow, telling her to leave and never return.

Julie cried herself out, then washed her face. She poured herself cold coffee from the kitchenette carafe, picking up the phone to call Barry.

Barry had moved a month before to Denmark with her new husband, Bruce Peake. There was a tiny Church community there in Copenhagen and they were working to get it going. While Julie didn't relish living in a country which spoke a different language, she figured it would be her best option. Besides, Barry had offered her a place in their home a couple of months back. Julie hadn't been able to get away from work long enough to take a real trip. Well, she had plenty of time now.

She heard the double ring once. She hoped Barry was home. She was reminded of the call George had answered, ages ago in another lifetime, which had resulted in her move to California.

It rang again, and she heard a click.

"Goomourn?"

What? Oh, it must be Danish. "May I speak to Barry?"

"This is Barry, who is this?"

"This is Julie. I am *so* glad it's you."

"Julie, what's wrong? Are you alright?"

"I lost my job this morning. Chas fired me over a payroll error." Barry had gotten many tearful stories about how much she hated her payroll duties, so this would come as no surprise to her friend.

"Well, then, you'll have to come and stay with us now, won't you? Have you enough money for a flight? Let me know when you've made arrangements, and I'll pick you up at the airport." Barry said all this rapid-fire, in a tone which allowed for no argument. Julie was glad she wasn't looking for one.

"Barry, you are the best friend a girl can have. Thank you so much. Are you sure Bruce won't mind?" She sniffed mightily, trying to hold back the tears that threatened to take over.

"He won't mind in the slightest, but even if he did, I'd make him change his mind. Do you have much stuff to bring with you? I can arrange for shipping if you'd like?"

"No, no, I pared my stuff down when I moved to Scotland. I've got clothes and art stuff."

"Well, call when you know your details. Chin up, girl. I can't wait to see how big you've gotten."

Barry had always been positive and supportive about her situation, making jokes to lighten her mood when she got morose about it. Relief washed over her, hearing the smile in Barry's voice.

"I'll do it as soon as I know."

After she hung up, Julie gave into the sobs. She was an emotional wreck. When she had cried herself out, she decided a walk down the street to the travel agent would be easier than trying to buy a ticket on the phone, despite the difficulty walking places. She also had the suspicion her pregnant state might be an issue, but she hoped it was a short enough flight that it wouldn't be.

Luckily, it wasn't an issue. She found an inexpensive flight. It wasn't even direct, but flew first down to London, then to Copenhagen. She gathered her belongings, packed up what she wanted and left the rest. Her roommates, whom she never saw anyhow, could have the lot. It was a load of trash anyway.

Like so many times before, she took a taxi to the airport for her flight, leaving that chapter of her life without so much as a backwards glance.

8 – A STAR IS BORN

1969, Copenhagen, Denmark

Julie believed every door in her life was slamming in her face. Barry would have kept her as a guest forever, had she been able to. However, the fact was she had needed to ask Julie to move out for a week, to a hotel. Bruce's parents were visiting, so they needed the spare room to accommodate them, of course. It was only logical, it was not a rejection, or a dismissal. Julie reminded herself over and over.

She had heard of post-partum depression. Was there such a thing as pre-partum depression? She was due any day now, so was awkward, unsightly, disgusting. She had only been in town a few weeks, and had made few friends. She didn't like going out in her current state, since most people rode bikes to get around town. A bike was pretty much impossible at the moment. Her back ached when she walked for too long, but both Barry and Bruce were busy daily at their jobs. She wasn't in any shape to help. She had drawn and sketched everything around the tidy suburban house several times. She was going utterly stir-crazy.

Now she was sitting in a dingy hotel room, reminiscent of the room she had rented in Washington, D.C. Had she come so far in two years? She had enjoyed many adventures, but also experienced much heartache. She remembered of Paul and Roger, but then veered away from the painful subject. She was about to get her permanent souvenir from those dalliances. She still wasn't sure if she would give up the child for adoption or not.

Julie pushed herself up from the bed with a great effort, grunted, pressing her hands to the small of her back. She bundled herself up against the frigid February weather and scooped up a pad and her pencils. She waddled to the back stairs, as the elevator was always scary and bumpy. She walked out of the hotel, finding the nearby park. At least the hotel was a change of scenery. She had new things to draw and create.

It was bright and brilliant out, which helped her mood. The white snow sparkled in the sunlight as she picked her way to the park. It was a delightful park, even in the blanket of winter. She was sure it would be sublime in the spring, when the flowers bloomed and the trees offered shade. Now it was stark and monochromatic, a beauty of a different type. A beauty well-suited to pencil work and charcoal.

She sat at a bench, drawing the skeletal trees reaching above her, like creeping hands extended to tear the flesh from her bones. My, how morbid. She attempted to lighten the mood of her piece, but it still came to her as haunting and sinister. So be it. She sketched the bones of the trees, the random patterns of branch and twig, against the faultless sky.

Sometime later, her butt had frozen to the bench seat. She decided it would be the better part of wisdom to extract herself and head back to the hotel. As she did so, she almost slipped on icy sidewalk under her boot, but she caught the arm of the bench before she tumbled. It scared her, as she was alone in the park. A fall now could not only be dangerous for her and the baby, she could be out here for hours before someone came by. Humbled by her mortality, she waddled back to the hotel.

Most of the staff in the hotel spoke no English, but there was one young bellhop on the day staff who had some. Sometimes she chatted with him, but he was off today. She sat in the lobby café for hot chocolate. Perhaps soup would be wise to thaw her inside and out.

Julie relaxed in the warm seat, enjoying the strange fruit soup on offer, called sødsuppe, and her hot chocolate. She wished for little mini-marshmallows she would have gotten at home, but settled for the thick whipped cream they offered.

As she was finishing the last of her soup, Barry came in, dressed in a long red wool jacket and red hat, looking around for her. She waved her over to the table, but didn't bother trying to stand up, as this was a process which would have taken several minutes and considerable effort.

"Julie. How are you doing? I was on my way home from the office, so I decided I'd drop in to see how you're doing. Enjoying the warmth?"

"Yeah, I was out drawing and got chilled. Would you like some?"

"Oh, no, I can't stay long. I wanted to let you know Bruce's parents were here until the seventeenth, so you can come back after. Will this work for you?"

"It would be fine, Barry. Though I may be in hospital by then, you know. I'm due any day now, according to the folks back at the Royal Infirmary."

"Haven't you gone to the hospital here for an update?"

"Of course I have, but they don't speak much English. The best information I have is from the Edinburgh staff." Julie made a rueful face. "It's not anything you think about much, but I've been able to make myself more or less understood when I've needed it. There are a lot more words which are

231

similar between Danish and English than I would have believed. Those Germanic roots sometimes rear their ugly heads."

"Well, be careful. Let me know when you know anything. And if nothing has happened yet, I'll come by on the seventeenth to help you with your stuff."

"Sounds good. Sure you won't stay for a cup of chocolate?"

"No, the parents are expecting me. Let me give you a hug. No, don't get up." Barry wrapped her arms around Julie in an awkward embrace, due to her size and sitting position, but it was warm and she held it for a while. Then she stood up and left in a flurry of scarf and long jacket.

*****

Julie couldn't sleep. Her back ached, she was hot and flushed, despite cracking the window in the hotel room. She couldn't sleep on her side or her back with comfort. She decided to try to sit up instead, perhaps read her novel.

She got up, put on a robe, rifling through her papers and books to find it. Where was the bloody thing? She heard a thunk on the floor to her left, spying the paperback, which had fallen from within a stack of sketchpads. She about managed to bend to pick it up, and stopped.

That was a new pain. It wasn't simply discomfort. Maybe she had better sit down for a while.

She eased herself into the big armchair next to the bed, breathing hard a couple times, to get through the pain. It was deep in her belly, like a horrible gas pain. Breathing didn't seem to help much, but she kept doing it. Then she saw her belly ripple, as the pain returned. That had to be a contraction. Okay, little Angel. It's show time.

When it passed, she pushed herself up from the chair ... and plunked right down again. She took a couple breaths and tried again. Succeeding this time, she made her way to the dresser, taking out a loose outfit. It seemed like it took forever, but she managed to change her pajamas into an acceptable outfit for outside. She wrapped up in boots, coat, hat, and was grabbing for her sketchbook and novel when another contraction hit. She bent over double, using the bed as a brace, until the pain passed.

She got outside with her bag, which also had a spare outfit, carefully navigating the stairs. She looked around for her English-speaking bellhop friend, but he was nowhere to be seen. She made her way to the front desk, getting the attention of the tiny blond woman behind the counter.

"Do you speak English?"

"Ingen Engelsk." The woman shook her head. This meant 'no English.'

"I need a taxi to the hospital ... the hospitalet?" Julie thought it was the word for hospital, but she wasn't certain at that moment. Her mind seemed to be foggy and drifting.

Another contraction hit, so she bent over, holding the counter for balance. The blond woman shrieked to someone out of sight, picking up the telephone.

The contraction passed. Julie did her best to demonstrate, with sign language, that she was having a baby. The heavy coat she was wearing did a lot to hide her condition, but she motioned with her hands downward, to indicate 'coming out and down.' The woman seemed to understand, waving Julie to a bench near the door. The blond woman motioned for her to sit and wait.

Two contractions later, a taxi pulled up. Julie pushed and shoved until she was on her feet, waddling outside to get in. The driver saw her, hastening out to help her. He held her arm so she wouldn't slip on the icy pavement, making sure she was settled before he got into the driver's seat. He sped off at what Julie considered a reckless and insane speed on the pre-dawn, icy February streets of Copenhagen.

Was he taking every corner in the city? Julie was thrown back and forth, side to side, as the taxi driver took hairpin turns at was breakneck speed. Then she paid little attention as another contraction took her. She was wet and slimy and disgusting, realizing her water must have broken. She was horrified at this, but forbade saying anything. The driver had no English, it seemed. He would discover what had happened soon enough.

They screeched into the emergency bay at the Copenhagen College Hospital, the Rigshospitalet. The driver came around to help her out. She handed her bag out first, then slid over the leather seat in her slimy state. As she got out, looking down at her soaked clothing, she looked in horror at the driver. He was smiling, almost laughing, as he was helping her out. This must not have been the first time someone had done this in his taxi.

She had to stop halfway into the door, as another pain shot through her. The driver yelled at someone in Danish. It was effective, as an orderly rushed up with a wheelchair. She fumbled for her purse to pay the taxi driver, but he waved it away, smiling, saying goodbye. It was one of the few phrases she had picked up—farvel.

Farvel. Farvel to my old life. Farvel to being single. I would have a baby soon. Life would be different. Hello, Angel.

Life was completely different then, as they gave her an epidural. The situation became fuzzy and unfocused. She was floating, but there was a tremendous pressure on her midsection. She wasn't sure why at the moment, but she must push, she must bear down. She did, over and over again, pushing and breathing, floating and dreaming. Eventually she must have done what she needed, because the ring of strangers around her stopped telling her to push. She heard a thin wailing, then she drifted off to sleep, dreaming dreams she forgot.

When she woke, the nurse brought her beer to drink. She didn't care for beer, trying to refuse it, but then the nurse brought a doctor who spoke a little English.

"The beer, it is good for milk. You drink, then you nurse," the doctor mimed her drinking then holding a baby to her breast. She had heard worse theories. She drank the beer—Carlsberg, she noticed, a Danish brand—and tamped down on her gag reflex. She had forgotten how bitter beer was, so wasn't prepared for the taste.

"The baby, is it ok?"

"Ya, the baby is good. You wish to see?"

"Please."

The doctor motioned to one of the nurses, who brought a swaddled bundle. Julie wondered how long she had been out, as the baby was cleaned and bundled. It appeared asleep.

"Is it a boy or a girl?"

"A little girl. What name would you like?"

Julie had tried not to think of a name, in case she decided to give the child up for adoption, but as she held the baby in her arms, it was no longer an option.

"Kristen, please," she had always liked the name.

"Christian? It is a boy's name. No good for girls." The doctor seemed confused.

"No, Kristen—it's a girl's name." Julie enunciated the name.

"Kirsten, ya, okay." The doctor scribbled on her chart, leaving with the nurse, leaving Julie to hold her precious bundle.

The baby was red and tiny and had her eyes closed against the new, bright, scary world. Julie held her in her arms, knowing she'd never again be alone in the world. She had a daughter now. At least she now knew who the father was.

*****

2000, Miami, Florida

Kirsten had enjoyed her long weekend off after tax season. Most CPA firms gave a 'Tax Recovery Day' on the sixteenth of April, after the personal tax returns were either filed or extended. Of course, the sixteenth was a Saturday, so everyone had taken Monday off instead. The first day back at work wasn't light, though—now they had to work on all the first quarter payroll tax returns they had shoved to the back burner during the first half of the month. Kirsten bent to her work, surprised to see the day fly by.

She was able to go home at a reasonable time, though, arriving at her house while it was still daylight. This was a sensation she savored and enjoyed. She picked up the mail, walking into her house. Her boyfriend was already at home, since he worked an earlier shift at the hospital.

Almost as soon as she walked in, she heard the phone ring.

"Hello, this is Kirsten."

"Hello, Kirsten? This is Sharon Henderson."

Fuzzy with the last several weeks' worth of hard work, Kirsten had to search her brain for the connection, but when it did, she snapped alert.

"Ms. Henderson? Then you got my letter? I had wondered, as I'd not heard from you. I thought perhaps it had been an old address." This had happened many times before in her research requests over the years. Most people didn't update their addresses when they moved, making contact much more difficult.

"Oh, call me Sharon, please. No, I got it, you bet, but I had to track down information for you. You see, my Uncle Fred Stein happens to be your Great-Uncle Fred Stein. He had to find someone who had your dad's information, you see. I have it all here."

Kirsten caught her breath. She seemed to be having difficulty breathing. She tried again, and it almost came out like a sob. Was her quest over? Oh, God, it can't be.

"Are you alright, Kirsten?"

"I'm … I'm fine, Sharon, I'm … this has been an extensive search, so I can't believe I've found anything."

Kirsten could hear the smile in Sharon's voice. "You have indeed. I've got your dad's address and phone number, he's in California. I also have your grandparents' phone number and address, both in Minnesota and in their winter place in Arizona. And Kirsten?"

Kirsten could only make a strangled noise which she hoped sounded like "uh-huh?"

"If, for whatever reason, your father cannot or will not acknowledge you, please know you have cousins who are happy to welcome you into the family, my dear."

She was outright sobbing now, trying hard to hide it from the phone, but the efforts were futile.

"Thank you, Sharon. Thank you so very, very much. For this, for everything." She put the phone down for a second, blowing her nose hard, trying to clear her eyes enough to see the paper. "I'm ... I've got a pencil. What are the addresses?"

*****

Kirsten sat, holding the phone, for a long time. She looked at the addresses and phone numbers she had written down, taking several long, deep breaths. Well, why not. Might as well go for it. You've got the data, use it. It would be so much wasted effort if she were to stop now, out of simple fear.

She hesitated. Perhaps she should let her mother know first. Yes, it would help calm her.

"Hello, this is Julie."

"Hi, Mom, how are you?"

"Kirsten! I'm doing great, how about you? Recovering from tax season yet?"

"Pretty much, but I've another puzzle to occupy my mind at the moment. Have you got a minute to talk?"

"Of course, my dear. For you, anytime. What's wrong?" Julie sounded worried at this gambit.

"Nothing's wrong, precisely, but ... I've got information, but I wanted to let you know before I used it."

"Well, nothing like ominous innuendo to begin your day. This could be anything from nuclear launch codes to proof of alien life. Can you be a bit more specific? "

"I have my father's phone number. His address, too. And his parents'."

"Oh. I see." This quelled Julie's joking tone.

"I am going to try to call him. I wanted you to know first."

"Why should I know first?"

"What if he … what if he wants to get in touch with you? Would you mind if I gave him your phone number? He may want to … verify things, perhaps."

"Well, if he asks for it, I don't mind if you share my number. But I doubt he will. You realize this may upset his family, perhaps derail his life, right? And you still want to go through with it?"

"I do, Mom. I must know. I must find out what he's like. I wish you could understand how essential this is to me."

"I don't precisely understand, not in the way you mean, but I do understand why you might need to know. Tread carefully, will you? Other lives are affected."

"I'll do my best, Mom. Do you have any message for him?"

Julie took in a deep breath. Kirsten heard her let it go with a big woosh. "No, no message. I said all I needed to the last time we spoke. If he wants to talk to me, that's fine, but I won't initiate contact. But do let me know how it goes, will you?"

Kirsten smiled. "I will, Mom, I will. Wish me luck."

"Good luck, my special child. Good luck with everything."

*****

1969, Copenhagen, Denmark

Despite her insistence at the hospital, the doctor had written the child's name as Kirsten, not Kristen, but it would be fine. Both were names she'd heard before. Sometimes fate had its own way, despite her best efforts. She didn't care. She had this joyous creature to herself now.

It had been several days now that she had been ensconced back in Barry's guest room. It was a bright, cheerful little room, painted white with red trim. Barry had been kind enough to find a crib for Kirsten to sleep in. Julie fell into a routine of napping whenever she could, as the baby only slept a couple hours at a time, waking in furious anger, demanding to be fed. Julie didn't know if the beer had helped, but at least she wasn't having a problem nursing the child. Her adequate cleavage had burst into abundance over the last months of her pregnancy.

Barry had brought artwork to her for the local branch of the Church, whose needs were much smaller than the large organization in the UK, so at least she could keep her mind busy as she cared for the little girl. She still never got enough sleep, but nothing she had going on required much intense concentration, so she skated on.

One bright March morning, the sun was shining so bright on the snow, Julie decided she must get out. This was no simple task any longer. She bundled up the baby until the poor thing couldn't move, putting her into the homemade sling Barry had fashioned for her, which let her carry the baby without using her arms. She bundled herself up as well, grabbed her sketching stuff, going out for a walk.

Julie reveled in the sunlight, face up and eyes closed, absorbing the light and the bright as well she could, knowing the short daylight hours of winter for a precious resource. She walked, sat where she could, wandered. She didn't even stop to draw, so intent she was in catching as much sun as she could, like a spring blossom searching for the summer.

When she returned to the house, she arrived at the same time Barry did. Barry put her bicycle back into the shed, so they sat at the table together after disrobing their multiple layers.

"It is so glorious outside, I had to go and enjoy it." Julie needed to explain the outing, for some reason.

"I don't blame you, my dear. Enjoy the bright days, there are few enough of them."

The short days and long nights had left their impression on Julie. She commiserated with Barry about them. Of course, summer would bring long days and short nights, but it seemed so long away, it was a dream and a promise.

"Barry, is there going to be any permanent work for me here, do you think? I know I've overstayed my welcome." Julie was conscious of how long she had been living off the couple.

"To be perfectly honest, Julie ... no. I mean, there will always be piece work, but full time, or permanent? This tiny place doesn't need it yet. But you, my dear, are the mother of our Goddaughter, so will always have a place here. Don't you worry about it." Another of Barry's famous hair flings accompanied her words, with a dramatic flounce this time.

Julie giggled, "You know I worry about it, Barry. Besides, it isn't fair to keep my parents in the dark. I should return to them, introduce them to their grandchild. Their first grandchild." Julie smiled, thinking of her tiny girl. Then she frowned, thinking of her father's reaction to his first grandchild, bastard that she was.

"Hey, none of that. No frowning permitted."

"I know I need to go back, Barry, but I'm really not looking forward to telling my father about this. I have no idea how he will react. Mom, no problem. She may be shocked at first, but she will love the baby, I'm certain. Dad? He's a right stubborn ass sometimes."

"Well, you can't travel overseas yet, anyhow. Doesn't Kirsten need to be eight weeks before a flight so long? You've time to decide how you're going to play it, at any rate."

"I suppose so. "Julie got up then, running the tap into the tea pot. "Would you like tea? I'm making myself some."

"Tea would be fantastic. You know, I never liked the stuff until I moved to Scotland. For them, tea is the answer to everything."

"I know what you mean. I will always prefer coffee, but tea does fine in a pinch, I've found."

*****

"Julie? Julie, wake up, hon. There's a phone call for you. It's your mom." Someone was shaking her shoulder. She opened her eyes to see Bruce's face above her own, eyes full of concern.

"Bruce? What's wrong?" He was a quiet, taciturn man, good-natured, but never talkative. Julie heard a rumbling in the distance, realizing it was thunder, not a distant train. She shivered.

"I don't know, Julie, your mother didn't say, but she sounded ... strained."

Julie got her robe on, thrusting her feet into the slippers. The house was still freezing cold in the morning, the hardwood floors retaining none of the heat of the day. She shuffled into the kitchen, where the phone was mounted on the wall near the door.

"Mom? It's Julie."

There was a delay as the signal bounced to the States and back. She heard her mother's voice, hoarse and harsh. Thunder boomed again in the distance.

"Julie, is it you? Julie, there's been an accident. It's your sister. She's in the hospital, her car was hit by a train. How soon can you get home? We need you here, Julie."

Julie caught her breath. Had she heard right? Katy, in the hospital? Oh, God, she couldn't get home. Now wasn't the time to tell her mother why, either.

"Mom, I can't, I can't come home right now. Do ... do you have the number to the hospital? Can I call Katy?"

"She's not conscious, Julie. She hasn't been since the crash. What in the world is so important you can't come home? Is it money? I can buy you the ticket, just get home."

"Mom, I CAN'T! I wish I could, oh, damnit. I ... I can't tell you why now, but I can't. Mom?"

"Well, if that's your decision, then it is what it is. I hope you can live with it." Julie heard her mother sob before the loud click of her disconnecting. Julie stared at the phone for a while, unable to place it on the cradle. Bruce came up behind her, startling her back to the present.

"Julie? Is everything okay?"

"No, and there isn't a damn thing I can do about it from here. Damn! Shit!" She looked up at Barry, not noticing the tears dripping down her cheeks. "My sister was in a train crash. She's in the hospital, lying in a coma, and I can't fly yet." She pounded one fist on the wall in frustration, welcoming the pain which radiated up her arm. She cradled it, sobbing. A bright light flashed and the crash made them all jump. Julie let out a shriek of real fear.

Bruce pulled her into a hug and rocked her like a child, comforting her and making noises.

Julie pulled away and stomped into her room, looking down at the sweet, innocent baby, burbling in her sleep.

"You! It's all your fault. If it wasn't for you I could be with Katy. Damn you!"

Kirsten woke up at these imprecations, smiling with bright eyes Into her mother's face.

Julie sobbed and snatched the baby up to cradle her, rocking. How could she stay mad at this tiny wonder? She tried, but her heart wasn't in it any longer. She comforted herself by rocking the child back and forth, feeding her. She burped her and rocked her back to sleep once more, back and forth, back and forth. The thunder booms got farther and farther away, as the constant sound of rain on the roof soothed her. Morpheus came, in time, so she slept in the rocking chair, runnels of dried tears still on her cheeks.

*****

March 20, 1969

Dear Julie:

Your sister Katy died yesterday. She recovered from her coma only briefly before she passed away. She was able to tell us the story of the accident. She had been on her way to the airport to fly to London, to meet with her fiancé. The car she was in was borrowed, a Volkswagen from her friend, Karen. The car evidently stalled on a train tracks near Monroe Avenue. The train came, and she panicked. She fumbled with the door locks, but did manage to escape from the car before the train hit it. However, the debris from the crash hit her. She was taken to the hospital on March 25th. She died April 5th. We will be holding services on April 12th.

We know you loved your sister dearly, so we do not understand why you could not return to be with your sister on her last days. There is nothing to be done about it now.

Your mother,

Carol Jensen

Julie spent the afternoon crying again. Except for the times Kirsten cried as well, when she would rock the baby against her breast. She cried for her absence from Katy, for being unable to be with her sister, her best friend, her other half, her closest confidante. She cried until she got the hiccups, then cried more. She dozed in and out, but when she woke, she cried again.

When Barry got home from work, she found Julie sleeping in the rocking chair, with the baby in her arms, tear-stained cheeks and red eyes giving testament to her misery. She saw the crumpled letter on the floor where Julie had thrown it earlier, and, suffering no guilt, read it. She was crying herself by the time she finished.

Not wanting to wake her from any respite sleep might be bringing, she covered the two with an afghan, closing the door behind her. She did her best to keep quiet, preparing soup. When they awoke, they'd need nourishment. It wouldn't help much, but it might help.

*****

When Bruce came home, an hour later, Barry didn't reach the door in time to warn him to be quiet. He shut the door hard, rattling the house enough to wake the sleepers. Groggy from sleep and despair, Julie set the still-sleeping infant in her crib, venturing out into the kitchen. If she was not interested in sustenance, her stomach was. It recognized the tantalizing odors coming from the kitchen as a necessity.

Julie saw Barry's face, knowing without asking she had read the letter. It had been, after all, no longer crumpled on her floor, but flattened and left on the desk in her room. Julie's eyes prickled with tears again, but she fought the urge to give in to them. She sat at the table, while Barry, wordless, came over and hugged her hard. She then ate the soup which was handed to her, after cradling the warmth of the bowl. The heat leeched into her frozen hands. Despite herself, she did feel better after eating.

"When will you be able to travel home?" Barry wasn't trying to get rid of her, but trying to help.

"The doctor said not until next week. I wish I could have gone ... before ..." The tears were threatening to return. The soup was a lump in her stomach. She swallowed several times, taking a sip of the ice water Bruce had brought her.

"Shhh, shhh. It'll be fine. You will go back, and your parents will understand why you couldn't travel. It's not the sort of news you could tell them on the phone, now, is it?" Barry was peering at her, using one finger to pull her chin up so she could look into her eyes.

Julie took a deep sigh, "Exactly. They have enough to deal with at the moment. I couldn't give them that bad news as well. They'll know soon enough, I guess. And when they do … they'll … I don't know what they'll do, really. Mom … Mom will come around eventually, I'm sure, but Dad …?" She didn't relish thinking of what her father's reaction would be. He was angry enough she had quit her degree. To show up on her doorstep, unmarried and with a bastard child in her arms, it might send him over the edge.

What would he do? He would yell, of course, he would curse her. He had been a navy sergeant in World War II. He knew a lot of colorful curses. She had heard many of them before, but she didn't think she had gotten the full spectrum yet. She would, though.

Would he send her away? Disown her? Julie was not at all sure. She had to give it a try. As difficult as it would be, swallowing her pride and moving back to her parents' house was her best option. She had thought of moving in with Katy before … before. But Katy was gone. The tears were back, so she swallowed more ice water. She choked on a chunk of ice.

Bruce swatted her on the back, dislodging it. She dabbed her eyes with a napkin, sniffed, looking at Barry.

"Can you take me to the travel agent tomorrow? I might as well make the arrangements. Time to face the music, as it were.

"Of course, whatever you need. What else can we do to help?"

"Can you ship my boxes home? I'll have my hands full with baby stuff, so will want the art supplies and sketchbooks sent separate. I don't fancy carrying everything while moving through the airports and home."

Bruce put his hand on her shoulder.

"Consider it done, Julie. And Julie? Good luck. Whatever we can do to help, call us. We cherish you, and our Goddaughter, of course."

* * * * *

2000, Miami, Florida

The phone rung once. Kirsten's heart was in her throat, swallowing hard to keep it down.

A second ring. Perhaps he wasn't home yet? It was six pm in Florida. He was in California, so it would only be three pm. Surely he had a job.

A third ring and a click. Hello, you have reached the Starship Enterprise. The bridge crew is not here to receive your hail. Please leave your name, hailing frequency, and planet of origin, and a member of the bridge crew will get back to you as soon as possible. BEEP!"

Well, at least he had a sense of humor. And he was a science fiction geek, which was all good.

She thought fast. She didn't want to come off as a kook and scare him off.

"Hello, my name is Kirsten. I have been doing family research, and I think we might be related. Can you please give me a call?" She gave her number, hung up the phone, letting out a huge breath of relief. This was a pretty safe message. Now she waited.

He sounded fun. Not like a stiff or a like a redneck. And Kirsten had grown up loving Star Trek and other science fiction and fantasy books, movies, films. She had had little choice, as her mother had loved those as well.

She had grown up reading Tolkien and Asimov, Heinlein and Anne McCaffrey. She had loved dragons as a child, fantasizing about finding a dragon egg to impress her personal dragon steed. Or of going into space to colonize Mars. It was one reason she had studied Computer Science, so she could be part of the space program. A failure to pass Physics had convinced her to switch to Accounting instead. At least Accounting still had puzzles for her to solve, her true passion.

Nothing to do now but wait. And waiting was hard. She had waited her whole life. She hadn't thought of it this way, but she had. She was almost thirty, and she had found a man she was willing to marry, her boyfriend, Jason. She wondered if she had held off until she found her father, found the last bit of her background. After all, no fairy tale wedding would be complete without the father bringing his princess down the aisle, would it?

She busied herself with computer work, so when the phone rang, it startled her. She dropped the mouse on the tile floor with a loud clatter. She picked up the phone.

Her heart was beating so fast, she imagined it could race in the Kentucky Derby and win.

"Hello, this is Kirsten?" It was more of a question than a statement.

"Hello, Kirsten. This is Paul Stein. You left a message on my machine about genealogical research?"

"I did, yes." She forced herself to modulate her voice, keeping it from being shrill. "Let me first ensure I have the right Paul Stein, okay?"

"Sure. Which one are you looking for?"

"One who lived in East Grinstead, England during 1968, and worked at the Church there."

"Yes, sounds like me. Unless I had a twin running around, but I never caught sight of him."

Breathe.

"And do you remember a young lady named Julie Jensen?"

Silence for a moment. Breathe.

"It has been thirty years. I don't remember the name, but perhaps you could describe her?"

"She was about twenty-five years old, 5'4", thick, long brown hair, with grey eyes. She was a quiet woman, loved music. She did artwork for the Church."

"Oh! Yes, I do remember her, with great fondness."

Breathe again. C'mon, you can do it.

"Well, she's my mother ... and she says you're my father."

Kirsten waited through the long pause, forgetting to breathe completely.

"Wow."

She let go of the breath she had held, but then forgot again.

"Wow. How come she never told me?"

Kirsten hadn't expected this to be the first question. She had been expecting "How does she know" or "Can she prove it". This instant acceptance of the fact was a surprise. She wasn't sure how to answer it right away.

"She ... she said you had been married, so she didn't want to mess it up. Besides, she didn't know until you had left, back to your ... wife."

There was more silence on the other end of the line. Kirsten began to wonder if he had hung up the phone.

"I suppose she was wise, at that. I wouldn't have been a good father at that point. Shoot, I probably wouldn't be a good one now." He let out a brief laugh, nervous.

Kirsten giggled, but tried to hide it. "So I don't have any brothers or sisters?"

"No, well, none who I've heard from. I didn't know about you five minutes ago, after all. Annie and I divorced about ten years ago, by the way."

"Oh! I'm sorry to hear it." Her response was automatic.

"It was amicable, we're still good friends. We were better as friends than as a couple. I've always managed to be good friends with women. Your mother was one, as well. How is she, by the way? I remember she was nice

255

company."

"She's fine. She lives in Miami. She didn't ... she never got married. She raised me on her own."

"Would she be amenable to, perhaps, hearing from me?"

"I cleared it before I called you, actually. She said she wouldn't mind." Kirsten grinned.

They talked, then. They talked about all sorts of things. They compared photographs via email, and Kirsten could see her face in her father's. It was as if someone had cut and pasted the features, especially the eyes and mouth.

They compared favorite books and movies. They discovered they both loved travel and languages, puzzles and math. They both collected dragons. They had a joy in history, and even in puns. They laughed and cried. It was as if she was talking to an old friend who had been lost for years. Perhaps that's exactly what it was.

After a couple hours, exhausted with relief and effort, Kirsten said goodbye to this new man in her life. Her father, at long last.

9 - ORIGINS

1969, Detroit, Michigan

Please let it be Mom. Mom, not Dad, only Mom. She had chanted this, almost like a meditation, most of the flight across the Atlantic. She hoped against hope her mother was picking her up from the airport, so she could explain to her first, before having to face her father. Having her mother as an ally would make things easier.

Her mother, Carol, worked as an art teacher three days a week at Edsel Ford High School. The other days she sometimes worked as a substitute. She had taught all sorts of things this way—everything from Algebra to Spanish, History to Music. But she loved teaching art, it was her vocation. It was from her mother she got her own talent and passion for art, as did Katy. Her mother's mother was named Wilda, but everyone called her Meema. She was an artist as well, who used to teach oil painting in private classes. She hadn't worked full time, of course, not in her generation, but she enjoyed the teaching of art. Her father, Jerry, wasn't artistic, but he was an engineer, combining creativity with mathematics in a way which mystified her.

Julie had never gotten the teaching bug. She enjoyed making art, but not the passing of the knowledge to others. Her passion was in the solitude of creativity, the sublime otherworld where she transported herself to while in the throes of her muse. She would paint or draw for hours, with no attention paid to the outside world. It was almost like a trance, an Eastern Yogi meditation. It wasn't anything she could instill in someone else, or even make most people understand. Katy had understood.

Julie took another sip of the miniature Coke can the stewardess had left with her, using the dying carbonation to fight her tears. She had no wish to let her seatmates see her misery. It was none of their business.

She was sandwiched in the middle seat of the middle section, between a large, sweaty man with shoulders broad enough for a football team and a young boy, around age ten. The child belonged to a woman across the aisle, busy with two other younger children, who seldom checked on the boy. The man had dozed most of the flight, though he kept leaning into her, his beefy shoulders pushing her into the child's space. She had eyed the boy when she boarded, Kirsten in her arms, but he had been angelic, busy coloring his activity books throughout the eight hour flight. Kirsten had been good as well, though Julie had to get up to stand in the galley to feed her twice.

As she had many times in the last nine months, she conjured up the scene of confronting her father with the baby, playing it in her mind as if it was a stage production. Each time it was different, as she imagined the setting, the reactions, what she would say to him, how he would respond. However, they almost always ended with him kicking her out of his home and his life.

As the plane descended into Detroit, Kirsten woke up and whimpered. Her ears were hurting from the descent. She made popping sounds with her mouth, to get Kirsten to copy her, distract her from the pain. It worked for a while, but the whimper became a whine, turning into full-blown tantrum.

She couldn't get up, but she bounced the fretful child on her knee as the plane got closer to landing, praying it would be over soon, giving frantic, apologetic glances to those around her. There wasn't anything she could do to keep the baby from crying, but her overriding guilt kept her trying.

The large man next to her was helpful in retrieving her bags from the overhead bin, a process made impossible with Kirsten in her arms. He smiled at the baby, nodding to her, then walked down the aisle after the retreating forms of the other passengers.

When Julie came out onto the concourse, she looked around, hoping to see her mother's face among those gathered to meet the arrivals. She held Kirsten close to her, face into her chest, to mask identification to a casual look. She did not look for her father's face. However, she did see a familiar smiling face, crowned with a halo of fuzzy, curly light brown hair—her brother Larry. He was waving like a clown, and next to him ... all she could see was her mother's dark wavy hair, with a glimpse of her loud turquoise floral dress. No father. Julie breathed in a huge sigh of relief, waved at Larry so he would stop his crazy gesticulations, then hefted her bags.

As she made her way around the ropes, Larry went to hug her tight, but stopped when she put her hand on his chest. He was prone to unthinking enthusiasm, and she didn't want him hurting Kirsten. He looked at her, puzzled. Silent, she unfolded her arm, revealing the gurgling infant to him and their mother.

Larry looked at the baby, then at Julie, then back to the baby, his mouth open in an O, looking like nothing so much as a goldfish with an afro. Julie smiled at the image, looking to see her mother's reaction.

Understanding and sympathy warred with disappointment on her mother's face, but the former won.

"Julie ... this is why you couldn't come for Katy, is it? Why didn't you tell me? Oh, my dear, sweet, special girl ..." She came to Julie and gave her a hug, loose in the front but tight around her shoulders. Larry joined the hug as well. Why was she so prone to tears now? She never was before. Was it motherhood or Katy's death? Julie blinked several times, determined not to let them take over again.

"I didn't think it was the sort of thing I should tell you over the phone, mom. You had ... so many other things to worry about. And I didn't want Dad to know yet." Julie looked down into Kirsten's face, sticking out her finger for the child to grab onto. She looked up again.

"And what is my grandchild's name?" Her mom was smiling at the child, putting her finger out as well, touching the baby-soft cheek.

"Her name is Kirsten. She was born on February 16th."

Larry, with awkward acuity, cut in, "Wait ... did you get married without telling us?"

Julie looked at him hard, a look which had quelled him as a child, but worked less so now he was nineteen. "No, I'm not married," she said, willing him not to ask further embarrassing questions. She straightened her spine to look defiant. She didn't think she managed it.

They exchanged looks. To avoid looking at them, Julie looked back at Kirsten.

"Well, shall we get ourselves out of this madhouse and to someplace quiet to eat, where we can talk?" They would need to talk before facing her father. Perhaps a restaurant would be a good, neutral ground.

"That's a good idea, Julie. Larry, grab her bags. Let's see if we can find

260

the car."

*****

They sat around a wooden table at a restaurant named New Hellas in Greek Town. It had been one of Julie's favorites when she was young. They were enjoying saganaki and moussaka. While she munched the flavorful morsels, she told her mother and brother the story of Paul, and why he didn't know anything about the baby. She told of her job disaster in Edinburgh, of her loneliness. She hadn't meant to unload all of this on them, not as soon as she returned, but having someone she trusted, someone she knew, someone she could talk to was such an incredible relief. As helpful as Barry and Bruce had been, their own fertility issues had kept her from confiding much in them.

"Well, I'm delighted to meet my granddaughter, and welcome her into the family. I think we will install you in the upstairs room. Your father has built out the large attic space, you know. It's now two rooms and a bathroom—perfect for you and Kirsten."

"But what about Dad?" Her mother didn't seem to be taking his reaction into consideration.

Her mom, fussing with her short hair, paused before she answered. "Your father has been ... different since Katy passed on." Julie could see the tears threatening in her mother's eyes, now, offering her a glass of water from her side of the table. Carol took it, smiling.

"He's much quieter, not given to his normal tempers, you see. It's as if his soul was removed. He read a poem at the funeral. He cried as he read it." Julie's own eyes were burning, as she glanced at her brother to see his reddened eyes. They all stopped for a few moments, in mutual agreement, eating a few more bites of lunch to regain control.

"I think he would welcome new life into the family, my dear. Truly, I do."

*****

Her mother had been right. Other than a few clipped questions about the origins of the child, her father had accepted them without a great deal of fuss. There was no thunderstorm of reaction and tears, which she had been expecting, dreading, since she found had discovered her condition. It was almost sad, pathetic. The loss of fire in her father was a little bit scary. It was almost as if he had given up on life.

But soon, Julie discovered, the spark showed again. Her father built things, which had always been his passion and his therapy. He built a crib and a huge dollhouse for the baby. He bought a play set and erected it in the backyard, even though she was much too young to use it yet. He played with the child, often while she was safe in her playpen, when no one was looking. If anyone came In, of course, or made a noise, he would pretend he had been checking up on the child, but a few rare moments of tenderness were apparent.

Life settled into an uneasy routine. Her father went to work every day in Detroit, where he worked as an engineer for Chrysler. Her mother went to work most days, though she took fewer substitute jobs to help take care of the baby. Julie missed Katy with an ache which settled into her bones. She kept seeing things in the house which reminded her of her sister, flashes of memory which hit her at random times, like a punch in the gut.

Julie and Kirsten settled into the upstairs rooms, while her parents ran the house downstairs. If she had guests, they stayed upstairs, so she had her own little suite, in effect. The front door opened onto a landing, with the stairs to the right and the living room to the left, so she even had privacy in this aspect.

Not that she entertained so much. She was too guilty to enjoy herself overmuch. Julie was keenly aware she was now living on her parents' charity and good will. She hadn't yet been able to find a job, at least not one which offered enough money she could afford someone to look after the baby while she was gone. Months went by. Though she had gotten temporary gigs at places like Greenfield Village, demonstrating crafts on school trip days, she hadn't found anything permanent.

It was like a fencing match. Her father was on one side, sullen and taciturn, going about his daily tasks without so much as talking to her, even at dinner. His silence was his reproach for her lack of college degree, employment, as well as her fall from grace. Julie was on the other side, torn between caring for her baby and trying to impress her father with her value. With Katy gone, she was more of a disappointment. Katy had been the golden child, excelling at everything she tried. Julie was a poor shadow, the remnants of the goddess who was forever gone. Her mother, as always, was torn in the middle, a referee trying to make everyone happy. Because no one was happy, she was unhappy herself.

At least she had been able to hang out more with Gail now she had a baby. Gail had two children by now, Ross and Kelly. She had her hands full with caring for them, though Ross was six now, able to help out. Julie enjoyed visiting them when she could, letting the three children play together.

She had made friends again with Sandy, who, though fierce of temper and quick with criticism, was also willing to forgive, given time and plenty of encouragement. She lived in downtown Detroit, though, so it was more difficult for Julie to get there, as she didn't drive. Her apartment wasn't much classier than her place in New York had been, though her neighbor had young children for Kirsten to play with.

Her room was pretty large, as it took a full third of the second floor. Another room, just as large, was set up for Kirsten. There was hallway, a half bathroom (no tub or shower), as well as leftover attic space. The ceiling had an odd garret slope which got low near the edge, except for the window bay. She had decided she loved deep, dark reds when she decorated. She haunted the thrift stores for curtains, bedspread, and rugs to fill this craving. She had arranged trinkets she had gotten as gifts on her travels, precious pieces Katy had made, with a light wind chime near the window made with large round pieces of frosted glass.

Kirsten's room was more of a mishmash, but for now it had her crib and playpen. There was also a big wooden box her grandfather had constructed, which was filling with toys at an alarming rate. He was still working on the dollhouse, though it was larger than she was yet.

Julie looked into the full-length mirror in her room, trying to pull in her stomach so the slacks weren't so pouched in the middle. Then she let out her breath, watching her tummy pouf out again, grimacing. She hadn't been able to get rid of much of her pregnancy fat, so she was self-conscious about it.

She was trying to get ready for a job interview, at a local needlework shop. They needed a clerk who could also paint patterns onto needlepoint canvas. It was part-time, and a couple of blocks away, so she could ride her bike. She abandoned the pants and tried on a long skirt instead.

This was better, as it bloused out and didn't show her belly and hips in relief. She fluffed her hair, now cut short for ease of care, touched up her make-up, gathering Kirsten and the playpen to take them downstairs. Julie left Kirsten with a kiss on her sleepy cheek, thanking her mother for watching the child during the interview.

It was a nice, bright day outside. It was downright sultry. She was glad it was close, for if the store had been too much farther away, she would have arrived in a sweaty mess. She made her way down the block to the corner where Pete's Grocery Store stood, turned right onto Monroe, down two blocks to the shop. She stashed her bike next to the front door, checked her hair in the glass window before entering.

The place was a magpie's nest, but a glorious one. There were yarns of all descriptions in baskets, hanging in skeins and dripping from the ceiling. There was a huge rack along one wall which had hundreds of painted needlepoint canvases. At a tiny counter near the back, an older lady reading a novel. She looked up as the front door chimed, giving a nod to Julie as she looked around her in wonder.

Needlepoint wasn't a passion with Julie, but her mother had always loved the craft. The valences above the large bay windows in the living room and dining room were covered with a huge needlepoint of the Blue Willow oriental pattern, all done by her mother. Julie calculated it must have cost a fortune in time and materials, but Carol loved her Blue Willow.

Julie was a few minutes early, so she took time to look around. She hadn't been here before, so was fascinated by the variety on offer in the narrow little storefront. The lady at the counter went back to reading her novel. She had on glasses with pointy ends, covered in lavish rhinestones. Her greying hair was pulled back into a huge bun, looking about forty.

When Julie wended her way to the back, the lady looked up with inquiry.

"Hello, I've an appointment with Shay at noon?" Julie tried to sound professional and calm.

"I'm Shay, you must be Julie. How do you like our little store?" Shay managed to both shake Julie's hand and gesture with her other, encompassing her little world in one wave.

"It's overwhelming. I'd done needlework, but had no idea the variety available." Julie smile, though she was still nervous enough that her stomach was ready to fly away with the butterflies. She hoped what she had said wasn't a bad answer.

"It can be at first, I'm sure. We try to stuff as much into a tiny space as we can. So, you are Carol's daughter, then? I don't think we've met before."

Julie had no idea how Shay knew this. Her mother must have mentioned it. "Well, yes, I am. I'd been away at Art School, then living abroad for several years." She decided this was the most innocuous way to describe her adventures to the curious. Her adventures were on the wild side for most of Suburbia.

"And what sort of art did you study?"

"Mostly two dimensional design—painting, drawing, that sort of thing. I'd done courses in sculpture, but it wasn't my focus. I've dabbled in lots of areas, though."

"Excellent. And have you ever painted on canvas before, for needlepoint?"

Julie smiled, "I helped my mother with her Blue Willow canvas preparations. She painted it, then I helped her with the rest. We completed the project together. There was a lot of it. Have you seen them?"

Shay smiled, showing a missing eyetooth among her yellow teeth, "I have indeed. She bought most of the supplies from here, I daresay. She's always been an excellent customer. I would be happy to welcome her daughter to my fold. Can you begin tomorrow at ten? I'll show you the ropes, staying with you a couple days before I leave you on your own, okay? The pay is $1.50 per hour."

Julie almost couldn't breathe, she was relieved. "Oh, that would be fantastic! Thank you." She pumped Shay's hand. Realizing how much the older lady was jiggling, she gentled her handshake. After so many months, she was thrilled to have a job, any job. One which was artistic was a dream.

"Carol also mentioned you have a young child? An infant?" Shay's question brought Julie back to earth with a thud, as her stomach began fluttering again.

"Yes, Kirsten. She's five months old." Was Shay going to decide not to hire her after all? A disgraced single mother?

"Well, you are welcome to bring her with you unless we've got a class going on. If you bring a playpen, she still sounds young enough to not be too much bother. Does it sound acceptable?"

Julie let out her held breath with a WOOSH, giving Shay a look of sheer gratitude.

"I was once a single mother, my dear. Well, widowed, from the war, you see, but my child was young and it was no picnic. I do understand." Shay reached out and took Julie's hand in both of hers, holding it. She held Julie's eyes. "I try to help out others in your situation when I can"

Blinking back tears, Julie managed to mumble a "thank you", dropping her eyes, but Shay wouldn't relinquish her hand yet.

"Be strong, my dear. Plenty of people will assume the worst of you, but remember, you are strong. You are yourself. The opinions of others are meaningless. Do not give them such power."

With a final squeeze of her hand, Shay let go.

"I'll see you tomorrow, then. Is that your bicycle outside? Bring it around the back tomorrow, so we can keep it inside the storage area, to keep it from being stolen or hit in the alleyway." She bustled around with items under the counter, so Julie made her escape.

She hadn't counted on such kindness. It made her spirits soar as she flew home on the bike. Previous job interviews *had* met with the sort of judgment Shay had mentioned. Women and men alike had looked upon her with disdain. This wasn't a big city, so some had already heard of her situation. Even those who were ignorant could read on applications she hadn't finished college. This gave them plenty of ammunition. When Julie asked about the hours, the fact she had an infant came up. That was usually the end of the interview.

She looked forward to working at Needle Arts. At least she had found a kindred spirit in Shay, someone who had an inkling into her struggles, both past and future.

*****

1970, Dearborn, Michigan

Julie juggled her covered dish and the baby while she attempted to get into the car, gave up, placing the dish in the back seat before trying again.

"Can you hold Kirsten? I have to go back and get her playpen." She handed the infant to Gail in the driver's seat and rushed back into the house. She emerged, laden with a collapsed playpen and a huge quilted bag of supplies and toys. While she walked to the car, Gail popped open the back of her woody station wagon so the items could be stashed away.

"How many people do you think we'll have to feed?" Julie was worried she hadn't made enough of her dish, a strange concoction her mother called City Chicken. It wasn't chicken, but pork cooked on skewers, with onions and peppers, smothered in chicken gravy. It was sort of a poor man's chicken shish-ka-bob, a family recipe.

"I don't know, though at least thirty. The whole block is invited, but a few are away on vacation. Don't worry, there's always plenty of food. Jan has the barbecue fired up in the front yard, so there will be a constant stream of meat coming from the other neighbors." Jan and Gail threw block parties every summer. They erected barricades on either end of the block to keep the traffic out, taking over the street with games, tables to sit around and drink chilled beer in the hot sunshine.

Kirsten would be ensconced in her playpen in Gail's house, with a couple other infants her age. Julie would be hanging out in the dining room, with its large bay window overlooking the street, in easy view of both the party and the babies. Jan would be out in the yard, playing the Barbecue King, drinking beer, being the loudest person on the block. Julie smiled at the idea—he loved being the center of attention. He told fantastic stories, reveling in a party atmosphere. Gail was often by his side, helping out with the bits of story he forgets. Julie envied their relationship and partnership.

She was very much looking forward to a day of relaxation, drinking and socializing with people her own age. While she loved working at the shop, most of the customers were women her mother's age or older. She wasn't comfortable socializing with them in a shop setting. Even when there was a class going, and social interaction was encouraged, it wasn't a friendship setting, it was a class setting.

But this, with people of all ages in a party environment, with the wholesome family atmosphere—she had missed this since her days living in East Grinstead. It was a craving for camaraderie, a sense of community she craved.

Julie sipped her soda, as she still couldn't stand the taste of beer, watching Jan gesticulating outside. The windows were open, screens keeping the bugs at bay, so she could hear the subject of his dissertation, on the merits of his method of barbecue, complete with vinegar-based marinade in the barbecue sauce. She smiled at the rapt attention of his audience, a group of six younger men, all awaiting the first taste of the chicken which was on the verge of burning. The buffet table nearby had all manner of covered dishes. Most were almost empty now, though, except her offering, which was barely touched. She wasn't a great cook, but it still sort of hurt to see.

Kirsten was gurgling, playing in her pen, though she had managed to crumple the blanket up into the corner. Julie believed she had made it into a cave, hiding her toys in it, then pulling them out as if making a great discovery. Julie smiled at her young girl, so happy to have her in her life. She was such a sweet child, when she wasn't crying bloody murder. The child was learning, though, crying or fussing when grandpa was around wasn't acceptable. He had made it clear he had already raised his children, so wouldn't tolerate a screaming baby in his house. A firm look from him would quell any fussiness in the baby. At least she had a father figure in her life. She veered away from such ideas, looking out at the party again.

Gail returned from bringing Jan a fresh Pabst Blue Ribbon beer from the huge cooler, settling into the chair next to Julie and their friend, Helen.

"God, it's great to relax today. I've been run off my feet with the kids. Jan is in fine fettle out there, isn't he?"

"Indeed, he is. He's in his element. He must not get to socialize much at his job, I imagine. He's normally stuck under an engine, covered in grease. It's hard to fascinate the multitude from under there." Julie grinned at the vision.

Once again, Julie's mind strayed to the partnership with Paul she had enjoyed, letting out a huge sigh.

"Do you miss him?" Helen had always had the uncanny ability to follow her thoughts.

"I do, of course I do. But there's nothing to be done about it, really."

"You could find someone else?" Helen offered this option, as if it was so easy.

"I've tried, now and then, but no one measures up. I mean, I was at home with Paul, completely natural. No pretense needed, no mask, no acting. It was the two of us, which was wonderful. Who else could measure up to that?"

"At least you've a bit of him to keep with you in Kirsten?" It was more of a question than an encouragement.

"Yes, at least I've got Kirsten. I hope it will be enough to sustain me in my spinsterhood." She was bitter, old and full of despair.

"Hey, none of that. You've a delightful little girl to fill your life with joy. It's a blessing, my friend. You keep that in mind."

"Yes, mother." Julie stuck her tongue out at her friend.

*****

2000, Miami, Florida

Julie reflected on what she might say when Paul called. Kirsten had called her last night, to let her know she had talked to him. He had expressed an interest in contacting her. Kirsten had also mentioned he was divorced. Julie was so nervous. Would he sound the same? Would she be silly? She had no idea.

She had things she needed to do, cleaning around the house, but as she went about her duties, she found herself hovering near the phone. She caught herself sweeping the same part of the living room floor a third time, before she made herself move on to the hallway.

When the phone did ring, it startled her, so she stopped, stunned into rigid inaction. On the second ring, she dropped the broom with a loud clatter on the tile floor, running to the phone. She waited, then, to catch her breath, so she wouldn't sound panicked when she answered. After the third ring, she picked up the handset. With a deliberate, even voice, forcing herself to sound as normal as possible, she answered.

"Hello, this is Julie."

"Julie? This is Paul. Our daughter called me, saying you wouldn't mind a call from me."

Julie took a deep breath, trying to speak. It came out as an unintelligible grunt. Horrified, she cleared her throat and spoke again.

"Hello, Paul. Yes, she mentioned she had found you." She did her best to sound nonchalant and light-hearted. It came off as hysterical.

"She did indeed. It's quite a little detective you have raised. I do thank you for her."

Julie's heart skipped a beat. She had no clue whatsoever what to say to him. She had imagined for years finding him again, speaking to him, but it was never on the phone. It had always been someplace random, running into him at the grocery store, or at the movies. A wild, chance encounter which would result in a romantic reunion and running away together. But this, this was an unknown, not a scene she had ever considered.

"Julie? Are you still there?"

"I'm here, Paul. I'm at a loss as to what to say."

"Well, how about I talk, then. I've always been pretty good at it, you might remember. I'll begin by saying I'm sorry. I had no idea you had our daughter. If I had, I would have helped, I promise you. But you were wise not to let me know. I don't think I would have been able to handle the responsibility at the time."

"It sounds about right." She sounded bitter. She didn't want to sound bitter, but it came out that way.

"I don't blame you for being upset. How can I make this up to you?"

"Can you ... would you like to ... be a part of her life? Fill in the void she grew up with? It's all I could ask of you, but it would mean the world to her."

"That is already going to happen. I was shocked and amazed when she called, but I was also thrilled. I'd never had any other children, you know. Annie and I had discussed it, then decided we would rather be the rich Aunt and Uncle than the poor parents. I'd gotten a vasectomy five years after I knew you."

"So you have no other children?"

"No, only Kirsten. And I am so glad she found me." He was, too. She could hear the pride and joy in his voice, the smile in his words. She found herself smiling in reaction to his obvious delight.

"I'm glad, too."

"I know it can't have been easy, raising her on your own. I'm proud of you, as well. I would love to become your friend again. Would you be amenable to this?"

"I think we can give it a try, for Kirsten's sake if no other reason."

"I seem to recall enjoying your company. I can't see why I wouldn't enjoy it now. Unless you've objections?"

"Well, it's not convenient to go out for a walk when we're three thousand miles apart." Julie said with acerbity.

Paul laughed, sounding nervous. "Fair enough, but we can at least get to know each other again, through phone calls and emails. I'm sure I'll be making a visit out there in the coming months, to meet my lovely new daughter. I should like to meet you again, as well."

"That would be … a good plan."

They were past the fencing stage then, so began to chat with more ease. They talked about things which had happened in their lives in the missing thirty years, about how their hopes and dreams had turned into lives and careers. Julie told of her career as a secretary, occasional artist and property manager, now working for an architect. How she had never married nor had any other children. Paul described his career in electronics, then computers, teaching classes in Linux and Red Hat for Hewlett Packard. His job sent him to teach seminars all around the country, sometimes around the world. He had a planned work trip in Orlando in September, so they made arrangements for him to come out a week earlier, so they could all enjoy time together.

As she hung up the phone, Julie sat down, trying to collect her feelings. This was a curve ball she hadn't considered before, what happened after the imagined chance meeting in the grocery store or at the movies. What would happen next? Would they fall into the easy friendship and affection they had enjoyed before? Or would it be awkward and strange. Perhaps it was both.

*****

1970, Dearborn, Michigan

"I told you to keep your screeching brat upstairs, Julie. I will not tolerate her running around, screaming like a fucking banshee through the dining room when I'm working on my designs. March yourself upstairs, take that hellion baby, and keep her quiet." Jerry had a large frame and a barrel chest, so his deep voice carried far when he yelled. Julie had a vision of a hurricane blowing from his mouth, pushing her and the child in her arms back against the wall. However, she had had enough.

"She wasn't screeching! She was laughing, which you never learned to do. If you weren't such a gloomy sourpuss, perhaps you'd recognize joy when you heard it."

Her father seemed to loom even larger, inflating like a puffer fish with rage and vitriol. Her mother did her best to intervene.

"Now, Jerry, dear, I'm sure Julie will keep the child quiet. Julie, take her upstairs with you, won't you, darling? Jerry, come, let me brew you coffee. I've fresh cookies baking now, those will be delicious." She managed to hustle the hulking form of her father into the dining room while Julie made her escape to the stairs. As she was leaving, she heard her father argue again, despite her mother's imprecations.

"She's living under our roof, she's got to live by our rules. She's a fucking charity case, and I won't have her disobeying me. Carol, stop trying to shove that cup into my hands."

"Dear, she's got a job, she's not mooching. Relax, your face is all red. Remember what the doctor said about your blood pressure. Now, drink your coffee ..." Her voice trailed off when Julie reached the top of the stairs. She brought the child into her room, calming her. She had become upset with all the noise and tempers. In calming Kirsten, she calmed herself. It became a game of peek-a-boo, until she managed to coax out a waterfall giggle.

This wasn't the first argument she'd had with her father. She was sure it wouldn't be the last. She managed to escape most Saturdays when her dad was home working on his plans. However, today Gail was away with friends in Ohio, and she couldn't get to Sandy's, who now lived in Detroit. She bore the creeping despair, the sensation of being trapped began again, but she tamped it down. She would have to bear it until Kirsten was old enough to go to school. Perhaps then she could think about moving away, someplace where she could take a full time job, when the child didn't take so much constant care.

She grabbed what she could, bundling Kirsten and her baby bag together. She grabbed her bike, heading for the Angelo's Pizzeria. It was her escape place when none of her friends were available, so she headed there for lunch and respite.

As she bicycled along the suburban street, seeing houses and manicured lawns, she imagined what life might have been like without a child, able to live where she liked, as she had in San Francisco. And where did it get me? Involved with a married man and with child. Perhaps she wasn't mature enough to control her own life, after all.

She pulled up behind the restaurant, parking her bike. She hefted the baby and bag, walking into the rear entrance as she always did. She walked by the counter bar on the left, finding an empty booth on the right. The maroon vinyl and sparkling silver table tops gleaming in the afternoon sun as it came through the glass frontage.

Hal came up and asked her if she wanted her usual slice and a coke, so she said yes. She settled Kirsten into her seat, giving her a bottle to keep her occupied. Then she pulled out her book. She needed escape, even if it was only into a vicarious world. She was reading the new book by Irwin Shaw, called Rich Man, Poor Man. It spoke of Americans living abroad, escaping the McCarthyism she remembered from her youth. It seemed to her it paralleled her own life in many ways.

She remembered a conversation she had had with Katy one time, about the political machinations of the government. How they were harming the people in their attempt to protect them. The memory brought pride for her sister's intelligence and clarity, rage at her death, sadness at her absence. Her lunch came, but Hal knew better than to chat with her while she was reading, so he left her to her solitude.

Julie wished she had brought sketching materials, but she hadn't had much time for art. The baby took up so much of her time, and the job had her working long hours. What free time she did have was spent in her room, reading or listening to records. She withdrew into herself. That was all there was, only herself and her daughter.

*****

2000, Miami, Florida

They communicated through email and phone over the next several months, all three of them. They exchanged photographs, obsessions, interests, dislikes, hobbies. They talked about family, friends, and memories. When Kirsten saw her father's high school picture, comparing it to her own, she was looking into a strange, distorted carnival mirror. The eyes, the nose and the mouth all looked the same. She had the same wispy, thin hair as her father. She had always believed she looked like her mother, but she now saw she was much closer to her father in looks, as well as in many of his hobbies and interests.

Julie and Paul emailed frequently, long letters where they talked of the past and the present, of memories and impressions. They became friends again. Because of the distance between them, it was slow, but perhaps less awkward because it was, by necessity, an intellectual and emotional reunion at the moment. If they had been together physically, it would have taken longer and been more tentative, but the safety of distance made them both bold. The formal separation of pen-pals evolved into an intimate correspondence.

10 – FULL CIRCLE

Julie got off the plane in San Francisco. She was more nervous than she had expected herself to be. After all, she was a grown woman, almost fifty-five years old now. She considered turning around and getting back on the plane, even knowing it was futile. She was heavier, older, more settled and less attractive than she had been at age twenty-five. Everyone was, that was nature. Paul would be, as well. They had exchanged recent pictures, of course, he would be expecting it, but still, she was almost terrified that he wouldn't like her any longer.

Recognizing someone you hadn't seen in years was a tricky business, even if you had known them well. You form an image of them in your mind, even if you know that they've aged, or if you've seen recent photos. That person is still in your mind as they were years ago, young and vital, trapped in their younger self by your memories. When you see them again, older and grey, the two images merging. This new, older stranger melds with the younger memories, so they become one in your mind. Sometimes this is instant, sometimes it takes longer.

He had invited her for a two week visit, as his friend was getting married. This would give them time to explore their relationship again. She looked around the crowded airport, with masses of people drifting in and out, swirling like eddies in a stream filled with rapids. She took a deep breath, forcing her legs to move towards the exit.

Would she recognize him from his photos? She doubted that, as she scanned the faces of the people waiting in the arrivals area. Then she saw a stocky man with wispy, thin greyish hair, holding up a sign that simply said 'Julie.' She looked at the man's face, remembering the warm, brown eyes that smiled. She doubted no longer.

She walked up to him, and he dropped the sign. They hugged hard, holding on for an eternity. She trembled in his arms, so he squeezed her tight, murmuring comforting sounds in her hair, smoothing it with one hand.

After eons, they parted, and she looked into his eyes again. He was grinning wide. Her own face ached because she was doing the same. They hugged again, quickly. He picked up her bag and offered an arm, as they walked out of the raucous lounge.

*****

She was enjoying her vacation with Paul. He had taken her to see his room, in the basement of a friend's house. Well, it was his house as well, they had bought it together, but he took the basement as his part of the living quarters, as he owned a smaller share, while Joy and her daughter, Christine, lived upstairs. They were sweet folk, welcoming to her, embracing her with open arms and tears. They knew the whole story, of course. Paul had told them and they were so happy for him. Joy was the one getting married, to her groom, Stephan, next week. Julie offered to help with the decorations, so was put to work in her free time, making wedding favors and table decorations.

During the day, Paul would take her sightseeing, to the Japanese gardens, or to Muir Woods. Julie remembered her time there with George, smiling at the memory. That seemed so long ago, a lifetime away, during a more innocent, more adventurous time. She was glad she had experienced San Francisco at that time. It had been a lot of work raising Kirsten, but at least she had enjoyed fun first.

The city was different, of course, from when she was there in the sixties. The buildings, the people, the vibe, it was as if her previous time had been in a dreamland, a place out of an almost-forgotten book of fairy tales from her childhood, or a half-remembered dream. Haight Ashbury was so changed. Gone were the twisted jellybean fonts of her day. It had a few shops that catered to its history, but most were new, glitzy, with ethnic restaurants and clothing shops.

Evenings were spent with Paul, Joy and Christine, sometimes Stephan. They seemed determined to show her every interesting restaurant in Alameda, of which there were plenty. Indian food, Chinese, Japanese, Thai, she could have had a different curry every night and still never repeated a meal. She enjoyed the flavors, but couldn't handle very much spice, so Paul had made a game of trying to find dishes that didn't burn her mouth.

Nights she spent on the couch. They took their time rekindling their friendship, simply holding hands at first. He even stole a few kisses lakeside at the Japanese Gardens. Julie and Paul rediscovered their affection for each other, as well as their passion. It was slow at first, clumsy. This wasn't anything she'd even done since him, after all. But, like riding a bicycle, it wasn't a skill you ever lost.

After an exotic meal of Ethiopian food in San Francisco, the whole group made it back to the house, retiring to the dining room for board games. They played for a couple of hours, until, one by one, each player decided it was time to go to bed. Soon, only Paul and Julie were left. By mutual agreement, they headed down into Paul's basement.

When they got into his room, he put on music. It was slow music, Celtic. Perhaps it was Clannad? She wasn't sure. She did know it was ethereal and slow, rhythmic and primal. They danced close, as she closed her eyes, enjoying the shape of the music, of his hand around her waist. They danced closer as he nuzzled her neck. Her back shivered. She bent her neck, to give him more room. She didn't want him to stop.

He didn't stop, but he did change locations. He kissed her shoulder, down her arm to the inside of her elbow. They had stopped dancing now, but her eyes were still closed. She gasped at the sensation of butterfly kisses on her skin, sensitive with the night and the music.

He pulled her wrist up, kissing the soft skin inside, the palm of her hand. She put her hand up to his face, caressing the rough stubble of his short beard, shot with bits of grey and white. She opened her eyes to look at the wiry hair, as she touched it, exploring it with her fingers, stroking along his chin line.

He caught up both her hands then, placing them around his waist. He then stroked her hair, bending her head back for a long, lingering kiss. Was the music still playing? She had no idea. Time seemed to stand still. It was like she had been waiting for this kiss her whole life. She had, really. For thirty years, at any rate. She stopped thinking and enjoyed the kiss.

He led her to the bed, reveling in the fact that they were, at long last, able to enjoy their affections in a real bed, and not a Victorian bathtub.

*****

Julie didn't relish this confrontation one bit, but it had to be done. She was torn between telling Sandy right away, like ripping off a Band-Aid, or trying to build up to it. She didn't think she had the talent for the slow approach. Sandy was never a person to pussy-foot around things. She would realize something was wrong right away, and draw it out of her. That would be worse. Very well, time to dive in.

They were having lunch in a tiny café they liked in South Miami, called Swensen's. While they served sandwiches and soups, they were known for their ice cream, complex sundaes you could create at their counter. The windows were stained glass in art nouveau patterns, the booths made of dark wood and red leather.

Julie stared, glum, into her hot fudge sundae with strawberries, while Sandy devoured frozen yoghurt with single-minded intent. Julie took a deep breath and dove in. One simple phrase would be all that was needed. Sandy was intelligent enough to know the whys and wherefores.

"I'm moving to California next month."

Sandy froze for a couple moments, as if time had stood still. Then she looked up from her dish and looked at Julie a long moment.

The heat of Sandy's anger hit her like a firestorm.

"You are a bitch, you know that? We were supposed to grow old together, best friends forever, but as soon as that jerk waves his hand, you go off and leave me here to die alone."

"Like you're full of sweet and innocence? Like stealing Jeffrey?"

Sandy rolled her eyes. "Why do you bring that up every time we fight, Julie? That was decades ago. He's long gone."

"It was still a betrayal. Far worse than what I'm doing."

"Well, fuck you very much, Julie. You go run after your little man. I'll do fine on my own."

Sandy threw her spoon down on the marble-top table. It made a loud clatter, which got the attention of everyone who wasn't already listening due to Sandy's tirade. Sandy grabbed her purse, stomping off as well as she could in heeled boots. Julie was despondent, but there was little else she could have done. Sandy would have been furious regardless.

They had planned to grow old together. While Sandy had dated many men, neither of them had ever gotten serious about getting married. They had lived together ever since they moved down from Michigan, twenty-three years earlier. Sandy had helped raise Kirsten, being the father figure for the most part, as she was stern and tough with the child. Julie had always had a difficult time being strong, and her child was strong-willed. Sandy had been a good partner.

And, after all that, she was abandoning her friend. How could she have done that? But then again, why would she put someone else's happiness above her own? She had postponed her own happiness most of her life. She deserved her long-awaited reward. She still regretted Sandy's rejection. She hoped her best friend would forgive her someday, relent and understand. She didn't think it likely, though.

Paul had asked her to come live with him in California a couple weeks earlier, and she had said yes. He was selling his stake in the house that he shared with Joy to Stephan, then buying a trailer outright.

She finished her sundae in miserable silence, getting on her bike to go back home. She might as well pack. Sandy wouldn't be making this easy.

*****

September, 2000, Miami, Florida

Kirsten was fidgety and nervous. She had a mental image of her father, as she had seen photos of him, but seeing him for the first time was sure to be different.

Most of her life, her mental image of her father had been nebulous and shifting. He had had dark hair, dark eyes, and sang, but that was about it. Her mother, artist though she be, was never great at describing him. Kirsten had come across an old photo at one point, thinking it may have been her father. The photo showed a handsome man with dark eyes and a thick mop of dark hair, in a black turtleneck shirt, perhaps a formal high school photo. She held it in a special box where she kept keepsakes, imagining him as he was now. However, her mother found it, saying it was an old friend named George that she had known in San Francisco, not her father.

Her mother had gone out to San Francisco a couple months earlier, to visit her father, allowing them to become reacquainted. That had to be awkward, but it seemed to have worked out well. Now, her father had a business trip in Orlando, so they had all arranged a meeting, with several days in EPCOT and

Disneyworld, to know each other. Her parents (that sounded so strange to say!) were driving up from Miami to meet Kirsten and Jason. They would travel up to Orlando from there.

There was a car outside. Was it them? Kirsten rushed to the window, saw a blue car pull in, hearing the whoosh of the tires on the gravel driveway. She watched as her mother pulled herself out of the passenger seat, forcing herself to look at the driver's side.

He was shorter than she had imagined, but then again, don't we always see our fathers as tall? He had thin, grey, wispy hair, being ruffled by the wind as he walked to the front door. He was heavy set in the belly, wearing a t-shirt with an HP logo on it, the company he worked for. He was putting on a baseball cap as he approached. Kirsten backed away from the window, not wanting to be seen watching them approach. She positioned herself near the door, poised to open it.

The knock startled her, despite all that. She opened the door to see her father for the first time.

They both looked at each other. He then drew her in for a long, solid hug. The tears burned her face. Looking up, she saw her mother had beaten her to it. She swallowed a couple of times to keep down the tears, and decided not to bother. Her father was doing the same. They broke the hug, looking at each other again.

"Hello, my daughter. I am incredibly happy to meet you."

"I've waited my whole life to hear that." The tears were unstoppable now.

They both hugged again, as Julie joined them. They stood like that for a while.

*****

October, 2001, West Palm Beach, Florida

Julie and Paul had arrived the night before, helping each other get ready. Julie was wearing a medieval-style dress she had made, with dark, floral velvets and gold lace trim. Paul was wearing a light tunic with a crown on it, of course. He had to play the king, after all.

They gathered their stuff, making their way to the Friends of the Police Hall in Palm Beach. The place was bedecked with strands of silk ivy, dark green tablecloths, and centerpieces with dried flowers in purples and greens. There was a buffet for lunch set up along one wall, with a huge cake shaped like a three-tiered castle in the middle. It looked beautiful.

There were only a few people here, so far. She saw Kirsten in a dark purple dress, with long, drooping sleeves and a train, with purple grape trim along the edges. Jason was next to her, resplendent in a medieval shirt of velvet, forest green and dark purple. Guests were trickling in, all in medieval garb.

It was a medieval wedding, so all of the guests were dressed in garb. Well, all except for Jerry, Julie's dad. He had an excuse, he said, as he was old and needed a walker now. Her mother, Carol, however, had done her best and was decked out in a long, flowing dress reminiscent of the Lady of Shalot. Her brother, Larry, was wearing a tunic that looked too small for him, while his wife, Pat, looked sweet in a light purple and gold dress with sleeves that hung to the floor. Even Jason's young niece, Nakomis, was fluttering around in a fairy outfit, complete with wings, her long blond hair floating as she bounced around from table to table.

The wedding itself was held outdoors, in the pine forest behind the hall. There were candles and glamorous costumes everywhere. It was October. The weather was overcast, but cool enough for comfort. Julie beamed with pride to see her precious daughter walking down the aisle with her father, the king giving away the princess.

Her hair had darkened from the blond she had as a child. It was now a mousy brown, still flyaway and thin, like her father's. She tended to dye it red, as it was now, which suited her freckles. Those she got from her father, as well. They were so alike, standing next to each other. Julie began to feel the prickle of tears behind her eyes, seeing her family together at long last. She pulled out the tissues she had brought.

The ceremony went as planned, with a few giggles and hiccups here and there. She held Paul's hand tight as the vows were made. She wondered if Kirsten had waited so long to get married because her father wasn't around. She was thirty, after all, which was old for a first marriage. But she hadn't met Jason until two years ago. It was a matter of timing that she was able to have her father give her away the year after she found him.

Julie wished Sandy could have been here, her parting words that day had been prophetic. Sandy couldn't have known at the time that she was going to get uterine cancer later that year. Nor could Julie have ever predicted that Sandy would ignore the diagnosis, spend all her money, dying alone before Julie heard of it. She had a heavy sense of responsibility for leaving her best friend, leaving her to die alone. She had failed her, like she had failed Katy. Katy would have loved this ceremony.

She wondered if either of them could see it where they were. But Katy never knew Kirsten. She saw flashes of Katy in her daughter—a style of drawing, or a glance with her eyes, when her hair was red, like Katy's. It was as if her sister's ghost came and touched her daughter once in a while.

*****

December 23, 2004, Las Vegas, Nevada

Kirsten and Jason rustled about the posh hotel room in Las Vegas, getting out their costumes. Kirsten's red velvet shirt was a reasonable facsimile of a Starfleet uniform when paired with black slacks. Jason's uniform shirt was borrowed from Paul. He even had a couple of Captain's pips to attach to the sleeves. They heard a knock on the door.

"Are you two ready? They should be starting soon." Kirsten's Uncle Larry came in, leaping around in his uniform like a gazelle. "Look at me. Beam me up, Scotty!"

Kirsten had always liked her Uncle Larry. He was the fun one, the silly man that always made her laugh. He and Jason got along well—they had done their best to drink each other under the table at the rehearsal party the night before, almost succeeding.

"We're about set. Are mom and dad already downstairs?"

"They're talking to the Admiral as we speak. Pat's already down there, but I don't think all of your dad's friends have arrived."

"Okay, let's do this." Kirsten took Jason's arm, motioning for Larry to lead the way. They made their way down to the elevator and into the Hilton's lobby. Turning to the right, they found the entrance to the Star Trek Experience Exhibition. The place was impressive, with props from all of the various Star Trek series franchises in place. There was a replica of the Enterprise hanging above them at the entrance, as well as doorways and walls reminiscent of the inside of the ship in its different incarnations. The place reminded Kirsten of a mix between Disney and NASA.

"Do we go in? Or is there a special entrance we go into? I remember there was a lot of other stuff before we arrived at the Bridge when we did the tour." There wasn't anyone outside the entrance at the moment to help them, much less her mom and dad or anyone she recognized.

At that moment, a tall woman dressed like a Klingon came out. "What are you humans doing in here? You're supposed to be inside already." She waved a dismissive hand at an unmarked door along one wall. Julie looked at Larry and shrugged. They all went through.

They came into an empty, dark hallway, but there was a door open to one end, with golden light streaming in. They got to the door, seeing the Bridge before them. The Admiral was in front, with her mother and father, in costume, chatting and laughing. They looked up as Kirsten, Jason and Larry came in.

The bridge was set up for Star Trek: The Next Generation. Jason went straight to Mr. Worf's station, posing for a photo at his hero's spot.

"Are you all ready for this, mom? Dad?" Julie looked at both of them, searching their eyes for nervousness.

Paul took Julie's hands, looked into her eyes, saying, "I've been ready for years." Kirsten had never seen her mom this happy before. She blinked back her own tears, taking her place as Matron of Honor, by her mother's side on the Bridge.

As odd as the setting was, with a Klingon and a Ferengi as witness, on the Bridge of the Starship Enterprise, the wedding was short and sweet. It was, however, full of emotions as well as history. Even Larry was tearing up, seeing his big sister wed at long last.

The party afterwards, at Quark's Bar and Grill, was raucous and genial. The Klingons came in, knocking people's water glasses, while Paul corrected their Klingon grammar, him being fluent in the made-up language. Jason and Larry once again tried to out-drink each other, while Pat and Kirsten laughed at their attempts.

It had been an epic journey, but she got the man she loved, The One, so to speak. She had to create her own detective to do the job, but it happened. She was ecstatic, but no longer scared, nervous, or worried.

EPILOGUE

The next year, Julie looked at the mess of boxes in the garage, despairing that they'd ever work their way through them all.

When Kirsten and Jason looked for a new house in Gainesville, Paul had expressed interest in retiring from his job and moving to Gainesville, to get to know his daughter. Jason had suggested that they could afford a bigger house if they all moved in together. As noble a gesture as that was, they had a time of it finding a house that would work. This one, though, had four bedrooms, one of which was in a mother-in-law suite in the back, with its own bathroom and kitchenette. That would work for Kirsten and Jason, while Paul and Julie occupied the front 'wing', with a guest room for others.

She hoped it would work, four strong personalities thrown together. She needed to remember that Jason was proprietary about the kitchen. And that they needed to go through all these boxes. Paul was a packrat, a trait he had passed onto his daughter. Julie and Jason were both pretty accumulative as well. It resulted in LOTS of boxes.

She saw a dot-matrix printer on top of a box. She sighed—yes, that's what it was. They had no computers capable of interfacing with it. But Paul had saved it, nevertheless.

Sighing with anticipation, she opened the next box, calling out to Paul.

"This one is full of Star Trek Books."

"Put that in the attic. We'll have to go through all those later."

Much later.

AUTHOR'S NOTE

This novel is based on my parent's true love story, and my own journey in finding my father. It was serendipity that my parents fell back in love with each other after my discovery. While the basic details are true, I had to make up a lot of individuals and scenes to flesh out the full story. Oddly enough, some things I had made up and my mother, upon reading the manuscript, said they were more true than she had ever told me.

A part of my life became complete when I found my father, a part I always knew was missing. It was only after I found him that I realized what a large hole had been left.

To anyone who has had a child, please do your best to be part of that child's life. Even if it is only a little bit, allow your child to know you, the person you are, your faults and virtues. It helps the child map their own soul, and to see what parts they inherit from each parent. It is a kindness and a beautiful duty.

ABOUT THE AUTHOR

My name is Christy Nicholas, also known as Green Dragon. I do many things, including digital art, beaded jewelry, writing and photography. In real life I'm a CPA, but having grown up with art all around me (my mother, grandmother and great-grandmother are/were all artists), it sort of infected me, as it were. I love to draw and to create things. It's more of an obsession than a hobby. I like looking up into the sky and seeing a beautiful sunset, or a fragrant blossom, a dramatic seaside. I then wish to take a picture or create a piece of jewelry to share this serenity, this joy, this beauty with others. Sometimes this sharing requires explanation — and thus I write. Combine this love of beauty with a bit of financial sense and you get an art business. I do local art and craft shows, as well as sending my art to various science fiction conventions throughout the country and abroad.

I live in the country with my husband, Jason, a dog named Dax, cats named Mallory, Cyril and Lana, and two sugar gliders, Sansa and Arya.

Made in the USA
Middletown, DE
25 October 2017